A BOY CALLED BRACKEN

Bracken, the gypsy boy, was a wizard with animals, especially sick ones. Anything wild, lost or injured ended up in his hands. Perhaps that was why he understood the world-weary reporter Jake, who had been given only a few months to live. The gypsy boy recognised his suffering and decided to do what he could for the sick man. In Bracken's thoughtful care, Jake was able to discover a new world, and gradually he was able to find the peace of mind which had always eluded him.

A BOY CALLED BRACKEN

A Boy Called Bracken

by
Elizabeth Webster

MAGNA PRINT BOOKS
Long Preston, North Yorkshire,
England.

British Library Cataloguing in Publication Data.

Webster, Elizabeth
A boy called Bracken.
1. Title
823'.914 (F)   PR6073.E2/

ISBN 1-85057-113-9
ISBN 1-85057-114-7 Pbk

First Published in Great Britain by Judy Piatkus (Publishers) Ltd, 1984.

Published in Large Print 1987 by arrangement with Judy Piatkus (Publishers) Ltd, London, and St. Martins' Press Inc., New York.

Printed and bound in Great Britain by
Redwood Burn Limited, Trowbridge, Wiltshire.

The leaf twirled down and fell at his feet. He stopped and picked it up, and held it between his fingers. Even a tree must die, he thought... then he looked at the leaf—and it was green. Young and new and green—torn off by some passing bird or a small, tugging breeze. It must be spring then, he thought. Not autumn at all...not the dying year...

He realised suddenly that he never really noticed the seasons—dashing about across the world to this or that far-flung assignment, coming home to the busy Fleet Street office full of stale air and clattering typewriters. Was it really spring? The seasons were different, out there in the field...Rain fell for months on end...or the sun burned on endlessly in an unforgiving sky. Dust or mud encompassed him, and hot dry winds pursued him while he chased after news.... He never had time to stop and look at a leaf...

But here? Here, the sky was soft, and the leaf in his hand was green.

He looked up and found himself opposite one of the huge old city plane trees that stood in the centre of the square. Traffic roared past in

7

a remorseless stream, but the tree stood unmoved. He stretched out a hand and touched the bark. It was dry and flaky with age, but beneath the peeling shell there was firm, strong growth....Life, he thought, pressing his palm against the trunk. Life...?

He moved on, and his feet took him automatically across a side street and down an alley to Fleet Street. He climbed the stairs to the busy newsroom, nodding to the doorman as he went.

'Morning, George.'

The doorman looked up from his desk and smiled. 'Morning, Mr Farrant, sir.' He liked Jake Farrant. Most people did. And though he was so famous on the telly screens of the world, covering each new crisis as it came along, he never forgot to greet George by name when he came home.

Jake paused inside the newsroom, looking round him with a curious sense of unreality. Phones rang, teleprinters clacked, heads stooped over desks.... No-one really noticed him much—they were too busy.

He gave a rueful shrug, and went on across the big, noisy room towards the news editor's inner sanctum. The door stood open, and he could see him inside, dictating a stream of what appeared to be crisp and angry words to some unfortunate recipient at the other end of the line.

Jake cocked an eyebrow in his direction and enquired of the harassed journalist at the end desk, who happened to be a friend of his: 'Bob busy?'

Bill Franklyn, who liked Jake more than most, gave a despairing grin. 'Christ—when isn't he?' Then, seeing something strange in Jake's face, he added: 'He'll see *you*, though.... Anything I can do?'

Jake smiled and shook his head. 'Not now.... Come for a drink after?'

'After what?' asked Bill.

But Jake had already gone inside and shut the door.

'Morning, Jake,' said his editor, finishing his decisive tirade and slamming down the phone. 'Did I send for you?'

'No.' Jake was smiling a little. 'Own free will....Bob—I hope you won't take this amiss. I want to resign.'

'Resign?' said his editor, searching on his desk for a recalcitrant paper. 'Nonsense! Where the devil did I—?' But something in Jake's voice made him look up sharply. 'Are you serious?'

'Perfectly.'

'But—' he sounded totally nonplussed,

'you're my most senior foreign correspondent—the best I ever had—you know that!'

'Sorry,' said Jake, sounding as if he meant it.

'What is it? More money?'

'No. Nothing like that.' He stood looking down at Bob Harris with affection and regret.

'Don't I send you to enough glamorous places?'

He laughed. 'Plenty!' He picked up a pencil from Bob's desk and absently started to turn it in his fingers. 'It's just...I need a breather...' It sounded lame enough. But how did you tell his sort of news to a man like Bob?

'Writing another book?'

He hesitated. 'Maybe.'

Bob looked at him searchingly. Something in Jake's face disturbed him. It was as lean and brown and good-looking as ever—perhaps a little thinner than usual? And his eyes—which Bob knew from past assignments saw an awful lot—were as steady and clear as ever....And as deep a grey—or were they even darker? No, he couldn't put his finger on it, but there was something about him this time...something almost...fragile?

'Family troubles?' he asked abruptly.

Jake grinned. 'Not on your life! You know very well my dear ex-wife and her children live very comfortably at my expense...and I scarcely

10

ever see them.'

'They're your children too, Jake.'

He sighed. 'Are they? They're grown up now, Bob. Flown. They live their lives—rather opulent ones, I admit—and I live mine....And never the twain shall meet. At least, when I'm home we do meet occasionally and they usually do an Oliver Twist on me! But I've been away too long, and I've seen too much of real poverty and hardship to have much patience with them! We're strangers now.'

Bob nodded, thinking it out. 'Then—if it's not family—what's biting you?'

Jake paused. 'I just...like I said...I want to go away and think.'

'Go away where?'

Once again his shoulders lifted in a shrug. 'I don't know...just away...I need some time alone....

Time, he thought. I need time...

Beside him, he heard Bob saying: '...won't accept....'

'What?'

'I said you can take as long leave as you like, but your resignation I won't accept!'

Suddenly Jake smiled. It was a fairly blinding experience, and Bob blinked. 'You're a good friend, Bob. But—' he changed his mind and went on: 'All right. We'll leave it like that....'

'You can stay on full salary till you let me know your plans.'

Jake looked embarrassed. 'A retainer would be better,' he said, and then added a little awkwardly: 'I—may not have any plans.'

'Don't be absurd,' said Bob briskly. 'Everyone has plans. In any case, what would you do for money?'

'Live on my savings...I don't need much.'

Bob snorted. 'A likely story!'

'And an advance on my next book—?'

'You'll be lucky!'

They both laughed, and Jake turned to go.

For some reason that he could not explain, Bob got to his feet and grasped him by the arm. 'Take care of yourself!' he said.

Jake's eyebrows shot up at this unusual demonstration. But he made no comment. 'I'll be in touch,' he said.

After he had gone, Bob sat staring at nothing for quite two minutes before he got back to work.

Outside in the main newsroom, Jake's friend Bill Franklyn took one look at his face and got up and followed him outside. They were joined on the way downstairs by Manny Feldman— another of Jake's closest colleagues—and they

12

all went down to the pub together. It was the place where everyone met at lunchtime, and greetings were hurled at Jake from all sides as he pushed his way in.

'Didn't know you were back, you old sod! Have a drink?' said one.

'Come and join us, Jake!' shouted another.

Jake made a face at Bill and elbowed his way past the crowds to the small snug at the back.

'Quieter in here,' he said, and bought them all a drink.

'You come into money or something?' asked Manny, grinning.

But Bill did not smile. He settled his long legs under the table and said: 'What's all this in aid of, Jake?'

'All what?' asked Jake, trying to sound both casual and innocent at the same time.

'All this about resigning.' Bill's voice was flat.

Jake looked at him severely. 'You've been eavesdropping again!'

'Walls have ears,' said Bill darkly.

There was silence for a moment while his two friends picked up their beer mugs and looked at him covertly over the top.

What can I say to them, Jake was thinking. How can I tell my friends I am going to die? It sounds so absurd....How can I say I'm not

13

good old Jake any more—safe in the field—resourceful in danger and reliable in a crisis—gets the news back and never makes a fuss.... Good old Jake who keeps all the press boys happy and always lends a hand in an emergency, Jake, the experienced campaigner, the good companion that everyone can trust....It isn't true anymore. I've got to leave my work now to someone else—someone who isn't going to be a nuisance or a liability...someone who isn't going to die on their hands....But I can't tell them, he thought....What's the use? It would only embarrass them profoundly...and in any case, we're all going to die one day....It's only a question of time....

Time, he thought. That's it, really....Plenty of time for them...not much for me...*morituri te salutant*... But that's a bit theatrical. He lifted his glass to his friends.

'What's that?' said Manny. '...*salut?*' And he lifted his glass in response.

Jake realised then that he must have murmured the last word of his toast aloud.

'No,' said Bill distinctly. 'He said *"salutant"*...' and he looked at Jake very hard.

'D'you know Bill—' Jake was staring into his glass, 'I didn't even notice it was spring!'

'So?' Bill's voice was rough with some unexplained emotion.

'So—I'm going away....'

'Going away *where?*' asked Manny, unconsciously echoing his boss.

'I don't know. Somewhere quiet....' He felt suddenly a little dizzy and took a quiet gulp of his drink.

'My sister's got a cottage she doesn't use,' said Bill slowly.

'Where?'

'Gloucestershire....Deep in some valley in the Cotswolds....'

'Hills...' murmured Jake dreamily. 'And an English spring!'

'You're going soft at the edges!' said Manny. 'I'm going to buy you a whisky.'

Jake laughed.

'I'll give you the address,' went on Bill severely, 'on one condition.'

'What's that?'

'You keep in touch. You hear?'

'Oh, I will,' agreed Jake. 'I will.'

When he left them, with a whisky inside him and the address of the cottage in his pocket, his two friends looked after him with concern.

'What's on his mind?' asked Manny, his long, mobile face looking unusually troubled.

'Hell, I don't know,' answered Bill, sounding even more troubled than Manny looked. 'But I suppose he'll tell us in his own good time.'

15

The cottage stood half-way down the valley with its back to the beech woods, facing south west. Below its tangled garden and the broken boundary wall was a steep grassy slope leading down to the valley floor. Here, threading through sedges and kingcups and flowery water meadows was a meandering stream which opened out into a small reed-fringed lake. The brown water was so still that the moorhens and coots chugging across it made little arrows on the surface. Around it the hills climbed in springy rises of turf and wedges of beech wood. It was very quiet and very beautiful.

The cottage itself was small and square, built of honey-coloured stone, and its windows reflected the setting sun.

Jake set down his bag and sighed with pleasure. Such stillness and such peace! Surely here he could come to terms with what he had to face?

He had left his car at the top of the lane and walked down the stony track to the cottage gate. Even that small walk had made him suddenly tired....His limbs felt heavy and slow....

He closed his eyes for a moment in silent rebellion. He wasn't used to weakness. Until now, his body had always obeyed him—accepted every challenge and every hardship without complaint....But now?

Resolutely, he opened his eyes, and found himself looking into the face of a merry brown boy peering at him from the bushes.

'Hallo?' he said.

The face vanished.

He stood looking at the new green of the hawthorn hedge for a moment in surprise. Then, shrugging, he picked up his bag, opened the garden gate and went inside.

'Staying long?' said a voice behind him.

He swung round. The merry boy was perched on the gate, swinging a leg and smiling.

'Maybe,' said Jake.

'The key's under the stone by the door....'

'Yes,' agreed Jake. 'I know.' He stooped down and found the key, and held it in his hand.

'Could get you some milk?' suggested the boy.

Jake nodded. 'Good idea.'

'And eggs?'

'Why not?'

'Bacon's more difficult. Unless they kills a pig.'

Jake's stomach heaved uneasily. 'No bacon, thanks.'

The boy looked pleased. He slid off the gate and stood poised on one leg. He cast a practised eye at the clear sky above the westering sun. 'Be fine tomorrow.'

'That's good,' said Jake, and opened the front door with his key. He stooped to pick up his bag and set it down inside. When he turned round, the boy was gone.

Inside, the cottage was very simple. There was one big living room with rough stone walls, and a small kitchen at the back. The large room—clearly two knocked into one—had an old-fashioned iron grate with bars and a hob at the side. The two windows looked out over the valley towards the setting sun. The furniture was simple—dark oak and brown homespun with two rag rugs on the polished wood floor. Upstairs there were two smallish bedrooms both looking out over the sloping hillside down to the little lake below. And behind the head of the stairs, along the slanting roof wall, was a narrow strip of a bathroom with a white porcelain bath and a shower attachment.

Jake looked round approvingly, and chose the bedroom with the widest view from its window. It was furnished sparsely—a bed, a chest of drawers, a chair, and a hanging rail behind a curtain. There was one soft brown wool rug on the floor, the rest was bare board.

There was running water in the cottage, but

no electricity—presumably it was too far from the road and the main supply route. But there was a small calor gas cooker in the kitchen, and the bath water appeared to be heated by the living room fire. What happened in summer, he wondered...cold baths, he supposed. In any case...he might not be there by the summer....

Before his thoughts could progress further down that unprofitable track, there was a knock at the door.

The brown boy stood there, carrying a metal cannister of milk and a basket of eggs. Under his arm he had tucked a loaf of home-made bread.

'Farmer's wife—Mrs Bayliss—says pay at the end of the week.'

'Good,' nodded Jake.

'Firewood's in the shed,' added the boy, smiling up at him. He seemed all brown and gold, standing there in the setting sun. His hair was tousled and brown, his eyes were brown flecked with gold and warm with laughter— and the freckles on his nose made a light dusting of brown-gold on his tanned skin. Even his clothes were a faded earthy brown....

'Could show you a coot's nest,' he said over his shoulder as he went. 'Tomorrow?'

'I'd like that,' agreed Jake, smiling too.

Already, he thought, I'm looking forward to

something. Bob said everyone made plans.... And Manny said I'm going soft at the edges!

He smiled to himself, and took a last look at the setting sun before he went indoors. The short turf glowed in the evening light. Each blade of grass, each stone, seemed to shine with interior radiance....So did the first pale leaves on the beech trees behind the house...a sheen of gold lay on the surface of the little lake....

Why, it's beautiful! he thought.

He glancd up the darkening track towards the brow of the hill. There was no sign of the boy.

He woke early. At first he thought it was the light—pure and bright—streaming in through the uncurtained windows...or the silence... the calm, unbroken silence of the slumbering valley....

No, not the silence....Already a few sleepy birds were beginning to murmur....He didn't know all their voices yet, but wasn't that a drowsy woodpigeon? And there was a different, more wide-awake bird outside the window, trying out some clear fluted notes and whistles. A blackbird, he was sure....

But it wasn't the light or the silence—or the awakening birds. As he lay listening, a small shower of pebbles hit his window.

He got out of bed, trying not to notice his growing slowness and heaviness, and went to look out of the window. Undoing the old-fashioned catch, he leant out into the cool morning.

Below him, looking up with a grin of welcome, was the boy.

'Come on,' he said. 'Best time of day!'

Jake came down into a new-washed world. Dew lay on every leaf and flower, and Jake's feet made silver footprints on the grass....

'That's my blackbird,' said the boy, with a jerk of his thumb towards the top of the pear tree.

'Yours?'

'Fell out of the nest last year...never thought I'd rear him....Everyone told me to wring his neck....'

His eyes crinkled with laughter. 'But he lived, all right! I used to give 'im bread and milk at first....then it was chick-feed. He used to sit on my shoulder and put his head on my hair and go to sleep....'

'In your *hair?*'

The boy rubbed a rueful hand over his brown curly head. 'Thought I was 'is mum, I expect.... One day I came back and found 'im banging to and fro against 'is cage, trying to get out. I knew it was time then, so I let 'im out...but he used to come down to eat if I banged a spoon on a cup. Still does, come to that....' He looked up into the creamy blossom on the pear tree and whistled at the bird. It whistled back.

'See? He knows me still...kept 'im alive all through the winter...' he went on reminiscently. 'Lived in your shed. We'd a lot of snow come January...lanes all drifted up. Real hard, it was...hard on the birds, too. Nothing to eat. I used to bring him something every day....' He put his hand in his pocket and brought out some stale bread which he crumbled between his fingers and tossed on the ground. 'Got a mate now—and a nest with five eggs—I seen it.....Soon have a lot of mouths to feed....'

The blackbird in the pear tree cocked a beady eye in their direction and let out a little joyous frill of song. Then it flew down out of the tree and landed quite close to them and started to investigate the scattered crumbs.

'Tame, 'e is...' commented the boy. 'Morning, Beaky. You're right, it's a grand old day...' and he gave a little skip of sheer delight and went on across the springy turf with Jake beside him.

I must be bewitched, Jake was thinking. I don't know this boy. I haven't asked him a

22

single question—not even his name—and here I am at five in the morning, being led into mischief like a child!

And, what's more, I'm enjoying it!

They went on down the slope with—it seemed to Jake—all the birds of morning singing their hearts out round them. The little lake was still—not a ripple stirring. The boy put a finger to his lips and led Jake round by the thick reedbed at the head of the lake.... Out in the dark water, a fish jumped suddenly with a clear, neat plop.

Jake followed the boy and crouched down beside him among the green spears of the new reeds.

'There!' breathed the boy.

Jake found himself looking at the boy's hands. They were brown and slim and clever—and one was gently parting the tall, feathery reed-heads, while the other was pointing ahead. Jake's eyes moved on to the curious, untidy tussock of twigs that the boy was gazing at so intently. At first he could only see a muddly heap of stalks, grasses and bits of willow withy...but then his eyes grew accustomed to the dim green light of the reed bed, and he suddenly saw the smooth dark head and curved back of the mother bird on her nest.

As he caught sight of her, she turned her

head and looked at him out of a fierce yellow eye, but she did not move. Something else did, though. Out on the water, a furious uproar began. Wings flapped and splashed against the surface, and a coot's harsh, staccato call echoed again and again round the lake. It was an angry, scolding voice, filled with alarm and outrage—and the circling and slashing movements on the water got louder and louder.

'It's the father bird,' said the boy. 'Trying to get us away from the nest....Better go before he has a fit!'

He turned a smiling face to Jake, and crawled out of the reeds backwards on to the grassy bank.

But now the whole quiet world of the lake was disturbed, and a host of wild duck rose up from the reeds in a swift thrum of wings, calling to each other, skimming the water like clumsy speedboats, and making a frenzied clatter of conversation as they went.

Jake was enchanted. The air seemed to be alive with wings.

'Wait...' muttered the boy. 'The swans'll come soon....'

He waited. Strangely, all his preoccupations and fears seemed to dissolve and fall away from him in this dew-laden watery world.... He was suddenly aware that a whole life-cycle was going on around him, a life in which other creatures suffered acute anxieties and fears—and joys and ecstasies, too—as vital and important to them as his own were to him....And they would go on meeting and mating, breeding and growing, living and dying, concerned with their own affairs, unaware of his private griefs and despairs...And they would still be there in their joyous numbers long after he was gone....

'Listen...' whispered the boy. 'They're coming!'

And then he heard them. At first it was the faintest thrum in the wind...but it grew and grew, until the great wing-beats were music, were a whole symphony of glorious, throbbing sound. The noise of their passing washed over him, and he looked up and saw them against the morning light—five great white swans, their slender necks outstretched, their wings beating in perfect unison....

He stayed there a long time, spellbound in the grass. The boy seemed perfectly content to lie on his back, chewing a stalk and gazing at the sky. And as they remained still, peace gradually returned to the little lake...the coot stopped fussing about his nest...the mallard ducks went back to sleep or chugged happily in and out of the reeds in search of food....The five white swans had gone....

At last the boy stirred and reached out a hand. 'Come on,' he said. 'The sun's up....' He pulled Jake to his feet and smiled at him in the growing light of morning.

They wandered back through sunlight and slanting shadow, until they came to the cottage gate.

'Coming in to breakfast?' asked Jake.

The boy shook his head, an expression almost of regret crossing his face. But then he grinned cheerfully: 'Not today. Gotta go now... I could come tomorrow, though?'

Jake nodded, smiling too.

He wondered how he could thank the boy for the miracles he had shown him. But before he could think of a way, the boy had gone.

That first day, Jake spent his time getting in stores for the cottage, and exploring his small domain. He walked up the track beneath the new beech leaves and took his car to the village shop. He didn't feel like eating much these days...but there was the boy to consider.... He looked like being a frequent visitor...and boys were hungry creatures...

He loaded up his car, smiled at the village postmistress who also seemed to be the shopkeeper, made a mental note to stop and satisfy her curiosity next time—and drove back along the sun-dappled leafy road. On the way, a sudden wave of dizziness assailed him, and he stopped the car till he felt steadier. I'd better walk in future, he told himself...not too safe on the roads.... He wondered, vaguely, how long it would be before he was too weak even to walk...what then?

But the sun on the leaves beguiled him and he forgot to be anxious. He drove home gently, admiring the view.

He spent a peaceful afternoon arranging his few possessions—laying out his books and setting up his typewriter on a small table near the wide living-room windows. He had brought a small radio with him, and he put it on for the news. But already those world-shaking events in which his old life had been so inextricably embroiled seemed far away and unimportant. Outside the cottage, the evening sun was shining and the blackbird was calling...

He went out to have a look at his tangled garden.

It was spring. Maybe he should try to clear the ground and grow something? He would probably not be there to see the results...but all the same, his fingers itched to get at that jungle of greenery...

'I could scythe that old grass for you—' said

the boy's voice at his elbow. 'And we could clear a bit for veges.... But I like flowers best...'

He tugged at Jake's sleeve. 'Look! The snowdrops is over—but there's primroses under the leaves...and wild daffs, see? And the bluebells is just coming. Lots of wild daffs round here—they're special.... Everything's growing like mad!'

Jake stooped to look at the pale creamy stars of the primroses, and put one incredulous finger inside the golden throat of a small wild daffodil.

'So young...' he said obscurely.

The boy grinned. 'They're young all right. Only just come up. And it's a terrible old world they've come into.... Feet trampling about all over the place. And tractors, and them sprays everywhere. I sometimes wonder why they bothers to come up at all! But they're safe enough here.'

He spoke as if they were people he knew, Jake thought—innocent people looking for a safe, quiet place to live...doing no harm to anyone. He remembered the long lines of refugees struggling down the roads from the last battle he had seen....But this was a different battle on a different battleground, and he was part of it...

'It's worse for the creatures, though,' said

he boy, as if Jake had spoken.. 'Hounded too death, most of 'em....' His face was suddenly serious, and sparks of anger flickered in his gold-flecked eyes. 'Like the badgers. Used to be a lot round here...but they're nearly all gone now...gassed or dug out...'

'Because of this TB idea, I suppose?'

He snorted. 'Never proved it, have they? No-one ever gives the poor things a chance....They can't talk back, can they?'

Jake laughed. 'You're a good champion!'

He kicked a stone with his foot, sounding quite belligerent for once, and went on reminiscently: 'I had a fox cub last year. Found him curled up in a barn, half dead with cold... I s'pose someone shot the vixen. I kept him till he was strong enough to manage on his own—' He glanced up at Jake and added confidently: 'You can't keep wild creatures too long, you know...or they can't never go back...'

'What happened to him?'

The boy shrugged. 'I let him go—when he was ready. He might've survived, if the hunt didn't get him...or one of the farmers.... He was bound to pinch a chicken sometime—or a pheasant!' He grinned. 'Can't blame him, can you? Everything would be fair game to him, see? He used to come back to me for food at

29

first. But he forgot in the end...they usually do when they go back to the wild...'

His voice did not sound particularly sad. It was the way things were—and you had to accept it. 'Things live and things die...' he said philosophically. 'When I was little I used to cry about it. I don't any more.'

Jake had been looking at him strangely. Now he said, with something more than curiosity in his voice: 'Do you have a name?'

The boy laughed. 'Two or three...but you couldn't pronounce them.'

'Why not?'

He looked at Jake seriously. 'We're Travellers, you see.'

Travellers, thought Jake. I've been a Traveller too, for most of my working life...though not in your sense. But that might explain why I have this extraordinary sense of kinship—as if I'd known you all my days.... But aloud he only said: 'Romanies, you mean?'

The boy hesitated. 'We come from the Rom, yes, so our grandfather said....We came from Hungary—or it might have been Poland, he said—a long, long time ago. We were called the Musicians then, he told us...but even he couldn't remember that far back.... We keep the old names, though...some of them...'

'When did you come to England, then?'

He looked vague. 'A long time ago...even before my Da was born, I think. But we usually go south for the winter, after the hop--picking...'

'South? Back to Europe?'

He nodded. 'Spain...sometimes further. There's a big meeting of gypsies...all Romanies. Everyone gets together and talks, and there are *pashtivs* every night...' His voice was dreaming and quiet. 'Or sometimes it's Africa...like the swallows...where it's warm.... And we come back in the spring...we follow the sun, like the *vadni ratsa*, the wild geese....'

'But you stayed last winter through the snow? You told me about the blackbird in the shed...'

'Yes...' the boy sighed. 'One of us was sick, too sick to travel, so we stayed....And the weather got harder and harder, and we wished we'd gone earlier. It was terribly cold...' He shivered, remembering more than the hard winter. 'And then our grandmother died...she wouldn't go to hospital, she wanted to die among her own people...' He paused for a moment, dutifully remembering the dead. 'So we had to burn her *varda*. It was the last of the old *vardas* in our family.... They was too rickety and slow for travelling. Though I liked the horses better than engines! But we don't

31

use them any more…only, my Da keeps a few *grais*, 'cos he likes them best, too!'

For a moment the brown, gold-flecked eyes were sombre and far away. But at once he seemed to throw off the sadness and was his laughing self again. 'Anyways, now it's spring, and we have a new trailer, and the sun is shining!'

'Yes,' persisted Jake, fascinated, 'but what do they *call* you?'

The boy looked at him consideringly, head on one side. 'Sometimes it's Kazimir or Zoltan, an sometimes it's Jerczy…and sometimes it's "Come 'ere, you!" ' He was laughing again. 'The boys at one of the schools I used to go to called me Jumper—because of Jerczy, see?—and because I could jump high.' He gave a springy little leap into the air.

Jake grinned. 'So you do go to school occasionally?'

The boy looked out at the sun-laced beech trees on the brow of the hill. 'Sometimes—when we're in one place long enough…and if they've got room for us. If there isn't a horse fair—or it's a wet day!'

A conspiratorial grin passed between them. Jake was escaping from something, too…. But he told himself sternly that he ought to make responsible noises about the boy's future. 'You could learn things that might be useful?'

The boy stared out beyond him at the wide countryside, suddenly quite serious. 'I can read books—I do in the winter—and I can figure better than my Da...I'm a Scholar, he says!' But his eyes were still grave. 'But the way I sees it—where would I learn more than this?' And he swept a brown hand round from horizon to valley floor.

Where indeed? thought Jake. And seeing the boy's serious, committed face, he resolved to say no more.

'You still haven't told me what to call you!' he said, smiling.

The boy smiled back. 'One of my father's names is Petalo—that's Romany for Horseshoe —'cos he's good with *grais*.... And he's called Kazimir and Jerczy, too. But our family name is Bracsas. It means a Viola Player, my grandfather told us.... So the people round here call me That Bracken Boy!' He grinned at Jake with sudden mischief. 'And my Da says as I was born in the bracken, it suits me very well!'

Jake laughed. Then he tried it out, almost shyly: 'Bracken...?'

'It's the nearest they could get to Bracsas...' said the boy, half-dreaming again. 'Brown and curly, green and twirly...' and he fingered a curled-up frond of new fern buried in last year's rusty growth.

Jake was delighted. 'That sounds like you!'

The boy roused himself from his intent contemplation of the frond of fern, and gave a little twirl on his toes to show Jake that he saw the point. Then he cast a practised eye over the tangled wilderness that had once been a cherished cottage garden. 'I'll fetch that old sythe from your shed,' he said. 'I got a stone for sharpening...'

Then he paused and looked at Jake. 'You better watch this time. You can rake tomorrow when it's dried a bit...you done enough today.'

Jake's eyebrows shot up in astonishment. 'What—?'

The boy smiled and laid his brown fingers on Jake's arm. 'When a creature is tired, it rests,' he said gently. 'Stands to reason.' Then, seeing Jake's outraged face, he added, smiling even more angelically: 'Besides, I got a lot to show you yet!'

Before Jake could answer, he had darted off to the shed and returned with a rickety wooden chair and an ancient country scythe.

In a dream, Jake allowed himself to be settled in a small island of green while the boy worked round him in ever-widening circles.

At last, most of the jungle lay flat in pale cut

swathes, and the sweet scent of drying grass filled the air.

Jake went indoors and brought out two tall glasses of orange squash. He had come to realise that the boy would not enter the cottage, or eat with him—yet. That was something that had to be worked up to slowly.... But a cool drink after all that labour, he would probably accept.

'I left some round the edge,' said the boy, laying down his scythe and pushing the curly hair out of his eyes with a green-stained hand, 'because of butterflies. They likes weeds, especially nettles...'

He accepted the glass of squash and drained it quickly. 'Gotta go now,' he said. 'I come up to say we're moving the *grais* tomorrow, so I'll be wanted.... But I'll come the morning after... if that's all right?' He smiled and handed Jake the empty glass.

'Bracken?' said Jake, trying it out once more.

The boy looked at him enquiringly.

'Thanks.'

'What for?'

Jake looked at him incredulously. 'All this—' he said, and waved an arm to include the cut grass, the sunny hillside and the darkening lake below.

Bracken's smile grew strangely adult and

tender. 'Might as well enjoy life while you can,' he said, and went off into the twilight without another word.

The next time, Jake was awake before the shower of pebbles. Pain had assailed him in the night, and for a while he had been entirely occupied with trying to master it. He knew it would get worse—and he had been given a supply of painkillers to dull it as much as possible. He also knew that the time would come when he couldn't manage alone.... But he didn't want to think about that yet. He had other things to occupy his thoughts at the moment...and they were strangely comforting.

There was the boy, Bracken, for instance. His infectious joy of life—the glancing mischief of his smile, and his deep love of the countryside around him—the revelations Jake was experiencing in his company.... *'Things live and things die...'* said his tranquil voice in Jake's ear.... And, being with him, Jake began to realise that he was part of the pattern, too—and that death was not something terrible and final, but a natural sequence in the long, long life-cycle of the world around him. I don't believe I'm afraid of it any more, he said to himself with wonder....It will happen when it happens—and meanwhile, Bracken is right, I might as well enjoy myself while I can!

He fell to wondering about the boy himself. Where did he live? Hadn't he said something about a new *trailer?* A caravan, then. How many of them were there? What did they all do? And then there was Bracken's voice—light and lilting, not Welsh exactly—and certainly not Gloucestershire—but not foreign either... though his names—Kazimir Zoltan Jerczy Bracsas—were as much Polish as Hungarian, he thought. He knew, though, that the Romanies took their many names from the countries in which they travelled....Jake himself spoke smatterings of a good few languages picked up on his travels—including a little Polish and Hungarian. But, he suspected, Bracken and his family would not speak either nowadays, if they ever had. They had probably left those countries behind generations ago...Romany was their second language, he supposed, and even that was dying out nowadays. And yet there was something a little strange about the boy's voice—the way he spoke, which was sometimes quite educated and adult and sometimes carelessly childish; that gentle, laughter-laced voice, too quiet to frighten any creature, too full of music to be ordinary...sometimes serious, often brimming with gaiety, speaking tranquilly of things which Jake had scarcely dared to put into thought himself...

'I used to cry about it when I was little...I don't any more...'

No, said Jake. No tears. I'm going to live every day to the full...I'm going to look at everything, see everything, do everything... while I can...and be thankful.... The shower of pebbles came then—Bracken's voice called up from the garden, clear and lilting as ever: 'The light's growing...come on out!'

This time, Bracken did not take him to the lake. They went side by side into the beech-woods where the new young leaves were just beginning to unfurl. The light was still dim among the tall silver-grey trunks of the trees, and the air smelt of moss and last year's leaf-mould and fungus. But the ground was star-red with white wood anemones, and the green spikes of bluebell leaves were already thrusting through the soil. Above them, the birds were already trying out their morning songs. The treetops seemed alive with calling and answering voices, and deep in the woods the staccato cluck of a pheasant spoke suddenly and got a sharp reply from further off.... There was a cuckoo calling, too—quite close—calling and calling in the quiet morning. And one of the other birds seemed to be laughing...

'That's a yaffle!' said Bracken. 'A green woodpecker. See! There he is, on that tree!'

Jake saw the trim bird in his bright spring plumage—olive green and scarlet—and said softly: 'Isn't he handsome?'

But they did not stay in the woods. All this time they had been steadily climbing—past the tall rows of beeches, past ivy covered stumps of old fallen trees, and high sandy banks hollowed out under the roots of even older ones....

'That's a fox's earth...' said Bracken. 'Look! Bones and bits of fur...he's been having a feast, all right...'

Or: 'That's an old badger sett...see those blobs of grass and stuff? That's his old bedding...they always pulls the old stuff out and drag in a new lot...' He stooped to look at it, and shook his head sadly: 'Too old...no-one living there now...'

They went on upwards, sometimes holding on to small branches of elder or hazel to pull themselves up the steeper bits of bank. Several times, Bracken paused to give Jake time to breathe—and always covered it by pointing out some new thing for him to look at.... And though Jake wasn't fooled, he didn't seem to mind...

'Look!' said Bracken. 'There's a jay—see his

wings? It's the brightest blue there is, except a kingfisher.... Wait a minute—' and he ran off into the hawthorn thicket where the jay had been hidden before it flew out in a flash of colour. Jake saw the boy stoop and search along the ground and then come running back to him, triumphant and laughing: 'Here you are! A jay's feather is lucky!'

Jake held the smooth grey feather in his hand and exclaimed over the vivid azure bars that lay across it. 'So perfectly marked...you're right, it's a marvellous colour!'

He stuck the feather in the lapel of his jacket, and they walked on up the path.

'Nearly there!' said Bracken. 'Just in time for sunrise!'

Jake looked round him and saw that the trees were thinning, and beyond them was a clear grassy rise leading to the top of the hill.... They came out of the trees on to short, springy turf, and looked up to see a sky awash with pale rose, and a few flamingo clouds drifting high above the horizon.

Swiftly, Bracken pulled Jake after him to the crest of the hill and stood beside him on the highest point, looking out...

Around them lay fold on fold of Cotswold hill, blue in the distance, brown and green and golden on their nearer flanks. Jake seemed to

40

be standing on the edge of the world, and he could see the whole curve of the sky and the whole round bowl of the earth as it fell away from the rolling hills of the deep mist-filled valleys below. Great wedges of beechwoods gave way to gently-swelling pasture with clusters of white sheep upon them, and far away to the west he caught a glint of the silver Severn winding its way down to the sea...

'Not that way...' breathed the boy, 'over there! Over Swallow-tail Beacon!' and he pointed a long brown finger towards a tall rounded escarpment of hill facing east.... As he spoke a thin, brilliant line of light seemed to touch the smooth curve of the hill's brow... the sky above it flamed with fire...the line of light grew ever more vivid until the eye was dazzled...and the sun's bright disc rose over the rim of the world...

Jake had seen many sunrises on his travels... but somehow never one like this. The pure air, the blue, sleeping valleys, the white mist wreathing the lower slopes of the beech-woods...the pale bleached grasses of last year's summer still clinging to the dips and hollows of the downland, and the vibrant green of the new turf under his feet...the sound of an early lark spiralling upwards...and, above all, the great wash of fiery colour—the dazzling out-

41

pouring of light in the clear morning skies—
all this untouched, unspoilt beauty left him
breathless and enraptured. He felt like the lark,
still climbing on beating wings, still pouring out
ecstasy to the sky...except that he could not
sing.

But Bracken seemed to know his mind. He
knew it was hard to come down from the
skies.... After a while, he sat down cross-legged
on the grass and drew Jake down beside him
with a determined hand.

'We can watch the valley waking up...and
you can hear the dogs barking. It'll be warm
in the sun...'

Jake suddenly remembered something and
felt in his pockets. 'I brought some bread and
cheese...and some apples...' He glanced at the
boy, and added carelessly 'I get hungry in the
mornings...'

'So do I—' said Bracken, falling into the trap.

They looked at one another and laughed—
and Jake shared out the bread and cheese.

They sat together on the scented turf, happily munching and looking down at the valleys
and little hills below them, while the sun
climbed in the sky.

Back in London in the busy newsroom, Bill
Franklyn got up from his desk, looking

troubled but purposeful, and went in to see his editor.

'Bob,' he said, without preamble, 'I'm worried about Jake.'

His editor looked up and sighed. 'You're not the only one.'

'What ought we to do about it?'

'I don't think there's anything we can do,' said Bob Langley slowly. 'He's made up his mind to go off on his own. We've got to respect that.'

'Yes, but—he may need help.' Bill's kindly, worried eyes met his editor's in mute anxiety.

Bob nodded. 'So he may. But I don't think we can force him to accept it.'

Bill was not convinced. 'D'you know who his doctor is?' he asked bluntly.

'No. I daresay Margaret—his ex-wife— might...'

'Bill made a face. 'Would she care?'

'Not a lot.' Bob's voice was dry. 'But she might tell you the facts—if she knows them.'

Bill stood jingling the keys in his pocket while he considered. 'Yes. All right. I'll ask her.'

His editor looked at him in a friendly fashion. 'Let me know...' he said. 'Maybe we can do something useful...'

Bill agreed, and went to lunch, turning over

various possibilities in his mind. 'Flipping Trappist!' said Manny. 'Let us in! You'd make the proverbial clam seem like a garrulous gossip.'

'Who's a garrulous gossip?' asked a fellow journalist, sounding interested.

'Not Bill, at any rate,' said Manny. And seeing Bill's abstracted gaze, he began talking very fast to his inquisitive friend to cover Bill's unusual silence.

He waited till they were strolling back from the pub towards the office before he tried again.

'Bill? What's eating you? Come on—give!'

Bill came out of his abstraction and grinned at Manny apologetically. 'Sorry, I was thinking about Jake.'

'What about Jake?'

'What we can do for him—if anything.'

'Hm.' Manny sounded non-committal. 'Any ideas?'

'Bob thinks Margaret might help...?'

Manny laughed. 'That gold-plated harpy! You must be joking!'

'She might know the details...'

Manny shook his head decisively. 'I doubt it. Jake's painfully self-reliant. If he's in trouble, he wouldn't tell her a thing...'

'She may know the name of his doctor.'

Manny's indiarubber face became suddenly

grave. 'So...? I was afraid that was it...'

'I'm only guessing.'

Manny was silent for a moment. Then he said: 'If you're going to tackle Margaret...shall I come?'

Bill sighed with relief. 'I thought you'd never ask!'

They laughed, and went on up stairs to what Manny privately called yet another tame afternoon on the home front.

They called on Margaret Farrant that evening. She lived in a trim suburban villa—fairly large and opulent—with a willow tree in the front garden and two cars in the garage. The door was answered by a cool young blonde in a bright pink catsuit, who called out over her shoulder: 'Ma...I think you're wanted...' and then sized up Manny and Bill with a sharp, observant gaze that reminded them both a little of Jake when he was on the job...

'You're from my father's paper, aren't you?' said the girl in a crisp, hard little voice. 'I remember you,' she looked at Bill.

'Yes,' agreed Bill, and introduced himself and Manny.

'Is anything wrong?' she asked, catching Bill's expression.

'Er—that's what we came to find out...'

he began.

'It's no good asking her,' said the girl, tossing back her mane of blonde hair. 'Anything about my father is death.'

Bill's expression did not waver. 'Yes,' he said again. It may well be death.

The girl's eyes widened.

At least she's not stupid, Bill thought.

Beside him, Manny shifted his position slightly so that he stood ranged for battle, shoulders squared and almost touching Bill's. 'Do you think we could come in?' he asked in a deceptively mild tone.

'I shouldn't think so,' said the girl. 'Seeing who you are—' But her eyes lingered for a moment on Bill's face, almost with anxiety.

'Who is it, Beth?' said a woman's voice behind her, and Margaret Farrant came out into the hall. Light, music and laughter poured out after her, filling the enclosed space with noisy brilliance. 'Yes?' she said, looking at the two men with obvious impatience.

She was a tall, elegant woman, expensively dressed in midnight blue clinging silk jersey. Her hair was almost as blonde as her daughter's, but a good deal tamer and set in a gleaming coil on top of her head. She wore long, glittering earrings, and her eyes, Manny thought unkindly, were as cold and blue as a chunk of

Arctic ice.

Bill began again—pleasantly and kindly—but there was a hint of steel behind the quiet mild tone now.

'We're sorry to trouble you, Mrs Farrant. It's about Jake—'

'I have no wish to hear anything about my ex-husband,' she said, and her voice was as cold as her eyes.

'But—' began Bill.

'It's a simple enough request,' Manny intervened. 'We just wondered if you knew the name of his doctor.'

She paused. 'I do—if it is any business of yours.'

They did not reply to this, looking at her in silent disbelief. So she was forced to go on. 'Why? Is he ill?'

A glance passed between the two men. 'That's what we would like to find out.'

She stared at them, deliberately uncomprehending. 'I see. Well, I doubt if a doctor will tell an outsider anything about his patients.' She made the word 'outsider' sound as insulting as possible.

'No,' agreed Manny pleasantly. 'But he might tell his *friends* how they could help him.'

The air tingled with antagonism.

'Very well,' she said at last. 'It used to be

Lawson in Harley Street.... He used to see him occasionaly when he was home on leave. They were old friends, I believe...I don't think he had an ordinary GP. And, of course, I can't say whether he still sees Lawson or not...' She put her hand on the door, as if to push the intruders out as soon as possible. 'Is that all?'

'Don't you—?' Bill changed his mind hurriedly. 'He hasn't contacted you—about being ill or anything?' He was determined to get something out of her before the door closed on his face.

'My only contact with him is through my solicitors,' she said dryly. 'About money. We no longer discuss anything else.'

'But—don't you realise—' burst out Manny, 'he might be seriously ill?'

She looked him up and down. 'If you mean, he might default on his payments—it has been known to happen before. But thank you for warning me.'

'I didn't mean that!' said Manny, outraged.

Beth turned to him and said in a surprisingly sympathetic tone: 'You'd better go, you know.... You've got what you wanted...'

Behind them all, a tallish, laconic man, carrying a glass in one hand, sauntered up and laid his other arm possessively round Margaret's shoulders.

'Having trouble, darling?'

'No,' said Margaret. 'Just a business matter. We have quite finished. Good evening, gentlemen.'

As Bill had expected, the door closed in his face.

'God!' said Manny. 'Let's have a drink. I'm frozen to the marrow!'

Bill stood looking round the flowery suburb in despair. 'We'll never find a pub round here! Look at it! Let's get back to civilisation!'

They strolled on together, and presently hailed a passing taxi and made for the suburban line station.

'You know,' said Manny thoughtfully: 'it must've been a very bitter split-up for her to feel like that after all this time.... What actually happened, d'you know?'

Bill sighed. 'He didn't talk about it much. It was mostly because he was away such a lot. All those unending assignments. You know how it is. You can never tell how long a war will last...or a crisis...or a coup or something. She never knew when he would come back— or even *if* he would come back, I s'pose.'

'And so? Lots of press wives put up with it.'

'Yes,' agreed Bill, smiling. 'And there are lots of press divorces, too.'

'Anyway—our Margaret didn't like it?'

49

'I gather so.'

'Weren't there—er—compensations?'

'Oh yes.' Bill's voice was dry. 'Plenty...'

'I see...'

'That was probably one of 'em you met at the door!'

'But—?'

'Jake's fastidious,' said Bill bluntly. 'Doesn't care for left-overs.'

'Mm.... And she...felt justified—being lonely and bored?'

'Sound simple, doesn't it, put like that...'

'But of course it's not simple at all—especially with kids involved.'

Bill nodded. 'The girl, Beth—I thought she seemed a bit concerned?'

'So did I.... A shade less callous, at least!'

They laughed.

'Wasn't there a boy?' Manny asked.

'Yes.... At Oxford, I think...'

'Ho-ho! High-flown!'

Bill grinned at his sideways. 'Oh yes...Jake paid for good schools...'

'In fact, Jake paid.'

Bill sighed. 'He did.'

Manny was silent for a moment. 'Well,' he said at last. 'It's clear there's not much help forthcoming from that quarter. It's up to us now...'

They smiled at one another—companions in arms—and took the train back to London.

★ ★ ★ ★

Andrew Lawson was a great man by now, but he had been friends with Jake Farrant for a long time—since his young houseman days—and he agreed to see Bill and Manny informally over a drink.

'I must warn you, though,' he said, looking at them over the top of his discreet glass of sherry, 'I'm not at liberty to discuss a patient's condition with anyone else—however well-intentioned!'

Manny nodded. Of the two, he seemed the more at ease with this quietly authoritative man. Bill seemed unaccountably nervous in the great specialist's presence.... Or maybe he was just afraid of what was going to be said.

'We know that,' agreed Manny, screwing up his friendly face into a kind of lopsided smile. 'It's just that—we were worried about him—Jake, I mean.... He was so damned good at his job. The very best, you know, and he loved it. But what does he do? He suddenly chucks it all up and goes off and buries himself in a cottage in the country...'

It was Andrew Lawson's turn to nod. 'Yes...

51

that figures...'

'But—' said Bill, agonised with the attempt to discover the truth without asking the forbidden question, 'what we want to know is...' He paused, looking helplessly from Manny to Lawson.

'Is he likely to—er—need any help...in the near future?' Manny finished for him, making it as easy for Lawson as he could.

The specialist's grave look softened a little. 'Yes,' he said. 'I'm afraid he is...'

The two younger men looked at one another and sighed.

'H-how soon?' asked Bill.

Manny found himself thinking, almost irrelevantly: Lawson has a fine head—that high forehead and thatch of grey hair, and those steady, penetrating eyes, grey, too, like Jake's. And that straight mouth, no nonsense.... It's an incorruptible face—but kind, too.... He's trying hard to be kind.

'I should say...within the next three months...' said Andrew Lawson, his voice suddenly deep with compassion.

They understood him.

'I assume—' said Manny, after a pause, 'that everything possible has been done?'

Lawson looked at them both with pity. It always hurt him to give that kind of news to people. He always wished with all his heart that he could lie to them, or hold out some hope—and not see the look of sad acceptance grow in their faces...

'Yes,' he said. 'Of course...I'm afraid our friend Jake left things much too late.... But, of course, there are things like remission...one never knows what may happen...'

There was a small, heavy silence, and then Bill said awkwardly: 'Well—at least now we know where we are...'

Lawson permitted himself a slight smile. 'You've been very clever, you know. I suppose I should have been more on my guard with two experienced journalists like you! I've already told you more than I should...'

Bill saw his smile with relief, and relaxed a little, too.

'You will treat what I have told you with the strictest confidence, won't you?'

'Of course,' said Manny, and Bill echoed it.

'But—' Manny was pursuing his own line of thought, 'how the hell will we get him to let us be any help?'

The other two laughed.

'I agree,' said Andrew Lawson, smiling openly now. 'Jake is a very proud and self-contained man. But I'm sure you'll be able to get round him somehow! Only,' he grew grave again, 'do be careful....Remember, I see a lot of this, and sometimes a man's independence and privacy are all he has left.... One must allow him to keep that final dignity.'

'Yes,' said Bill sadly.

'Yes,' agreed Manny. And then—with sudden humility: 'But—he might be glad of some support...from a couple of old friends?'

'He might indeed,' Lawson nodded at them very kindly. 'You can but try.'

'Oh, we'll try all right!' said Bill sturdily.

'Yes,' echoed Manny. 'We'll try!'

Two evenings later, Bracken came back to Jake's garden. The blackbird sat in the pear tree and sang to him, and the evening sunlight lay like gold on the brown earth as he turned it with his spade.

Jake had raked up most of the long grass by this time—and it stood now in two sweet-smelling heaps at the end of the sloping lawn.

'Could do with this for the *grais*,' said Bracken, straightening up to smile at Jake.

'You take it,' Jake responded. 'What do I want with hay?'

'You might keep a grass-lark,' said Bracken, laughing at him in the sun.

'A what?'

'A grass-lark...a donkey.'

'Is that what they call it?'

'Round Worcester way, they do.... We go there sometimes for the hop-picking.... But we call it a long-eared *grai!*' He was still laughing. 'Look,' he added, reaching into the leather pouch he always wore on his belt, 'I brought you a few plants...'

Jake held the small green bundles in his hand and looked at Bracken severely. 'Where did you get them?'

The boy grinned. 'I didn't pinch 'em. Farmer gave 'em me.... I was planting for him all day...he runs a bit of a market garden on the side.... These was left over, see? I told him they was for you, and he said OK.'

Jake was ashamed of his suspicions. 'That was good of him. Tell me what they are...'

'These spindly dark ones is cabbage—and Brussels....Those floppy pale ones is lettuce—you'll get some of those ready quite soon, if you plant 'em now—and those with two grey leaves is broad beans, and those is runners....I might get you some peas and some carrot seed tomorrow, only he mostly sows them with a drill.... And you could have some radishes here—they're quick, too...' He grinned at Jake, his eyes full of dancing mischief. 'Then I'd have to make you a hug-a-day...'

'A what?'

'A hug-a-day—A scarecrow—to stop the birds scratching up all your seeds. I like making hug-a-days...the last one had a big swede for a head. It doesn't stop all the birds, mind... but it frightens the sparrows and bullfinches, and they're the worst about seeds...'

He turned back to the newly turned earth and showed Jake how to plant each fragile seedling in the ground.

'We'll leave that bit by the window,' he said, stooping to pull out an obstinate dock root. 'You can grow flowers there—something to look at—' He did not go on, though Jake glanced at him enquiringly. But Bracken was carefully clearing a breathing-space round a clump of primroses and did not look up.

After working for a while in silence, he said suddenly: 'Do you sleep much, nights?'

Jake looked at him, surprised. 'Not a lot, no. Why?'

The boy nodded his tousled head, as if confirming something. 'I just wondered...if you'd like to come badger-watching?'

'I'd love to...' Jake sounded really pleased.

'Not tonight, though...you done a lot today...' His quicksilver smile flashed out. 'You have a lay-in tomorrow. We'll go out at night instead.'

Jake felt a lurch of absurd disappointment.

He loved those early morning wanderings...'Oh but—' he began. Then he remembered that the boy already gave up a lot of his spare time on his account. 'Yes,' he said lamely. 'That'll be fine...'

Bracken looked at him consideringly, head on one side. He was not taken in one bit. 'All right then,' he said, smiling. 'We'll just go a short way in the morning...but you gotta rest in the daytime, mind!'

Jake found himself laughing—not at all annoyed at being bullied. He reflected that the boy only came in the early morning or late evening.... And he said he was planting for the farmer.... That must mean he was working hard all day...

'Don't you get tired?' he said.

Bracken laughed. 'Not me. I'm strong. I've only been sick once—and that was when I fell off a *grai* and broke some ribs.... And that was my own fault!... Listen!' he broke off suddenly.

Jake listened, and heard, beyond the blackbird's bubbling song, a strange, plaintive downward cry—wavering and sad—often repeated, coming from the tall ash trees across the field beyond his garden wall.

'What is it?' he asked.

Bracken was peering intently at the nearest

57

tree. 'I think it's a long-eared owl. They're the only ones I know who cry like that...sort of sorrowful.... Come on! If we go quietly, we might see him...'

They climbed over the broken golden stones of the wall and went very quietly around the edge of the field, keeping near the hedge, until they came to the foot of the first ash tree. The bird called again, almost directly above their heads, and Bracken pointed silently upwards with a slim brown hand.

Jake looked up. At first all he could see was the black tracery of the branches against the evening sky—and that was beautiful enough. But then he saw, on one of the thickest branches leaning towards the field, a dark, unexpectedly tall and slender shape. As he stared, the bird turned its head and seemed to be looking directly at him. Above the long, dark-brown body, there was a heart-shaped face, each lustrous golden eye ringed with pale feathers which extended downward to a kind of white bib below its beak. And above the dark-hued feathers of his forehead which gave the pale disc of its face a semblance of eyebrows arching in grave surprise, there were two long, pointed tufts of ears. It seemed to be gazing at these interlopers in its field with a certain mild disapproval—but it did not fly away.

'Lovely,' breathed Bracken. 'Doesn't he look serious? Never seen one so close before...'

The owl called again then, sadly—not like a hooting tawny owl and not like a screeching barn owl, but wavering and strange and desolate—and before long a second mournful voice answered it from further down the valley.... At this, the owl turned its head as if to listen, and then silently took off on wide, dark wings and sailed downhill towards that other wandering cry...

'Beautiful, those wings...' murmured Bracken. 'So *quiet...*'

He held Jake back a moment and pointed down the field. 'They won't come out now we're here—but if you watch on your own from your wall, you'll see the hares come out to play. They often do up here...'

Together, they turned back across the field and climbed the wall into the garden. It was almost dark now, and the first stars were winking between the branches of the pear tree.

'A cup of tea?' asked Jake, greatly daring.

Bracken hesitated. 'Can I sit out here on the step?' He didn't say: I don't like houses...they make me feel shut in...but Jake understood him.

He went inside and lit one of the lamps and boiled a kettle on his calor-gas cooker. Presently he carried two mugs of tea outside and sat down on the step beside Bracken to look out at the night.

He found himself gazing intently at the dried seed-head of some last-year's cow parsley silhouetted against the lamplight from the doorway. Its delicate filigree of stiff, perfect stars fascinated him.... He realised suddenly that he was looking at things with entirely new eyes since the boy came...everything seemed clearer and more vivid—and extraordinarily beautiful.... It was as if each day of his increasing weakness made him more aware of the world around him...so that even his illness brought him unexpected gifts...

'I like night-time,' said Bracken softly. 'You see shapes clearer against the dark...'

Against the dark, thought Jake...and turned to smile at Bracken.

But the empty mug lay on the step, and the boy had gone.

★ ★ ★ ★

In the night, Jake was woken by an extraordinary scream right below his window. For a moment his mind jumped with thoughts of muggings and murder—but then he remembered he was in the quiet countryside, not the

dark streets of London. Quiet? he thought...
and the scream came again, harsh and wild in
the night.... Then he heard the answering
sharp, metallic bark of the dog fox in the woods
beyond. It's a vixen calling, he thought. I know
about that...but I've never heard one before....
It's a dreadful, eerie sound.

The vixen screamed again, seeming right
under his window, and he got up and went to
have a look. Bright moonlight lay on the sleeping fields and dappled the garden with silver.
He was just in time to see the long, slender
body slide gracefully over his wall and go across
the field like liquid shadow...

Out in the field, she stopped for a moment
and turned her face back towards the cottage
garden. He caught a glimpse of her white throat
and underbelly before she turned away and
cried again to the dog fox within the darkness
of the beechwood.... Then she moved off in
the fox's peculiar gliding trot, and disappeared
into the black shadow of the trees...

Jake knew now when a bout of pain was coming. He went downstairs to make some milky
coffee, and took a couple of painkillers...they
would work soon.... He wandered in to have
a look at his typewriter and his books. A sheet
of paper, half-typed, stuck out of the
machine...he stooped to read it, and found that

his latest account of the course of a foreign war seemed utterly meaningless to him. What am I writing this stuff for? he thought.... It all seems so far away now.... Who will care what I say about the violent happenings on a distant shore?

Far better, he thought, to write about his actual world around him that was disclosing new wonders to him every day...and every night...

He took a new sheet of paper and wrote on it in his swift, decisive long-hand: 'Today, I saw the sunrise...and Bracken showed me a long-eared owl...and in the night I heard a vixen screaming...'

I will keep a diary, he thought. Each day I will set down the marvels I have seen...each day I have left will be a new voyage of discovery.... I will record each day, each living moment, as it comes...

He smiled remembering the boy's instant joy in every new thing that came his way—Look! A woodpecker! Listen! A long-eared owl! *You see shapes clearer against the dark...*

Yes, agreed Jake...you do. He looked out once more at the moonlight in the garden... then he went back to bed and fell asleep.

That morning it took two handfuls of gravel

to wake him. He was deep in a heavy, drugged sleep and it seemed impossible to drag himself out of it and pull himself to the surface. He felt slow and stupid, and there was an ache in all his limbs that seemed to hold him down...

But outside, the light was growing and the blackbird was practising a new bit of song.... And Braken's voice came to him clearly through the window.

'Tea's up....I brought a flask today! It's a pearly old morning...you coming out?'

Jake struggled to his feet and went to the window. Below him, the garden lay bathed in dew—it lay in drops along the branches of the trees and even on the bars of the gate. Outside the garden, the lower slopes of the valley were swathed in translucent wisps of mist.... It clung to the tops of the beeches and curled round the little hills, making veils and scarves of shimmering light. It was indeed a pearly morning.

Jake looked down into Bracken's upturned face. It was as joyous—as bright with welcome—as ever.

'Hang on,' he said. I'm coming...'

When he came down, Bracken took him firmly by the hand and perched him on the garden wall in the first rays of sun. Jake could see his own shadow on the silvered grass—and by this he knew it was later than usual, and he had overslept.

'Did I keep you waiting long?' he asked.

'Doesn't matter,' said Bracken, who was busy with a thermos and a package wrapped in newspaper. 'Try some of this...'

'What is it?'

'Herb tea. We dry the herbs ourselves... makes you feel all fresh, like the morning...' he grinned at Jake, and opened his packet and broke off a piece of yellow-brown cake and offered it to him. 'And this is sesame cake...'

Jake sipped the fragrant tea, wondering what strange leaves had gone into its making—and almost immediately felt better. The heaviness went from his body, and his head felt clear and tinglingly alert.... He bit into the sesame cake, and found it delicately spiced and pleasant on the tongue.

'Mm...' he said appreciatively. 'This is good!'

Companionably, they shared their early breakfast in the sun. The cuckoo was calling now, insistently, from the dark woods...but Bracken made no attempt to move on until he saw that Jake was ready.... He watched the brightness return to those shadowed, observant grey eyes, and the startling pallor recede from his skin as the warm tea and the sunshine revived him....To him, Jake was just another sick and exhausted creature who needed caring for and comforting—until he was strong enough to manage on his own. Many of the creatures that came through Bracken's gentle hands were bewildered and frightened half to death as well as injured...but this one was not frightened now—not even very bewildered any more. Only, Bracken knew, his injuries went deep and were probably past his curing...

He looked again at Jake's peaceful face as he sat sunning himself on the wall, and judged him to be about ready to wander off into the bright morning.

'Bracken...' said Jake suddenly: 'what would you have done if it rained?'

The boy threw back his head and laughed. 'Sat on your step, o' course, and handed you your tea in the kitchen!' He was still chuckling. 'You got a mack?'

Jake pointed to his own clothes—a thick, waterproof anorak with a hood, ancient cords and wellington boots, working gear on many a wild journey in the field. 'Ready for anything!' he said, smiling.

'Well then, what are you worrying about?' His smile was so infectious that Jake began to laugh, too.

'Mind, it does rain quite a bit down in this

valley—especially in spring...but it does the plants good.... Things can't grow without a drink, can they? You want to go and look at the mallards in the rain...they love it...' His eyes grew thoughtful as he looked down at the green valley and the glint of water below. 'I suppose...' he said slowly, 'people with roofs over their heads see things differently...'

Jake looked at him. 'Even a trailer has a roof!'

Bracken smiled. 'Yes, but...I mostly sleep out of doors...except if the weather's really bad. And you get sort of to feel like the creatures do—it's enough to be alive...and to get a bit to eat...and to lie down when you're tired. The seasons come round...in a kind of pattern...you get used to all kinds of weather...'

Jake thought once again of those long lines of refugees who had no roof over their heads, and who lived from day to day, walking in rain and sun.... Yes, he thought, we people with roofs are spoilt! We do see things differently— and we're mostly wrong!

'Anyways, it's fine today,' said the boy, his eyes changing like mercury and beginning to dance again, 'so what are we waiting for?' And he leapt down off the wall into the dew-laden waiting world beyond the garden.

'It's enough to be alive...and to get a bit to

eat...and to lie down when you're tired, thought Jake. What a marvellously simple philosophy! How lucky I am!

Bracken did not take Jake as far as the lake that day. He turned off along the stream and followed its course back up the hill till its shallow banks grew steeper and it came out into a small, hidden pool with a little waterfall at one end. Here, the boy cast a swift glance round the stooping willows and alders that leant over the water, and then sank quietly to the ground and drew Jake after him.

'We might see the kingfisher, if we wait...' he said.

At first all they saw was the gently tumbling waterfall and the widening ripples and eddies that it made on the quiet surface of the pool.... But there was plenty of life around them— kingfisher or no. A bank vole dropped with a plop into the still brown water and swam in a busy, thrusting vee towards the other side.... A yellow wagtail came down for a drink, dipping and flirting among the shallows, its wings a gleam of saffron in the sun...

In the pool itself, Jake saw the speckled lissom body of a fish, turning lazily among the weed—it might be a trout, he thought....He watched it move with a flick of its tail and glide through the eddying ripples of the waterfall into the deeper water beyond...

There were flowers all round his hidden sanctuary. He recognised most of them now—kingcups, pale lilac cuckoo-flowers, blue speedwell and creamy primroses; fragile wood anemones, rose-coloured in bud and transparently pale in full flower.... And, yes, there were the first bluebells under the skirts of the beechwoods on the slope above. Dog violets grew in little purple clumps at his feet, and the grass was starred with golden celandine...he knew them all now. They were like friends waiting to welcome him. He put out a hand to touch one...

'Look!' whispered Bracken, and clutched his arm. 'There he goes!'

A flash of blue—so vivid and so pure that it made him blink—shot past his eyes and vanished into a green tangle of bushes near the waterfall.

Jake held his breath.... Was it gone already? Was that brilliant, heart-stopping glimpse all he would ever see?

But the kingfisher came again, speeding low over the water like blue fire, and dived suddenly in a diamond sparkle after a shadow swimming below the surface. Almost at once it was out of the water and perched on a willow branch, with something small and silver caught in its razor-sharp beak. The sun glinted on its bright plumage—a blue so dazzling that it almost hurt his eyes, and a glowing orange-chestnut on its smooth, trim breast. The fish vanished in a single gulp, and the little bird sat there quite still, sunning itself above the quietly moving water...

Look thy last on all things lovely every hour said the treacherous voice in Jake's head.... But he shook it from him and looked at the brilliant little bird without sadness—with a delight as real and immediate as the joyous recognition in Bracken's sun-gilded eyes...

At last the kingfisher took fright at a sudden movement in the reeds and darted off, flashing blue lightning as it went, till it was lost among the trailing willow branches.

Bracken looked up at the sun and sighed a little. 'Better go now...I've been longer than I meant!'

They walked back side by side across the springy hillside. There were sheep on the hills, and young lambs' plaintive voices calling their mothers across the quiet valley.

'Will you get into trouble if you're late?' asked Jake—suddenly anxious about the boy.

Bracken laughed. 'No...I'll just have to get the work done faster—that's all!'

It sounded a sensible arrangement—and one

that required a minimum of nagging. Jake hoped for the boy's sake that it was true...

When they got to the garden gate, Bracken said gently: 'You gotta rest now, see? So's you'll be ready for tonight. I'll come just before dark...all right?'

'Fine,' said Jake. 'I'll be ready.'

He had meant to do as he was told and rest all day. In fact he did go back upstairs and lie down for a while. But he found that he could not keep still for long—it seemed such a waste of the day. So he went out into his garden and did a bit of weeding. But this made him feel suddenly dizzy, so he got himself a chair and sat in the gentle spring sunshine until he felt better. The cuckoo was still calling over the hill, and Bracken's blackbird was still singing away in the pear tree. The sun was warm on his face...Jake closed his eyes and slept...

He woke feeling rested, and even less inclined to sit about doing nothing. So he decided to walk up the lane and take his car to the village. He needed a few things, he decided and he ought to locate a chemist and the village doctor.... So far, he reflected, he had been singularly impractical in his deliberate isolation.... But now that the initial spate of shock and despair was over—over? he thought, astonished—and realised yet again how much the gentle company of the boy, Bracken, had already done for him. Grief and rage and towering pride had sent him away from his friends.... now, he could scarcely remember what had driven him to be so fiercely solitary.... Except that he had run, like a wounded animal, for cover...for sanctuary and peace...and he had found it.

So this time he returned to the village in a much less unapproachable mood—and Mary Willis in the General Store and Post Office seemed to sense this at once.

She was a round little woman with a round and cheerful face—and she was quick and light on her feet like a bird, darting to and from her shelves with instant helpfulness but absolutely no servility.

'You're Jake Farrant, aren't you?' She smiled at him rosily. 'I've seen you often on the telly. Staying at Mrs Cook's cottage, aren't you?'

Jake found himself smiling back, but cautiously. 'That's right, Bill Franklyn—Mrs Cook's brother—is a friend of mine...'

A sudden wave of nostalgia came over him for the hard, bright days in the field, and Bill's astringent company and irreverent laughter.... I miss him, he thought—and Manny—wry, sarcastic Manny with his shrewd tongue and the incurably warmhearted tenacity of the Jew....I miss them both, and I miss my work, and the brave, unspoken loyalty of my friends.

'I hear you've been out in the fields with our gypsy boy, Bracken?'

'Yes,' admitted Jake. He noted the 'our' gypsy boy.... Evidently, he was not unpopular in the village—like some gypsies were.

'I suppose everyone here knows him?' he asked.

Mary Willis smiled even more cheerfully. 'Bless your heart, course we do.... He's a wizard with animals, that boy—especially sick ones.... All the villagers take their pets to him...and anything wild or lost or injured lands up in his hands...'

'Yes, thought Jake. So they do...

'What about the rest of the family?'

'Oh, they're all right, too—as gypsies go.... They work on the farms come spring and summer: there's cherry-picking and later on the soft fruits down in the vale...and they go down Hereford way in August for the hop-picking.... But they're here most of the summer. They don't seem to steal nothing, and the boy's father is very good with horses...can cure anything—better than the vet, some say! Mind you,' she leaned over the counter to wag a

72

finger at Jake, 'there's still some as won't have a gypsy near the place, set the dogs on them even.... But that's prejudice, I say. This lot never did anyone any harm—and they'll be off again come winter...'

Jake's heart gave a curious lurch of dismay—off again come winter? But maybe he wouldn't need to consider that parting.... It might all be over by then...

'—the schools' officer—' Mary Willis was saying.

'What?'

'He tries to get the gypsy children to school—but they don't like it much. They hate houses, you see—and those crowded noisy town schools must be torture. I can understand it—I like a quiet life myself!'

Jake grinned. 'So do I!'

'Out here—' said Mary Willis, gazing beyond Jake at the single village street and its little grey-stone houses, 'we live close to the fields and such.... There used to be a nice little village school with a playground under the hill....I went there meself when I was a girl. We used to run off up the hill at dinner-time, and sometimes forgot to go back! Anyways, if it was fine, most of us had to help on the farms, especially harvest time.... The school mistress was used to us not being there half the time—

she never grumbled. But now, all the children have to go on the bus to the town—and the school there has hundreds of kids, and no-one really knows anyone else.... In our day, Miss Terry knew us all—and all our families, too...' She looked at Jake, her rosy face quite serious now. 'You can see why someone like the gypsy boy would hate it, can't you? And anyway, he works on the farm by day with the others—I expect they need the money...'

Jake nodded.

'But there I am, running on! What can I get for you, Mr Farrant, my dear?'

He gave her his list, and enquired about a chemist and the doctor.

'No chemist in the village, my dear, I'm sorry...but we take prescriptions and orders into Stroud or Gloucester for you and bring them back here.... If you give 'em to me, I'll see you get them as soon as I can. As to the doctor—he lives over in the next village, Sheepwick, and he has a surgery there every day. But he has one here for people as can't get over there twice a week. Dr Martin's a good man—been here years...he knows us all...' She looked searchingly into Jake's face and added, with unexpected diffidence: 'Been a bit under the weather, have you?'

'A bit,' said Jake. Then, taking a deep

breath, he added: 'Mrs Willis, I—er—I'd be grateful if you didn't let on to everyone who I am. I've come down for a bit of peace and quiet, you see...and—you know how it is—if your face has been on the box, people always want to stop and chat. They even come and ring your doorbell sometimes—in London, that is—' He smiled hopefully at the round, kindly face before him—and Mrs Willis became from that moment his ally and his friend.

'Of course, my dear,' she said in her warm, Gloucestershire voice, 'I understand.... If peace and quiet is what you want—you've come to the right place. Nobody'll bother you here...' She paused, and then added obscurely: 'And the Bracken boy'll take good care of you, I'm sure...'

Jake went out of the shop with his purchases and stood looking down the village street. Ashcombe was drowsing...sunlight lay like a charm on the golden stone of the cottage walls...daffodils nodded golden heads in the little gardens, and tubs and troughs of yellow polyanthus stood outside nearly every door.... At the end of the street stood the church, golden-grey stone, too, with a tall, slender spire topped by a golden weathercock. Dark green yews—sunflecked and glossy—flanked the churchyard whose ancient tombstones were carved from the same golden stone, now covered in yellow lichen. The whole village seemed bathed in gold…there was even an old yellow labrador sleeping the sun…

Peace, thought Jake…. Why do I feel my life increasing? Each day seems richer and more golden…what strange spell has this place cast on me?

'I thought you were supposed to be resting!' said a laughing voice at his elbow—and Jake turned to look into Bracken's smiling, up-turned face. The boy had a small wicker cage swinging from his hand, and inside it Jake could see a very ruffled bird looking at him with a glazed and baleful eye.

'What have you got there?'

'It's a young kestrel…winged with lead shot. But I think I can make him well…' He looked down at it, frowning and angry. 'People with guns…they never give a thought to what they hit—or what they miss!'

They strolled together along the street towards Jake's car. 'Want a lift?' Jake asked. He suddenly realised that he had no idea where the boy's camp was—or even which farm he fetched the eggs and milk from every day. But he had a strong instinct that he must not ask yet…the boy would tell him in his own good time… Meanwhile, he must just trust him to come and go as he pleased...

'Good idea,' said Bracken, and then—as an afterthought: 'Maybe you could help me with the bird...I shall need two pairs of hands...'

'Maybe I could,' agreed Jake, 'though you'll have to show me how.'

'Don't worry,' said Bracken, climbing into the car, 'I will!'

Back at the cottage, the boy asked for a bowl of water, a sponge, and perhaps a dash of disinfectant. 'Though I've got some herbs with me—self-heal and comfrey and sorrel and some nettles—they'll probably be better...'

They sat together on the step, and Bracken set down the cage between them. 'You'll have to hold him,' he said. 'But I don't think he'll peck...'

He opened the wicker cage and took the bird out, holding it gently between his hands. 'Like this—' he said. 'Both hands round his wings... then he can't flap.... He feels safer, too...'

Jake laid his hands round the rumpled feathers, and felt the warmth of the bird's body against his fingers. He could even hear its frantic heart beating unevenly—struggling to overcome its fright and the outrage to its torn and mangled flesh...

'Hold still now,' said the boy, 'and let me

look at you. How can I help you if you wriggle? That's it...gently does it.... You see? That didn't hurt a bit...'

Talking softly to it all the time in his caressing, lilting voice, he began to clean the matted feathers and small bleeding holes where the shot had entered the frail body. Jake held the bird firmly, but not too tight, he hoped.... All the time, its bright yellow-rimmed eyes were alert and open, and it turned its head from side to side trying to see what the boy was doing.... It made no attempt to attack Jake with its sharp, curved beak...

'There now...' said Bracken. 'That's got you clean. I don't know about the shot, though.... I'm not sure I can get it out without killing you with shock...'

'Should we take it to a vet?' asked Jake.

The boy shook his head. 'He would only say "Put it down", and an anaesthetic would probably kill it anyways...' He reached into his pocket and brought out a curious long thin probe. 'This here mitlet will do the trick if anything can.... But I'll have to be quick...too much handling will finish it off sooner then anything. Got a match?'

When Jake lit one, he held the thin steel blade in the flame for a second. He worked very fast then, probing and gently pulling on the fine

78

steel blade—and presently he had got out quite a row of small lead shot, laid carefully on the step beside him. The bird was still now—its golden eyes half-closed, but the brave, tired heart still laboured on...

'That's the best I can do...' muttered Bracken. 'Daren't do any more, I'll kill it else.... The trouble is, lead shot will kill it in the end as well.... Seems a shame...it's scarcely a year old yet, I should think, only just got the white tips on his black tail feathers—look!'

He paused, his hands gently stroking the damp feathers back into place. The bird opened its eyes and looked at him and parted its beak to let out a cry.... But no sound came.

'Never mind,' said the boy comfortingly, 'you can rest now...you'll feel better soon...' One brown finger stroked the chestnut mantle down and lingered lovingly on the blue-grey head. Then he looked up at Jake and said: 'We can put him back now. We'll try feeding him a bit later on...when he's got over the shock...'

'I've got a drop of brandy in the cottage,' said Jake. 'Would that help?'

'Might...' agreed Bracken. 'Watered down.... Too strong, it might choke him...'

Jake fetched the bottle and a spoon. Together they mixed a little of the spirit with water and Bracken forced some of it down the bird's un-

uncaring throat.

'That'll do now,' said the boy. 'We'll have to wait and see…'

Gently, he took the limp bundle of feathers from Jake's hands and laid it down on the dried grass on the floor of the wicker cage.

'If you don't mind,' he said, 'I'll leave him here with you for today…I don't want to move him about too much…'

'But—I shan't know what to do!' protested Jake, suddenly alarmed. What if it dies, here in my care—when I ought to have saved it if I'd known how?

'You needn't do anything,' said Bracken, smiling. 'We'll put him in the shed where it's dark. He'll sleep then…. If he's going to live, he'll wake up hungry…and I'll be back by then…'

So they carried the cage into the shed and left it standing on top of a rusty iron mangle. Bracken covered it with a piece of old sacking which he found in the corner.

'Be good now,' he said. 'And have a nice sleep…I'll be back to see you soon…'

He looked at Jake as he came out of the shed, and added, grinning: 'I was talking to the bird!'

Jake laughed.

In the late evening, when the twilight was

deepening in the valley, Jake came out to have another look at the bird.

Its body lay still, and his heart misgave him as he peered into the cage. Was it dead already? Dead of wounds and shock? But as he got closer, he saw the speckled breast still heaving and the golden eyes suddenly opened, the head turned within its feathery mantle to look at him.

'So you're alive!' he said. 'Congratulations! I don't know what you'd like to eat—but Bracken will be here soon.'

The bird seemed to listen to his voice, but it did not try to rise.

He went out of the shed and stood looking down the field beyond his garden wall. A sudden movement caught his eye. Two grey brown shapes seemed to be dancing about on the grass. Yes—the hares were out—just as Bracken had said. He watched them, enchanted, while they leapt and played and galloped in swift circles round each other, leap-frogging and kicking out with their powerful legs. At one stage, the bigger of the two—the male, was it?—seemed to get too close and too rough, and the other hare stood up on its hind legs and gave him a hearty box on the nose...she stood there, boxing away, forelegs flailing the air, until her partner backed and turned and ran....

81

And then she ran after him, contrite, and the game began all over again.

'Just like a female!' said Bracken, close to his ear. 'Lead him on, and then box his ears! There's no pleasing 'em!' He was laughing again, and Jake found himself laughing, too.

'I brought the bird some supper,' said the boy, and held up a screw of bloodied paper containing a few lumps of raw mince, cut very fine.

'Don't suppose he can tackle much yet,' he said. 'But we'll try...'

When they got to the shed, the bird was sitting up and feebly pecking at the bars of its cage.

'Good!' said Bracken. 'Want to get out already, do you? But you're not ready yet, my friend—not by a long chalk.... That wing's got to heal first.... Here, try some of this...'

He put a couple of small pieces of mincemeat in the cage. But the wounded kestrel didn't seem to see it, so Bracken picked up a piece in his fingers and held it just in front of the bird's smooth head. The curved beak opened automatically, and Bracken dropped the bit of meat inside the pulsing throat.... Patiently, he did this with every separate morsel. The bird swallowed each mouthful with increasing eagerness...

'That's it now,' he said. 'You'll burst, else!

Next time, you'll be strong enough to pick it up yourself, I shouldn't wonder...' and he turned away and wiped his fingers on the side of his ancient brown jersey.

Outside, he looked up a the sky and said: 'The moon'll be up soon.... We'd best get into position first, then we won't scare them off. You ready?'

'Yes,' said Jake. 'I'm ready.' He told himself he didn't really feel tired at all.

For a time, Bracken led him steadily through the beechwoods, climbing obliquely higher and further from the cottage with every quiet step. He did not talk, and the woods seemed very still and dark. Behind them, Jake could still hear the thin voices of the lambs in the hillside meadows, and a late thrush was finishing his evening song on one of the tall beeches. Even the cuckoo called a couple of times in the deepening dusk as it flew home to roost.... But presently even they were silent, and Jake became aware of other sounds—rustlings and comings and goings—all round him in the woods.

At length they came to a clearing where a steep bank thrust upwards, displaying the gnarled and twisted roots of the beech trees which were standing in tall grey columns above. The bank was like a miniature quarry, sandy and scarred, with loose stones and golden-yellow shale in between the clinging roots, and various holes and heaps of scratched earth and trampled grass all round it...

'Here...' murmured Bracken. 'This is what I call Frith Wood Sett...it's still occupied, I know.... You can see the droppings over there, all in one place—see? Very clean creatures, badgers is...and there's the old bedding thrown out.... See them balls of grass and such? They've probably pulled in new beds today... the grass looks all torn up...'

Jake stood gazing at the holes in the sandy earth of the bank, and wondered what hidden tunnels and passages lay beneath them.

'Come on,' whispered Bracken. 'Best get under cover...down wind. Very keen scent, they have...they'll never come out if they smell you...'

He took Jake to the bottom of the clearing and hid him carefully in a clump of green alder bushes, then he slid in beside him and settled down to wait. He glanced at Jake once, anxiously assessing the tell-tale pallor of his face. But he said nothing then about his tiredness.... Maybe the wait would give him a breather... and when the badgers came, he only had to sit still and watch...

The darkness was coming swiftly now, and

before long he could scarcely see Jake's face at all…. But the moon would be up soon.

The first thing they saw was not badgers at all, but a vixen and her cubs. They came trotting out of the undergrowth and stopped to play and roll about and frolic on the brown carpet of last year's leaves. There were three cubs—one with black tips to his ears and cheekier than the others—but they were all fluffy golden-brown balls of mischief, and captivating to watch. The vixen seemed very good-natured and let them gallop and prance and wrestle all over her—and only once put out a swift, chastening paw when one set of baby teeth sank in too far…

One of the cubs stood up on his hindlegs to sniff at the base of a tall tree-trunk near the entrance to the sett…but something clearly startled him, and he dropped to all fours and scuttled away, followed by the whole fox family. The vixen went last, with one anxious glance over her shoulder—and as she left, a black and white snout emerged from the nearest badger exit…

It was the boar who came out first. He spent a long time sniffing suspiciously about, and then sat down to have a good scratch. That done, he had another sniff round, decided all was safe, and began to clean up his fur…. He was very meticulous about this, although he looked pretty spruce already with his neat black and white markings. Soon, his mate arrived behind him, and the two turned towards each other, nose to nose, grunting and squeaking in close communication.

All this time, a growing radiance was spreading through the trees from behind the hill as the moon rose in the sky. Soon it was light enough for Jake and Bracken to see the badger sett quite clearly. Black shadow and white moonlight lay in bars on the forest floor— and black and white fur gleamed on the sleek heads of the badgers as they rooted and scratched and talked.... At last the boar trundled off slowly through the undergrowth and left the sow behind—and now the young cubs came tumbling out of the sett and started to play round and round the clearing, rolling over, chasing each other, wrestling, grunting and squalling. Even mother joined in—and presently a couple more adults appeared from nowhere and got mixed up in the general fun, sometimes stopping to preen and comb their fur, sometimes surveying the youngsters from a convenient tree-stump, sometimes blundering into the chase as if they too felt the cubs' infectious spring fever on this heady, bluebell-scented night...

Jake and Bracken watched a long time, until their limbs were cramped and their eyes ached with staring into the flickering shadows.... But at last all the badgers were gone, and there was nothing left but the moonlight pouring through the tall, silent trees...

'All gone a-hunting...' murmured Bracken, and took Jake's hand and pulled him to his feet. 'Are you cold? I brought a flask...'

Cold? thought Jake. Am I? I've never been so enchanted in my life! I can't feel anything at all, except amazement.... Where have I been all my life, to have missed such wonders?

'No,' he said softly. 'I'm not cold...just stunned!'

Bracken looked at him in the moonlight and smiled.

★ ★ ★ ★

They wandered back across the sleeping fields through moonlight and shadow. Nothing seem-ed to be stirring now, except the night breeze among the leaves and the small clouds chasing the moon across the sky. Jake's long shadow and Bracken's smaller one went before them over the silver grass.... Bracken pointed a toe at his and stopped for a moment to dance with it...twirling about with sudden irrepressible mischief, like a playful cub himself.

When they got to the cottage path, he followed Jake in and went to fetch the sick bird from the shed. 'I'll take him home now,' he said. 'He'll need a lot of care yet, and it's not fair to leave him with you! But I'll bring him back to see you before I let him go...'

Jake nodded, smiling. He realised suddenly that he was very tired, and put out a surreptitious hand to steady himself against the doorway before he went inside.

'A long rest...' said Bracken, judicially, looking down at the bird. 'That's what you need...'

He stood there, holding the wicker cage in his hand and smiling in the moonlight.

Jake did not answer. He had his eyes closed and was trying to stop the world from spinning.

'...and dream of growing strong...' added the voice, softly below him.

But when he opened his eyes there was no-one on the step—only the bright moonlight burning on...

After considerable thought and some anxious consultations with Manny, Bill decided to go and see his sister, Carol.

She lived in a sunny flat in West Kensington, with her twin boys, Matthew and Mark. The household was always turbulent and full of comings and goings, football boots and home-work, but Carol was always glad to see him.

This time, the kitchen table was littered with exercise books and report forms at one end, while at the other Carol was putting the finishing touches to a garish-looking iced cake.

'Hi, Bill,' she said. 'Sit down...if you can find anywhere. It's the twins' birthday—I'm trying to get this done before they come home.'

'Where are they?'

'Playing squash.... They'll be ravenous when they get in. Are you staying to supper?'

'I might,' said Bill cautiously. 'Depends what you've got.'

Carol laughed. She was a bit like Bill, with her clear hazel eyes and ready laughter...but her hair, which was the same kind of hazel brown as her eyes, had two startling wings of silver at each side of her forehead. And her mouth, when it was not laughing, had a sad-dened downward curve...

Bill, observing the laughter and the sadness it covered, spoke abruptly: 'How's things?'

'Oh...pretty good, really. Except that I've got all the end of term reports to write...' She made a face at him.

'Boys all right?'

'They're fine, Bill. Doing quite well at

school, and actually enjoying every minute of it!'

'Money all right?'

Her eyes softened. 'Brother mine, you'll kill me with kindness before you've done! Yes, I'm managing very well...the rent's paid. My salary's just about enough to cover most things. We have enough to eat, and the twins haven't outgrown all their clothes yet. So what is there to worry about?'

'Holidays?'

Carol's smile faded a little. 'Yes, well—I thought I might send them on a pony-trekking holiday in Wales.... It's not too expensive...'

'And what about you?'

'I—er—think I'll wait and see how things work out...' She looked at Bill severely. 'And you're not to come up with any more pre-paid miracles! I won't have it!'

It was Bill's turn to laugh. 'Well, anyway— what's for supper? Shall I go down to the take-away?'

'No,' she frowned. 'Not yet anyway. You can tell me first what is on your mind.'

Bill looked astonished. 'What—?'

'There's no need to look so innocent...I know all the signs by now. What's bothering you?'

Bill sighed. 'Never could hide much from

you, could I? All right, then. It's Jake.'

'Jake Farrant? The one who's got my cottage?'

'That's the one.'

'What about him?'

'Well...I'm in a bit of a dilemma.... The thing is—he's ill...and I want to find out how he's managing, but I don't want to appear to be fussing unduly.'

'How ill?' asked Carol, seeing straight to the heart of the matter.

Bill was silent for a moment. Then he shook his head faintly and said: 'I think...it's about as bad as it could be...'

'I see...' She was looking at Bill now, with compassion and much kindness. 'You're very fond of him, aren't you?'

'Of course,' growled Bill. 'Old mate of mine.... Been together on assignments for years...'

'So—?' said Carol, after a pause. 'Where do I come in?'

Bill smiled. 'You're his landlady—I was wondering...couldn't you just...drop in to see how he is?'

'Bill dear—it's a hundred miles! I can't just "drop in" as you put it!'

Bill looked a trifle crestfallen. 'Well then— stay the night.'

'At the cottage? With your reluctant friend Jake who had gone away to *escape* from people? No thanks!'

Bill grinned. 'I don't think he'd be that reluctant!' Then he went on: 'No, but seriously —you were talking just now about the boys going to Wales.... Well, stay a night at the Farmer's Arms on the way. —I'll gladly—'

'No, you don't! You're at it again!' Carol glared at her brother. But she looked so outraged that he burst out laughing, and in a moment she was laughing, too. 'Honestly, Bill, you're incorrigible!'

'Yes, but it makes sense. I do need to find out how he is—and I don't want to distress him by asking! You could surely find a reason to call and see him—just for a few moments?' And when she still hesitated, he added in his most persuasive voice; *'Please?'*

Carol sighed and ran a hand through her hair. 'I hate you, Bill Franklyn. You know I can never say no to that pathetic face! All right, I'll go. But it'll have to be after the end of term...'

Before either of them could say any more, the twins burst into the room, squash racquets in hand, bringing with them an aura of sparkling energy and something of the freshness of the spring evening from the park, through which they had just been running madly to get home.

'Hi, Mum.... Hi, Uncle Bill,' they chorused, standing together and looking absurdly alike. 'What's new?'

They were both fairer than their mother, but their eyes were the same light-filled hazel. Only the set of their heads and the shape of their mouths was like their father's—firm and courageous, as Robert's had been till the day six years ago when a skidding lorry wiped him and his new car off the map...

But now the twins were twelve, and their mother, Carol, was beginning to look almost young again, and Bill's watchful eye wasn't nearly so necessary as it had been...

'New?' he said. 'Your birthday, for a start. I hadn't forgotten, in spite of what your mother thinks.... I brought one of you a camera and the other some binoculars. You'll have to fight it out between you.... Shall we go down and get something extra special to eat? I've brought a bottle of wine.'

'Great!' they said. 'Can't we get Chinese? Mum, can you bear Flied Rice?'

All at once, it was a party, and Bill clattered down the stairs with his two nephews, feeling absurdly cheerful and useful. It almost made him forget about Jake...

But Carol looked after him thoughtfully, and did not smile.

Jake stayed in bed a long time the next morning. Not because he was lazy, but because, to his horror, when he tried to get up, he couldn't.... There seemed to be no strength left in his body at all—and when he managed to haul himself upright and put his legs to the ground, they refused to hold him up and he fell over.

I won't be beaten! he said to himself, and crawled on hands and knees to the bathroom. There, he put his head under the cold tap and woke himself up.... After a time, the world steadied round him, and he heaved himself to his feet by holding on to the wash-basin...

This won't do, he thought. I can't go out with the boy if I'm going to collapse on his hands.... I've got to overcome this somehow...

After a little while, he managed to stagger back to bed, and lay there, thinking furiously. I suppose I'll have to see that doctor, he told himself...though I doubt if he can do much.... A sudden awful reluctance seized him...he didn't want any more hospitals and tests...he didn't want any more useless treatment.... Life was tranquil here, and he loved it...he wanted no disturbance, no interruption... The strange communion that was growing between him and the boy and the natural world around them was too fragile and too precious... He didn't want it spoilt by the sordid trappings of illness... No, he'd have to manage somehow on his own...

So he lay there a long time, waiting for his strength to return—and at last his legs felt firm enough to carry him downstairs to make a cup of tea.

It was a beautiful morning again. The sun was well up and the garden looked very inviting. The apple tree near the shed was suddenly a mass of pink blossom. Even his lettuces were growing in the newly turned earth of his vegetable plot...and there was a clump of white narcissi nodding at him by his own back door. He carried his mug of tea in one hand and went to sit on the step.

For a time he just dreamed in the sun, idly watching the bees at work on the yellow forsythia at his door. There was a rather battered looking butterfly, too...a peacock, he thought. Bracken had told him they sometimes overwintered indoors and came out, looking shabby, in the spring. The colours on its wings were a bit faded, and the edges looked ragged—but it was still lovely to look at. What did it do all winter? he wondered. Sleep? *When a creature is tired—it rests*, said Bracken's lilting voice in his head. Yes, he agreed. I am resting...I know what I have to do...it will be all right if I rest...

After a time, he became aware that the blackbird was not singing on the pear tree, but making its furious alarm call and flying about in little bursts of panic all over the front garden. So was his mate, the hen blackbird, and her danger call was even more strident and more urgent. 'Quick!' they seemed to be saying to him. 'Come quick! We need help! Help!'

'I wish I could understand you,' he said and found he had spoken aloud. 'Bracken would know, wouldn't he? What's wrong? What can I do?'

Their fierce cries got louder, and their dives to and fro over his head got more and more frantic, till he got up from the step and went rather groggily round the path towards his shed. *Lived in your shed all winter,* said Bracken's voice. *Gotta mate now…and a nest… more mouths to feed….* Where? he wondered. In the shed? Or above it, in the ash tree?

And then he saw the source of the trouble. A large, handsome black and white magpie was sitting on the roof of the shed, looking up at the neat little bunch of twigs in the fork of the tree.

'Robber! Egg-stealer!' screamed the blackbirds. 'Thug! Mugger! Go away! Our eggs! Our family! Help!'

He understood them now quite clearly.

'All right!' he said. 'I'll get rid of him. Don't worry! He's only a big bully. I'll soon scare him off!'

But the blackbirds screamed even louder.

He stooped down to look inside the shed for any sort of implement, and found an old tin tray lying in the corner. Seizing the little wood-chopping hatchet in one hand, he started beating furiously on the tray, and walked out of the shed, still beating, and stood right under the magpie on the roof.

'Clang! Clang! Clang! Clang!' The sound reverberated round the garden with sudden violence. The magpie shot up into the air and sailed away on outraged wings. He followed it slowly down the garden path, still beating, till he saw it disappear into the woods below. (I must be mad! he thought. I wonder what a passing stranger would think!)

Behind him, the blackbirds were still uttering their alarm call—but it was less shrill now. They fussed and clucked round for a bit, and then the hen bird flew up on to the roof of the shed, disappeared over the far side, and approached her nest from beyond. He saw her dark head grow still as she settled quietly down on her eggs...

The male blackbird still clucked a little, flashing his yellow beak in the sun.... Then he flew up into the pear tree, quite close to Jake's head, and let out a shrill little burst of song…

'OK, OK,' said Jake. 'So it's all right now. He's gone…'

The blackbird cocked his head on one side and looked at him out of a bright black eye. Then he let out another joyous trill.

'No need to thank me,' said Jake, smiling. 'Any time!'

But he was exhausted by this small incident…. He sat on the step again for a long time in the sun, waiting for strength to return…

After a bread-and-cheese lunch—the minimum of effort—he decided he ought to walk up the lane to his car and make an attempt to see the local doctor. Mrs Willis had told him the surgery times—he knew when he should get there. But when he stood at the bottom of the lane, it seemed to stretch for ever, and its curve was frighteningly steep.

I can't get up there! he thought. It's much too far! All the same, he started walking slowly up the path. Sunlight filtered through the leaves and dappled the stones with gold at his feet…and a yellow-hammer darted before him in and out of the hawthorn hedge as he approached. Even this small lane is full of life, he thought…beautiful and secret…. How many small birds have their nests here, I wonder?

And how many flowers and trees have their roots deep down in this stony soil? What small creatures are there, going about their daily business in this dappled shade?

He had reached this point in his reflections, when his strength suddenly gave out.... The trees, the hedgerows, the grassy banks of the lane and the stony path seemed to spin into a whirling spiral of colour, and then rise up and hit him. Sighing, he sank into a heap in the middle of the lane...

Jim, the postman, was coming down the lane on his bicylce, carrying a letter for the new man in Mrs Cook's cottage, when he saw the dark heap lying in front of him on the stony path...

He leapt off his bicycle, and went to stoop over the tired jumble of limbs, saying anxiously: 'Lordy, we're in trouble here, and no mistake.... Are you all right, Mr Farrant, sir? No, of course 'e isn't! Mr Farrant! Can you hear me?'

Dimly, Jake heard the voice calling him. He turned his head and muttered tiredly: 'All right in a minute...'

'Take you time...' said Jim. 'Here, let me help you up...that's it...gently does it.... Feeling a bit groggy, were you?'

'A bit....' said Jake faintly. 'The lane...too steep!'

'Ah, you can say that again! All the pitches round here are too steep...leastways, for a bicycle.... Shall I give you a hand back to the cottage?'

'Thanks...'Jake was upright now, but weaving on his feet. 'Better now...'

'O' course you are...just lean on me.... Tell you what, you sit on my bicycle and I'll wheel you down! Don't look fit to walk yet, to me!'

So they progressed, unsteadily, wobbling from side to side, until they got to the cottage gate. Here, Jake almost fell off the bicycle, and Jim the postman put a sturdy arm round him and helped him into the cottage.

'You'd better sit down,' he said, lowering Jake into the nearest chair. 'And rest awhile.... Anything I can get you?'

Jake smiled hazily. 'No thanks...except...a glass of water?'

The postman fetched it and stood looking at Jake anxiously while he drank it. 'Should I fetch the doctor?' he asked.

Jake shook his head. 'No thanks...there's nothing—I mean, it's not necessary...I'll be fine now...just overdid it a bit. Silly of me...'

The postman looked unconvinced. 'Well— I'm not sure he oughtn't to have a look at you...all on your own here, as you are...'

Jake's smile was growing less dim. 'Honestly,

I'm feeling much better now…I'm sorry I gave you such a fright…'

Jim grinned back. 'That's all right. Postmen are used to shocks! I once found an old lady in her nightgown lying in the coal shed!'

'Was she all right?'

'Oh yes…after a trip to hospital…spry as a cricket in a day or two…. Hadn't been eating properly, they said.' His face grew serious momentarily: 'Old folks are a problem, you know…especially out here in the country.'

'They're a problem anywhere,' said Jake, and thought, painfully: and so am I—or I'm becoming one.

Aloud, he said: 'There's a can of beer in the larder, if you'd like one?'

'Not me!' said Jim, his grin widening. 'Not on my rounds…I'd soon be falling off my bike on all the corners!' He took another assessing look at Jake, and added suddenly: 'That reminds me—I was bringing you a letter…. Here you are.'

Jake took it from him and looked at it curiously. No-one knew where he was except Bill Franklyn, and this was not Bill's writing.

'I'll be off now, then,' said Jim, 'if you're sure you're all right?'

'Yes—perfectly,' Jake assured him. 'And thanks for all your help…'

'You know,' said Jim, as he turned to the door, 'I was just thinking.... That's your car at the top of the lane, isn't it?'

'Yes.'

'Well, if you brought it down through the farm lane beyond the field...it's not so steep and not half so rough for the car as this one, and you'd only have to walk across that one field, just beyond your garden wall.... I'm sure Stan Bayliss wouldn't mind...'

'Is he the farmer?'

'Yes...I'll ask him, if you like. I'm going on there now...'

'Would you? That'd certainly save me a lot...'

Jim the postman nodded briskly. 'No point in wasting energy,' he said, and winked at Jake. Then he went out, leaving the cottage door open to the sunny garden, climbed on his bike and rode away.

But when he got back to the village after his rounds, he told Mary Willis at the Sub-Post Office all about it, and she agreed with him that Dr Martin ought to be told.

So, that evening, when Jake was feeling a bit stronger and had decided to type up some notes, there was a brisk knock on his door and a cheery voice called out: 'Can I come in?'

Dr Martin was getting on for sixty and had

been looking after this widespread country practice for most of his working life. He loved this countryside, and he loved the slow-moving, quiet people who lived in it. He even (almost) loved the summer visitors who invariably got ill a long way from home, though they mostly only needed reassuring until they could get back to see their own trusted GP. He was a squarish, patient, bluff kind of man, with keen blue eyes surrounded by lots of smile wrinkles, and a warm, firm voice that instilled confidence with every syllable.

But this visitor, he could see at a glance, was not the ordinary tourist with tummy trouble.... This was clearly something much more serious.

'Dr Martin,' he said, smiling and holding out his hand, 'I hope I'm not intruding? Jim Merrett was worried about you...'

Jake got to his feet and grasped the outstretched hand. 'It was good of you to come. I tried to tell him it wasn't necessary—'

Dr Martin was looking at him quietly, and when he spoke his voice was surprisingly gentle. 'Do you mean unnecessary—or not much use?'

Jake laughed. Then he gestured to a chair. 'Please sit down.... As a matter of fact, I was coming to see you when I—er—'

'Collapsed?'

Jake sighed. 'I suppose you'd call it that...'
He glanced up and saw those bright blue eyes
fixed on him in careful assessment. There was
knowledge in them already and sympathy.

'You see,' went on Jake, with some diffidence, 'I already know what's wrong....
There's nothing much anyone can do about it...
I've come to terms with that by now.... This
place—' He looked round at the cottage affectionately and his eyes strayed to the darkening
garden beyond. '—it's already taught me a lot
about acceptance.'

The doctor nodded. 'Yes...this countryside
does that.'

'But—you see, I came down here expecting
to be solitary...I mean to shut myself away and
let things take their course.... But now—I'm
enjoying myself so much...and I'm making use
of other people when I meant not to...so I want
to keep active as long as I can!' He looked
almost shame-faced. 'You wouldn't believe
how sorry for myself I was when I came—but
I'm not any more...I've discovered I'm damned lucky to be alive and living here.... The only
question is, can you help me to keep going...
just a bit longer?'

Dr Martin sighed. 'Hadn't you better tell me
where you stand?'

Jake hesitated. 'I've...got my medical notes

from Andrew Lawson...'

'Lawson!' said Dr Martin, startled. 'You do move in exalted circles! He's a very great man these days!'

Jake smiled. 'Yes, I know...but we've been friends for years—since he was a young house-man and I was a young reporter, in fact—so he doesn't mind dealing with me.... In any case, I've been abroad so much, I never really had an ordinary English GP, I wasn't home long enough...'

'So—what happened to you?'

'It was cancer, of course.... They diagnosed a tumour about three years ago. I had a lot of treatment, including an operation and both radiotherapy and chemotherapy, and every-thing seemed to be cleared up. We all thought I was cured....It took a longish time, of course, and my hair fell out and I had to wear a wig for a bit, but otherwise I seemed to be OK. I managed to keep quiet about it, too...only my boss knew I wasn't actually away on a job at the time...And even he only thought I'd been ordered a long rest! And after a while I went back to work and went on with my normal life... Then—a couple of months ago—I collaps-ed in the street. I was in London at the time, so I went back to see Andrew and he took me in for tests. It seems I have advanced leukemia.... Too bad now to correct...it's only a matter of time...'

David Martin nodded. He wasted no time in murmurs of commiseration. 'Much pain?'

'Oh—a bit of bone pain...it comes in bouts.... I know now in advance, so I can take enough painkillers to keep it within bounds.... But it's this sudden weakness that defeats me...'

He glanced at the doctor, trying to sound steady and practical—unaware that a wild, frightened appeal was looking out of his eyes.

'There's so much I want to do—' he said. 'So much to see...and so little time.... I just wondered if...there was anything I could take when I felt weak.... I don't want to be a nuisance, you see. I don't want to feel...that I can't risk going out...in case...'

'In case you fall down in a heap in the lane and Jim Merrett the Postman has to rescue you!'

'Exactly...'

Dr Martin considered. 'I hear you have been exploring a bit with our young gypsy, Bracken...'

Jake nodded. 'That's one of the reasons I was worried...'

'Yes. I see your point.' He sighed again, wishing—not for the first time—that he could work miracles. 'Well, before I make any suggestions, could I see those notes?'

'Of course.' Jake got up to fetch them, moving much more steadily than in the morning. He found the packet lying on the table by his typewriter, and beside it, the unopened letter that Jim the Postman had brought. He had felt so weak and faint after Jim had gone that he had laid it down and forgotten all about it. 'Here you are,' he said. 'Read all about it...' and then remembered that only a newspaper man would laugh at that joke.

But David Martin smiled at him very kindly and began to leaf through the notes.

Jake ran a finger down his letter and ripped it open.

'Dear Mr Farrant,' it said. 'First let me introduce myself. I am Bill Franklyn's sister, Carol—and your landlady. And by the way, thanks for the rent which Bill passed on to me.

'I am writing to say that the boys and I are coming down to Gloucestershire for a night on the way to a pony-trekking holiday in Wales—and I wondered whether you would mind if I called to collect a few things I put away in the spare room? Bill said you valued your privacy, so if you would rather be left in peace, please say so, and we will not trouble you. We will be at the Farmer's Arms for the night of the 26th April. If you would be kind enough to leave a message there—or at the village shop with Mary Willis—it will be sure to find me.

'I do hope you are enjoying the cottage and Gloucestershire. Yours sincerely, Carol Cook. P.S. The boys say their fishing rods are in the spare room cupboard and you can use them if you like!'

'Mm...' said David Martin, a note of respect and compassion in his deep voice. 'You do seem to have been through the mill. Now, what I suggest is this—I'll take a blood sample with me now, and I'll let you know the results when the lab have dealt with it. In the meantime, I'll get a few pills made up and send them down via Jim Merrett. He often acts as my courier, too. As for practical precautions: you must be careful of outside infections—though you're not likely to run into many down here! But you've practically no red blood cells left to fight with, so take care! And be careful of falls of any kind—even in the lane!' He grinned. 'You'll bruise much too easily, and you may set up internal haemorrhaging.... But the chief and most important thing is to know your own limitations...don't do anything too strenuous, don't take unnecessary risks, don't walk too far...' He stopped, seeing Jake's mutinous expression, and his own eyes softened. 'Yes, I know...it seems foolish to be too cautious....

But you may give yourself a chance of a little longer that way. I wish I could be more positive—and more optimistic—but beyond that, all I can really say is, rest as much as you can bear to—and enjoy yourself in between! Even a rest period can have its compensations, you know!' He laid a kind hand on Jake's arm. 'If things get really bad—we'll help you through, you know that.'

Jake nodded. 'I'm not afraid of that part.... It's just...staying mobile.... I suddenly looked up that lane today—it looked enormous— and I thought: I can't do it! I've never thought that before, and it scared me...I didn't know I was such a coward.'

'You're no coward,' said Dr Martin brusquely. 'I hope I'd face your future with as much courage and equanimity. Roll up your sleeve, will you?'

Jake obliged.

When David Martin was ready to go, Jake said suddenly: 'Do you know the owner of this cottage?'

'Carol Cook? Yes, why?'

'This letter says she's coming down...I wondered what she was like?'

David Martin grinned. 'She's a very nice woman—and a brave one. She has twin boys— her husband was killed in a car crash some six or seven years ago. She's a teacher, and she's bringing up those boys on her own. Apart from that, she has a consuming passion for this countryside—and so do I!' His smile grew wider. 'I think you'll like her.... She won't fuss.'

Jake nodded, surprised that the doctor knew at once what would trouble him about any outside visitors.

'Don't become too much of a recluse,' said David Martin, smiling. 'There's no need to be prickly, you know. People round here are naturally friendly, but they'll respect your privacy.... No-one'll bother you unless you ask them! By the way, do you play chess?'

'Chess?' Jake sounded bewildered. 'Yes, I do. Why?'

'Can't find anyone round here to play with. You might take pity on me some time?'

Jake almost began to refuse—but he caught the gleam of mischief in David Martin's eye, and smiled instead. 'Yes. I'd like that.'

'I'll let you know...' said the doctor, as he left. 'So you can go on gallivanting with that young scamp, Bracken, with a clear conscience!' He seemed, Jake thought, to be referring to more than just a game of chess.

'But take it easy, mind!'

'Yes,' agreed Jake dutifully. 'I will.'

Late that evening, while Jake was reading quietly in his chair, there was a soft knock at the door. When he went to open it, Bracken stood there on the step.

'I heard you wasn't well...' he said. 'I brought you some honey.'

'Will you come in?'

He hesitated, and then sat down on the step. 'You won't be cold, though?' he asked, looking up into Jake's face anxiously.

'Heavens, no. It's a warm spring night...'

'Are you better now?'

'Much better, thanks.'

'Did I take you too far last night?'

'No, of course not...it wasn't that, Bracken. I just...sort of...felt a bit dizzy, that's all...'

The boy looked at him levelly. 'Strength's not an easy thing to judge, is it?'

'No...that's the trouble...' He smiled at him. 'Would you like some tea?'

'If you'll have some.'

'Yes, I shall.... I've got something to tell you about your blackbirds, too.'

They sat together on the step, talking peacefully. Presently Bracken pointed to the smoky moon beyond the branches of the pear tree and said: 'There'll be a change tomorrow...but I think the morning'll be fine still...' He turned to look at Jake again. 'Maybe you should rest another day?'

Another day, thought Jake. And another... and how many more?

'No,' he said. 'Let's not waste the fine weather.... We needn't go too far.'

Bracken smiled happily. 'That's all right then. But I won't come too early! And by the way, the bird's getting on fine.'

'I'm glad of that,' said Jake. 'He looked almost a goner to me yesterday afternoon...'

'You'd be surprised what awful things they can put up with,' said Bracken. 'I think it's a kind of...will to live—if they want to badly enough, they can go on much longer than you'd think...' He did not look at Jake, but his voice was soft and full of gentle knowledge.

'Yes,' agreed Jake, very quietly. 'I believe you're right.'

The next morning they crossed the hares' field and went down into the pearly mists of the valley. The slope was gentler here—Jake suspected that Bracken had chosen it for that reason.

On the way down, Bracken turned aside into a little hidden field enclosed in honey-coloured drystone walls, and said: This is where the snake's heads grow...'

'The what?'

Bracken took him by the hand and led him over to a clump of flowers, their speckled heads nodding in the wind.

'Snake's head fritillaries, they're called...' he said. 'They only grows in this one field round here. It's a kind of secret...and all the villagers keep quiet about it, see? They're rare now, these are—though there used to be lots of 'em once...'

Jake knelt down in the spring grass to look at them more closely. He saw then that their pinky-purple mottled heads did indeed look like a snake's jewelled head with its special scaly markings...

'Lovely...' he murmured. 'So tall and graceful.... How many d'you think there are here?'

'Almost a hundred in this field...I counted 'em once. There used to be more, too...but I think the spray got to 'em.... And that's all that's left of 'em now, in this bit of countryside at least...'

Jake touched one swinging motley-patterned bell with his finger gently, and got to his feet. 'Thanks for showing me—I'll keep their secret for them.'

Bracken smiled. 'Knew you would. Wouldn't have shown you, else!'

Jake laughed. And they went on down the

mossy slopes of the valley.

'Even cowslips is getting rare now,' said Bracken reminiscently, stooping to look at one growing on the short turf at his feet. 'We used to make cowslip balls when I was little and sell them by the roadside....' He put his face down close to a clump of them and sniffed. 'They're the freshest-smelling things I know...'

Jake stooped to smell them too—and they went on side by side, their feet making no sound on the springy turf.

At last they came out a little below the big lake where the wild swans lived, and followed the stream down a series of smaller, deeper pools and shallow falls. At the deepest of these—a dark oval surrounded by tangled alders and willows—Bracken stopped.

'Might see the old grey heron down here.... D'you see them taller willows over yonder? There's a heronry in there. You can hear them calling sometimes—they make a lot of noise when they get talking!'

He drew Jake down on the flowery bank among the sedges and fragrant meadowsweat at the water's edge.

As Jake settled beside him, there was a sudden wind of movement in the willows and a great grey-white ghost flapped heavily into the air, almost at their feet. A cry, much harsher and stronger than the little coot's voice from the far end of the pool, rang out over the water as the beautiful bird rose into the air and planed effortlessly away to the clump of willows round the heronry.

'Old grey heron...' said Bracken softly, 'there you go!'

Jake watched, breathless, as the grey ghost-bird seemed to hover a moment above the willow trees and then sank out of sight behind their garnet branches—now glowing like jewels in the first rays of the early sun...

'Lord of the Marshes, they call him...' murmured Bracken. 'But the swans is prouder...'

The heron called again, harshly, from the willows, and was answered by several fierce, hard voices in reply. There was a brief flapping and stirring of wings, and then silence returned, except for the small excited 'Krrk!' of the coot among the reeds.

But that was not the end of the day's miracles. From the swaying tendrils of willow branches which the heron's flight had disturbed, there suddenly appeared a dark brown, questing head—alert and intelligent—looking round without haste to see if any danger threatened his small domain.

'An otter!' exclaimed Bracken very softly. 'A real live otter! I don't believe it!'

Silently, the two of them watched the sturdy little creature as it made its way through the reeds like a slim, energetic dog, and finally slid without a splash into the water.

Once there, it swam happily round the pool, diving and splashing, playing in the early morning sunshine. At one point it came quite close to them and Jake scarcely dared to breathe in case he scared it...but the wet, clever head reared up out of the water to look at these two strange interlopers on its territory. It seemed to be laughing at them a little—quite unafraid.... After a few moments of looking at them, the little otter clearly decided they were harmless, and began to dive and play again almost as if it were giving a special display for their benefit.

How beautiful it is in the water, thought Jake. Such perfect balance and grace—that dark wet skin as supple as silk. And how friendly and full of intelligence those bright eyes are, observing us from the middle of the pool.... He wanted to reach out a hand to it in greeting...but he knew he must not.

They stayed there a long time among the grasses and flowers at the pool's edge, watching the young otter play until he gave one final, exuberant swirling dive and disappeared into the reed bed at the top end of the pool...

'Where will he go?' asked Jake in a spell-bound voice.

'Probably upstream to the lake,' said Bracken. 'Though I've never sen him here before... I thought they'd all gone long ago...' He paused, thinking about it tranquilly. 'He might be a tame one from somebody's private lake.... There's a lot of big houses round about...they might easily keep a pet otter. He seemed extra friendly, didn't he?'

Jake agreed, smiling. 'He almost seemed to be laughing at us!'

'I expect he was. We must look very funny to him. All legs and no tail! He probably thinks we're awful clumsy.'

Jake felt awful clumsy himself, remembering that lissom wet body turning in the water...

'The bird, now,' said Bracken dreamily, 'the kestrel—he needs the sky to play in.... He'd sink like a stone in the water. I s'pose a man looks best walking upright.... But he can swim as well...'

'He can't fly, though!'

'Not by himself, he can't,' agreed Bracken, laughing. And then fell to watching the flight of a lone wild duck crossing from one pool to another, clean-cut against the morning sky.

'I sometimes wish I was a bird...' he said.

So do I, thought Jake. A bird, flying straight

for the sun, free of this heavy, mortal body...
with all the wide sky to play in...

'Come on,' said the boy gently. 'There's
more sky on the way back!'

That afternoon, as Bracken had predicted, the
weather broke. A grey pall of rain swept over
the valley, drenching the trees, drowning the
young flowers in the grass. Jake watched,
fascinated, from the cottage windows as the
light changed and grew dimmer, and a silvery
nimbus seemed to clothe every dripping leaf
and blade of grass.

As suddenly as it had come, the rain ceased
about teatime, and a small, brilliant rainbow
clung to the hills as the sun came through the
rain clouds.

The cuckoo called and called in the wet
woods, and a chorus of birds started up, including the blackbird who sat on the topmost
branch of the pear tree declaring his approval
of the new-washed world...

I must go out, thought Jake. It looks so green
and untouched...all the colours are brighter...

He was standing in his garden, gazing out
at the green beech woods when he heard the
whizz of a bicycle in the lane. Jim Merrett, the
postman, got off at his gate and came hesitantly
up the path.

'Evening, Mr Farrant. Dr Martin sent these down from the chemist for you…. And I had a word with Stan Bayliss at Wood End Farm— he says it's quite all right to use his lane, and if you give me the keys and trust him with your car, he'll run it down for you this evening and leave the keys in it for you to collect?'

'That sounds a wonderful idea,' said Jake. 'I'll fetch them for you.'

When he came back, he also had an envelope in his hand. 'I wonder…do you go anywhere near the Farmer's Arms on your travels?'

Jim laughed. 'Most days! And most nights, when I gets the chance!'

'Then—d'you think you could leave this for Mrs Cook when she comes at the weekend? The landlord will see she gets it, won't he?'

'Course he will…. At least, his missus will— Joe might forget!'

They stood at the gate talking for a moment or two, and then Jim got on his bike and went off to see Farmer Stan Bayliss at Wood End…

Later that evening, Jake thought he would stroll across the hares' field and see if his car had arrived. He was a bit worried about disturbing the hares. Would they be frightened away altogether? But he walked across the new wet grass and saw nothing stirring. He noticed, though, that the field was now starred with pale

119

yellow cowslips. At least they're not scarce here yet, he thought.... Their sweet scent rose to him in the air as he walked...

He climbed the gate at the far end of the field and found himself in another leafy lane like his own, but with a gentler slope and a less stoney surface. And there, neatly parked on a patch of grass at the side, was his car.

The keys were still in the ignition, and on the driver's seat was a package and a note which said: 'Hope this will be alright for you. It won't be in the way if you leave it here. The missus sent you some home-made cheese. S. Bayliss.'

Jake was touched. He had done nothing to deserve all these small kindnesses. He had even been morose and stand-offish when he first came.... And yet the quiet people of this valley seemed determined to help him one way or another.... He felt ashamed of his own self-centred pride and independence...why shouldn't they be friendly if they wanted to? He ought to be grateful—not afraid of kindness.

Or pity...

That was it, of course. He was afraid of pity. That's why he had run from all his friends and hidden himself away in this solitary place...

Only, it wasn't solitary at all...and it seemed he was not going to have it all his own way.... Especially if Bracken had any say in the matter!

He smiled a little, thinking of the boy, and strolled back across the field with his car keys in his pocket and the home-made cheese in his hand.

When he got back, Bracken was in his garden, hammering away at some sort of wooden frame. He looked up and smiled at Jake, and then said a little shyly: 'Will you mind? I'm making a kind of flying cage for the bird up here. He needs to exercise that damaged wing...he can't go free yet. He'd never last a day without something attacking him...'

'Why here?' asked Jake, not at all put out. 'Why not...at your camp?'

'It's the dogs,' said Bracken. 'They bark so...they scare him to death...'

Jake went to look at the bird, who sat sullenly in his cage and glared at Jake with a fierce, angry eye. Yes, my friend, thought Jake, you are proud and independent, too...aren't you? And you hate people trying to help you don't you? I know just how you feel...

The bird looked at him, scowling, and blinked his yellow eyes. He hated his captivity, hated the world, hated everyone!

'Have you given him a name yet?' asked Jake.

'Yes,' said Bracken, still hammering. 'Sky... because he belongs there.... I thought of it this morning when we was talking...'

'Sky?' said Jake to the bird. 'Yes, it suits you. Don't worry, my friend. It won't be long now. Poor, grounded Sky...be patient!'

Bracken had brought a roll of chicken wire with him, and now he erected the wooden frame he had been making, fixed it to the four posts he had already driven into the ground near the oldest apple tree behind the shed, and began to stretch the wire over the top and round the sides...

'Here, let me give you a hand,' said Jake. Together, they worked at the long cage until it was safe and enclosd. Bracken had carefully arranged it so that one gnarled branch of the apple tree stretched inside the wire, and he had also put an old twisted tree-trunk inside for a perch and scratching post.

'It's a regular little aviary,' said Jake, pleased with the result. 'I hope he likes it.'

'He won't,' said Bracken, hammering in the last of the staples. 'But it'll be better than nothing. At least he can fly about a bit...I want that wing to get strong.... He's got to be able to ride a storm and lie on the wind before he goes...'

Jake smiled at Bracken's poetic phrase. 'How long will that be, do you think?'

'Dunno...maybe a couple more weeks.... It's

healing nicely now. I thought it might go septic with all those holes and bits of lead shot...but it didn't. I kept bathing it with them herbs...it seemed to work...'

He turned to Jake, still a little shy about it. 'I ought to have asked you first...but I knew you wouldn't mind...'

'How will I feed it?'

'I'll come up morning and night...and I'll leave you some for mid-day. He likes raw meat...or a mouse or two. He ought to have a bit of fur and bones soon, for roughage, like. Don't you worry, though, I'll see to his supplies.'

'I'm glad of that!' said Jake, grinning. 'I don't think I'd be much good at catching mice and voles...'

'Did you know you'd got a *hotchi-witchi* in your garden?'

'A what?'

'A hedgehog...I found him curled up under that bush.'

'What did you call it?'

'A *hotchi-witchi*. That's our name for him...'

He took Jake over to the hawthorn bush and parted the thick thorny branches with a slim brown hand. Curled up underneath on a comfortable bed of dead leaves was a round brown ball, the quills lying flat and smooth, the little

snout tucked into its own soft, furry under-
side...

'There he is,' said Bracken, smiling. 'Little
hotchi-witchi, fast asleep....'

'Would Sky eat him?'

Bracken laughed. 'He'd have a job—with all
them prickles. No, a *hotchi-witchi* is too big for
a kestrel. Badgers eat them, though...they turn
'em inside out...' He glanced at Jake a trifle
warily. 'So do gypsies—they like them in a
stew.... But I won't eat 'em...they're such
friendly little souls...' His cheerful grin returned. 'Anyways, it's good luck to have one in
your garden—even a gypsy wouldn't harm him
in his own camp. So I hope he stays...if you
put down some bread and milk, he might...'

He went over to the bird's cage and picked
it up gently. 'Come on now, you're going to
feel much better in here...'

But when he go to the little frame door in
the aviary, he turned to Jake and said, smiling:
'Would you like to let him out?'

Jake looked at the boy, knowing yet another
gift was being given. 'How shall I do it?'

'Just...go inside. Put the cage down on the
floor, and open the door...then come out
fast.... He won't attack you, though...he's still
much too sick and scared...'

Jake did as he was told. He set the small

wicker cage down on the ground and carefully slid the piece of stick out of the fastening on the door. Quietly, he pushed the door open, and then backed away, reached the wire, slipped through the opening and let Bracken close it quickly behind him. Then he stopped to look at what Sky would do.

At first the injured kestrel did nothing at all. He sat staring at the open cage door as if he did not believe in even partial freedom any more. Life was over, he seemed to say, with every drooping feather.... He would never reach the wild free air again... But then something about that square of extra light intrigued him, and he took a hesitant step forward on his thin, scaley yellow legs...one step...and then another...a curious, nervous, uneven hop, with the damaged wing dragging a little on the ground and a desperate hope beginning to dawn in his golden eyes. And then he was out. Suspiciously, he turned his head this way and that within its feathery mantle, and then he made a scrabbling, ungainly dash for the upright tree-stump—his wing still dragging pitifully along the ground.... But he managed to lift himself in a fluttering heave of long wing feathers on to the top of the tree-trunk perch, where he sat very still, upright and wary, surveying his new, wider world.

Suddenly, he uttered a strange, fierce 'Kee!' and hurled himself across the open space to the branch of the apple tree at the other end of the wire. For one awful moment, Jake thought he was going to dash himself to pieces against the wire itself...but his lurching, unsteady flight just upheld him till he reached the tree.

'That's it,' said Bracken approvingly. 'Try again...you'll soon get stronger...'

Then he went quietly into the wire enclosure and laid some pieces of meat on the tree stump. The young kestrel seemed to know Bracken was a friend. He did not even shrink away when the boy went up to his branch and laid one extra piece of meat at his feet...

'There you are,' said Bracken. 'One piece to make you hungry...the rest you must go over and get for yourself...'

Like Jake, he retreated through the gap and closed the frame door, fastening it with a twist of wire.

Sky turned his head and looked at Bracken hard. Then he uttered another harsh 'Kee-kee!' and flew lopsidedly down to his tree stump and stood over his food, wings forward protectively.

Satisfied, Bracken turned away. 'He'll be all right now for a bit...but when he's really ready to go—we'll know it, I can tell you!'

Jake laughed. 'I can believe it!'

'Will you be able to feed him like that, midday?'

'Yes, I think so...'

'I thought...' the boy was suddenly shy again, 'I thought maybe he'd be company for you...? And I think he gets lonely, too, alone in the *hatchintan* all day...'

Jake was smiling a little at the boy's anxious face. 'Yes, it's all right. I shall enjoy watching him get better.... Look, Mrs Bayliss sent me some cheese. Why don't we sit down and eat it?'

He fetched them both a hunk of bread, and at the same time put on his kettle for their ritual cup of tea.

'It's hard when things is hurt and you don't know how to help them...' said Bracken, with his eye on the bird.

'Yes,' murmured Jake, busy pouring tea. 'It is...'

'But letting them go is harder,' said the boy, in a voice as soft as spring rain.

★ ★ ★ ★

Manny Feldman was sitting at his desk looking at his own political report with a jaundiced eye, when a junior reporter came up to him and said: 'Is Bill Franklyn about?'

'No,' said Manny. 'Gone out somewhere.

127

Can I help?'

'There's a girl here—says she's Jake Farrant's daughter...'

Manny got up from his chair very swiftly. 'Where?'

The reporter gestured vaguely towards the end of the big newsroom, and Manny saw the blonde mane of hair glimmering by the door.

He went across at once. 'I'm Manny Feldman, remember me? I'm afraid Bill's out just now...can I do anything?'

The girl, Beth, looked at him coolly. 'Maybe...I wanted to ask him about my father.'

Manny looked round at the busy office and said in a friendly sort of voice: 'I think we'd better go out and have some lunch...'

The girl nodded, still cool and off-hand. But Manny fancied this was a front and she was a trifle nervous.

He took her to a quietish dive he knew and bought her a drink and a salad.

'Now,' he said. 'Tell me what's on your mind?'

The girl hesitated, and took a gulp of her drink. 'I felt...we were rather...off-putting the other day....If he's really ill, I mean...maybe there's something we ought to do?'

Manny shook his head. 'I don't think there's much we can do.... He's gone off on his own somewhere.'

Beth nodded. 'He always did that...especially if there was trouble.... But if—' she broke off and added in a small, hard voice: 'Ma is always talking about money. She doesn't need it, you know.... Her new boyfriend—the one you saw —is very rich, and she's going to marry him.... I mean, she won't need all that from Jake now...and he might need it himself?'

Manny looked down into his glass. 'He might.... What about you—and your brother?'

'Oh, I've got a job now—with a travel agent up here. I'm independent, thank God...' A brief almost friendly smile touched the cool mouth. 'And as for Charles—he has a grant, though he's always head over ears in debt...'

Manny said slowly: 'What exactly do you want to do?'

'I don't know.... Maybe...see him?'

He looked at her curiously. 'You don't know Jake very well, do you?'

She laughed. 'How could I? He was always away...and when he came home, he wasn't exactly made welcome.... He didn't like rows, so he stayed away even longer...'

Manny nodded. 'Makes sense.'

'It does, doesn't it? After the divorce, he used to take us out now and then...but I think he kept out of the way on purpose.'

Yes. I'm sure he did. Tug-of-love situations, are bad for kids—I've heard him say it!'

Beth grinned. 'I used to think he didn't care a damn about us.... Now I'm not so sure...'

Manny sighed. 'So...? We can't force him to see you...and I don't think you ought to descend on him unannounced.'

'No,' agreed Beth. 'But I wish—I mean, if things are that bad, I'd just like him to know I felt friendly...?'

'I don't know,' said Manny doubtfully. 'I'm not sure.... Human relationships usually hurt, one way of another. Maybe it would be wrong to saddle him with them now...he may be only too glad to be free of them...'

The girl looked suddenly young and confused. 'Yes...I hadn't thought of it like that. Perhaps I'm just being selfish...'

At this point a shadow fell across their table and Bill's voice said: 'Oh, there you are—mind if I join you?'

Manny's eyebrows went up, but he merely said: 'Your detective work is good.... Have a drink?'

Beth turned to Bill as if he had been part of the conversation all along. 'What do you think I should do?'

Bill stretched his long legs under the table and said flatly: 'Wait.'

The others looked at him, Manny with a faintly sardonic grin, Beth with a certain pleading in her gaze.

'Wait?' she asked. 'What for?'

'I've arranged for my sister to stop by and have a look at him...' said Bill. 'Casually— though I expect he'll smell a rat...'

Manny snorted.

'And if she reports that he's in an approachable mood, maybe Manny and I will go down to see him.... If—' he glanced at the girl, totally unbending at present, 'I say, *if* he shows any interest in family ties at all—I could possibly mention that you'd like to see him. He may refuse. And if he does, I'm afraid you must respect it.'

'Yes,' said Beth, sounding humble. 'I will...of course...'

'What about your brother?' asked Manny, who was feeling a little kinder than Bill, though not much.

'Charles?' Beth made a contemptuous face. 'He's like Ma—the only person that matters to him is Charles Farrant.... But if—that is, supposing Jake does want to see us...Charles never listens to me—but maybe he might to you?'

Bill nodded briskly. 'If it comes to that—I'll see him.' He made it sound like a threat.

Manny realised then that Bill was still deeply

angry about Jake's family and their attitude. And deeply upset abut Jake himself. Bill always sounded toughest when he was most upset.

Beth heard the note of suppressed anger in Bill's voice. She got to her feet and said abruptly: 'I know you think I'm a callous bitch like my mother. But—but will you let me know if there's anything I can do? If it would be of any help to him, I mean?'

Bill's expression softened a little. 'Yes,' he said. 'All right. Better give me your phone number, then. I take it you're living up here now?'

Beth nodded. For a moment she stood looking down at them, almost shyly. She's just a child, really, thought Manny. And absurdly like Jake when she smiles.

But Bill thought bitterly, now—when it's too late—she wants to get all friendly and sentimental. What's the use? It will only hurt Jake more.

'OK then—thanks,' said Beth somewhat awkwardly, and wrote down her phone number for Bill on a scrap of paper. 'I'll wait to hear from you...'

Bill did not answer, though Manny smiled at her—so she turned away and went out of the bar alone.

'A bit hard on her, weren't you?' said

Manny.

Bill swore a little. 'Now!' he said fiercely. 'Now, she asks! What of the years Jake might have had?'

'All the same...' said Manny judiciously, 'we don't know what he wants.... It may be better than nothing?'

'Better than nothing, my arse!' said Bill rudely. 'I'd like to wring their necks—the whole gold-plated, selfish lot of 'em!' But he knew, really, that he was only angry because his old friend Jake was dying, and he could do nothing to prevent it.

★ ★ ★ ★

The next morning, Jake got up without being woken by a shower of pebbles, and without feeling exceptionally weak, and went out to look at the bird.

On the way, he stopped to inspect the saucer of bread and milk he had put down for the hedgehog. It was empty. But there was no sign of Bracken's little *hotchi-witchi*...

It was still very early, but Sky was awake, sitting alert and belligerent on his perch, turning his head from side to side beneath the smooth russet mantle, looking out at the world with the same angry stare...

'I know,' said Jake aloud. 'You want to be free and away. It's hard to wait.'

Sky turned his head in Jake's direction. He seemed to be listening.

'Never mind,' Jake went on comfortingly. 'Never mind, Sky, my friend. One day, when your wing is strong again, you'll find the door open...and you'll be away up there...soaring and hovering, sky-diving and sailing on the wind...' He looked up, dreaming, at the limitless spring sky above his head. The bird was still staring at him attentively out of its golden eyes...but now it seemed to follow his gaze and tilted its head up to look through the wire mesh at the empty air above...

Jake could feel the longing in the folded wings...the ache and pull of freedom stirring within that frail body...

'It won't be long now...' he said softly. 'Not long. Try not to grieve, my friend...'

The bird looked at him fiercely, as if to say: What do you know about it? How do you know what it feels like to be cooped up in here, weak and useless...when all the wide sky is above me, taunting me with its wind-driven spaces where I used to fly free...free as thistle-down?

But Jake knew...yes, he knew.... And he sighed because he could not make the bird understand that it would soon mend and fly free…. Even though Jake would not.

'There's ways and ways of flying free…' said Bracken's voice at his elbow.

And when Jake turned to look at him in astonishment, he only smiled and added: 'Look, I've brought him his breakfast…some meat and a real mouse…'

They watched Sky fly across to the food, and fancied his wing was a bit stronger already— the crumpled feathers looked smoother and glossier in the morning light.

'He's mending,' said Bracken gently. 'He's getting on. Let's go and look at the morning…'

That day they did not go far. Bracken took him to a little hill and sat beside him in the spring sunshine, admiring the view.

'Over there—' he said, waving an arm at the distant beeches below yet another hill crest, 'is an old quarry where the kestrels nest…. I expect Sky will go there when he's older, looking for a mate…'

'What's it called?'

'Hawkswood Quarry…and that's Hawks-wood—the big wedge of beeches yonder…'

Jake was getting used to the lie of the land a bit by now. 'Isn't that the wood where the badgers' sett is, over there?'

Bracken nodded. 'The one we went to—yes.

There's others, though.... There's a big one the other side of Hawkswood...' He looked a little troubled, and Jake felt he knew him well enough now to ask why.

'What's the matter?'

The boy did not answer at first. He was gazing intently out at the farthest beech woods, frowning a little. 'I dunno...something one of the farmer's said.... Over there, tother side of the hill, there's one of them rich dairy herds... and the owner doesn't like badgers.... Says they're a risk to his cows...' He paused, still frowning, and squinted up at the sun, assessing the time. 'We used to work for him once—we had our *hatchintan* on his land—but he threw us out one day.'

'Why?'

The boy shrugged. 'He said he wanted the pasture...but it wasn't pasture we was on—only a bit of old scrub—and he never touched it after we left. I looked.'

He sighed. 'I guess he just didn't like gypsys, lots of people don't.... And he said the *jukels*—our dogs—weren't reliable. But they are!'

Jake was silent. He could see the pattern of the age-old war between the caravan-dwellers and the settlers...it never came to an end...

'So...?' he said at last. 'What's worrying you?'

Bracken hesitated. 'I just think...the badgers is threatened.... You can't make that man see reason...I think they're in for trouble...'

'What will he do? Dig them out?'

'Probably...or put the dogs in. Or drive them out and club them to death, or shoot them. Now that gassing's been made illegal, they'll think of other ways to get at them—even traps. Poor things, they're never safe for long...and there's nothing much I can do about it, either...' he muttered, sounding quite fierce and upset. 'I wish there was!'

He stayed still for a while, brooding and silent, looking out at the smiling countryside with sombre eyes.... But then he seemed to throw off anxiety and turned back to Jake, full of cheerful energy.

'Come on...there's a squirrel's drey down yonder in that oak...I often watch them going in and out.... They gets extra playful in the spring...'

They clambered down the little hill, their feet springy on the turf, and went into a leafy dip filled with young fern and cuckoo flowers.

'Keep still!' whispered Bracken. 'I think they'll come out if we wait...'

Presently, as he had predicted, the first grey squirrel appeared with a whisk of its bushy tail and a swift dart up the branch of the nearest tree. Following him, came another—equally swift and equally bushy-tailed—chasing its mate round and round the huge gnarled trunk of the oak tree. For a time they played hide-and-seek happily up and down and round about the ancient tree, leaping from branch to branch, hiding and pouncing, running vertically upwards and downwards—never seeming to falter or tire.... It was a glorious game, and they were entirely given to the joy of the moment...

But in a little while, one of the squirrels ran down the trunk on to the ferny grass and began to search for grubs...or last year's hazel nuts. It went on deeper and deeper into the young bracken, and the other squirrel soon followed it, running in little bursts of joyous speed—stopping and starting—frolicking in and out of the shadows...

But suddenly, behind them, Jake saw a creeping shadow...and one of the farm cats came into view, flattened against the ground, stalking the nearest squirrel.... Nearer and nearer it came—and the two squirrels, intent on their own business, paid no attention, did not even seem to see it coming.

Jake turned an anxious face to Bracken beside him. Surely they ought to do something? Surely they should warn these beautiful little creatures of the danger creeping up on them?

'She'll catch them!'

'Not she!' whispered Bracken, smiling. 'They're much too quick! Watch!'

Smooth as silk, the cat inched forward—swiftly she pounced on the unsuspecting squirrels.... But she pounced on air. With a whisk of tail and whisker they streaked like lightning for the tree—ran up the branches, and sat there, perched high up among the swaying leaves, looking down in cheeky triumph at the frustrated cat below.

Jake let out a sigh of relief. They were so swift and perky, so full of mischief...so much too pretty to be eaten by a cat!

Bracken laughed softly. 'Told you! A cat would never catch them!'

'They're so fast! Like quicksilver!'

Bracken nodded. 'Vermin, the farmers call them...say they chew the trees. But I like 'em, meself.... They're cheerful creatures—always playing hide-and-seek like that!'

He got up, smiling, and Jake followed him. The farm cat looked at them with flat green eyes and turned away in disgust.

'There's a horse fair at Stow tomorrow,' said Bracken, as they strolled back towards home. 'So I'll be wanted all day...I'll come up to feed Sky tonight, though.... D'you think you could manage him yourself tomorrow? I'll be back the day after...'

Jake nodded, pleased that Bracken would entrust Sky's welfare to him.

Bracken looked up at the roof of the cottage as they came in through the gate and said: 'You've got jackdaws nesting in the chimney... d'you mind? They're noisy birds—and you'll likely get a few extra twigs in your fire!'

Jake laughed. 'I don't mind—if they don't!'

'By the way,' added Bracken, with seeming carelessness, 'can you ride a *grai?*'

'Yes,' Jake said absently, his eyes on the noisy jackdaws. 'I used to ride a lot at one time...'

'Bare-back? We don't use saddles on ours...'

He paused, smiling. 'Mm...yes, I have ridden bareback...horses...mules...and donkeys... I mean, grass-larks!'

'You mean long-eared *grais!*'

They were laughing now.

'I even rode a camel once or twice—but that was horrible!'

Bracken grinned, but his eyes were thoughtful.

'Wonderful with *grais,* my Da is...' he murmured. 'Can tell what they're thinking, almost...'

'Like you can with birds.'

He glanced at Jake, unsmiling now. 'You can usually tell what creatures is thinking,' he said, 'if you cares about them enough!'

Jake was silent, realising almost with terror how close his thoughts marched with the boy's these days...

'Yes...' he murmured at last. 'So you can...'

Jake went out to feed Sky by himself at midday. He followed the same procedure as Bracken—putting one tempting piece of meat close to the bird, and the rest as far away as possible...so that the damaged wing would get the maximum exercise...

Sky watched him, head on one side, seeming as angry and unapproachable as ever. When Jake had left the cage, the young kestrel let out a sudden sharp 'Kee!' and flew across to the new supply of food with an almost-balanced swoop.

'That's better,' said Jake. 'Keep trying!'

Sky stood with his two feet clutching the chunks of meat, his wings hunched forward, looking at Jake with the same baleful stare. Then he stooped his head and tore at the meat with his cruel beak.

For the first time, he looked what he was—a wild, savage bird of prey, compact and deadly —and somehow beautiful in his fierce, unbending pride...

Yes, thought Jake, you're getting better....

Your self-respect is coming back...you really look like a fighter now...

He went away and left the bird alone—sure somehow that it preferred to eat in solitude...

The rain came back in the afternoon and shrouded the valley in silver mist. But towards evening, the clouds lifted and the sun came out, laying long shadows on the hills and lighting the wet leaves with sudden radiance.

Jake went out to have a look at his garden and found Bracken stooping over his vegetable patch. As he went across to him, a blue-black shadow swooped and darted over his head, and he looked up to see the sky alive with wings.

'Yes,' said Bracken, smiling up at them joyously. 'They're back! The swallows are back! Summer's on the way!'

Summer already? thought Jake—and sternly repressed the small lurch of terror that assailed him. He looked up at the dark wings cleaving the sky, the long forked tails streaming out behind, the small white throats gleaming in the dusk.... Yes! he said, his heart lifting to their darting flight. You are beautiful, you carefree, high-flying wanderers—and I shall admire every swirl and dive while I can...and take no thought for the morrow! Welcome home!

'Let's go and feed Sky,' said Bracken, close

to him. He'll be sadder than ever, with all them wings above his head...'

The hares were out in the field when Jake and Bracken came back from the bird's pen. They stopped to watch the grey-brown shapes running and twisting and leaping over the cowslips in the short spring grass.... But all at once the sharp crack of a shot rang out from across the field, and the playful creatures suddenly froze, and then scattered wildly, streaking across the open ground to the safety of the dark hollows beneath the hedge.

Jake drew a swift breath. 'They *can't* shoot them!'

'Oh yes, they can!' said Bracken grimly. 'A nice tasty dinner, hares is...and you can get good money for 'em in the shops...'

Jake looked at him. 'You wouldn't—?'

'Oh, I wouldn't! But then I'm soft about animals! My people would eat hare, though— any day! And *hotchi-witchis*, too!' He sighed. 'It's a rough old world. There's Sky, now ...he'd eat a young leveret, if he could get one. And he'd eat a mole—or a mouse—or a rat even...lots of vermin, he'd kill. And yet someone shot him...' He looked up at the darkening sky above him. The swallows were still high up, chasing insects on the wing. 'Even they eat living things...you can't be too fussy, really, can you?' He smiled at Jake. 'If you grieved at everything that's killed, you'd be crying all day long!'

Jake nodded, smiling back.

It was nearly dark now, and the last of the old moon was climbing low over the horizon, hiding behind the crowns of the beech trees...

By common consent, they paused to watch it rise, and then Jake went in to put his kettle on.

'Tomorrow,' said Bracken softly from the step, 'it's going to be wet...I can smell rain on the wind.... You won't be missing much!'

Jake laughed, and brought him his mug of tea.

In the morning when Jake came down, he found that Bracken had been and gone. There were two packages on the step, and a note written in a clear, painstaking hand. 'I've fed Sky and left you some for 2 more feeds. The cake is for you. Back tomorrow. B.'

Jake opened the first packet and found a screw of paper wrapped in cool dock leaves, containing some chunks of raw meat and two small mice. The other package contained a large wedge of golden-yellow sesame cake. Smiling, Jake carried both packets inside and

144

put Sky's food away on a cool larder shelf.

He was tired this morning, and the alarming weakness had come back...so he took one of the doctor's new pills and tried to pretend that he didn't feel too bad...

It was a grey, wet morning, with a heavy drenching mist hanging over the valley and pressing down on the hills. The sky itself seemed to have come down lower, and Jake felt stifled, as if all the air had been cut off from the world by the low ceiling of cloud...

He went out to have a look at Sky, and found the young kestrel sulking bitterly, with his head turned aside, hidden under his good wing.

'I don't blame you,' said Jake. 'That's how I feel, too...but the sun will come back, you know.... And so will Bracken...'

Sky did not stir.

It was too wet to do much in the garden—though Jake saw with satisfaction that his plants were growing well and he would soon have a lettuce or two to pull—so he put on his anorak, pulled the hood over his ears and set off in the rain towards the woods. It would be quiet there in the leafy shade...and dryer, too, walking under the lofty canopy...

He walked a long time alone, and, because of Bracken's training, stopped to look at many things he might not otherwise have noticed. An

145

owl's pellets at the foot of a hollow tree…a scatter of hazelnut shells below a squirrel's drey…. He looked up then and caught a whisk of a tail as its owner climbed higher. He heard the yaffle laughing, and the cuckoo calling and calling, deep in the woods. He stood listening to a thrush singing its heart out on the topmost branch of a tall beech tree, and stopped to watch a cock pheasant strut by, glorious in his spring plumage…

But he was tired again now, so he sat down on a log and let the rain drip round him. The floor of the woodland was carpeted with bluebells, and their sweet, damp fragrance drifted across him as he sat there, dreaming…

He would not admit to himself that he was growing weaker…. He had just walked further today than on the last two mornings with Bracken. In a little while he would feel stronger, and then he would make for home.

Home…. It was extraordinary, he thought, how much the cottage and this wonderful countryside had come to mean to him. Already he cared far more about it than anywhere else he had lived for years past…

Briefly, then, his thoughts turned to Margaret and the early days of their marriage when the children were small. He had been away a lot even then, and when he had come home unexpectedly, he wished he hadn't.... So he had gone away again, rather sooner than need be.... There had not been much time to watch his children grow up. He had felt then that it was fairer to let them alone, their loyalties undivided...and always when he came home they seemed to have grown further away from him, prompted, he supposed, by their mother to be more hostile and more acquisitive.... Buy me this...I want that.... Never, we're glad to have you back...

His thoughts returned to Bracken, who never asked for anything—refused payment even for his gardening—and always came bringing Jake some gift or another...

It was difficult to know how to repay him.... He didn't think there was a way without offending him. He thought back to the small argument they had engaged in over the digging.

'You let the farmer pay you, don't you?'

'That's different.'

'Why?'

The glimmering smile, the grave, tranquil gaze. 'There's some things you do because you have to...and some you do because you want to...'

It was another gift given into his hands. He could not refuse it.

Smiling a little at his thoughts, he got slowly

to his feet and began the long walk home.

He just about made it to his gate, and almost fell in through his own front door.

'I'm a fool!' he told himself. 'I went too far!'

But he was not sorry. The woods were beautiful in the rain...and there was so much to see, so little time left for looking...

Sighing, he lay back in the brown armchair and dozed his exhaustion away. There were things he ought to do...there was Sky to feed... and there were papers he ought to deal with before it was too late.... But he was tired... tired...things would have to wait...

He was roused from a confused dream about the kestrel by a knock on the door...waking was always difficult. He felt sick and dizzy at first...but he struggled to his feet and went to see who was there. Standing outside on the step was a woman, with two cheerful-looking boys beside her.

Jake's hazy mind did a swift double-take. Of course! It was Carol Cook and her boys. He must have forgotten the day.

'I'm sorry—' he said, and smiled his most engaging smile. 'I'm afraid I was dozing...do come in...' and he turned back into the living-room and went across to his kitchen to put the kettle on. 'Could you do with a cup of tea? I know I could!'

Carol Cook spoke in a warm, friendly voice: 'Jake—I can't call you Mr Farrant after Bill's been going on about you so much!—are you quite sure you don't mind us coming?'

'No, of course I don't,' said Jake, busy with the teapot. 'And anyway, I'd like to hear news of Bill.'

Carol was looking at him quietly. She recognised the lean, ardent, good-looking face she had seen often on the television screen, reporting from some desperate battle-front or disaster area...talking to soldiers under fire, to civilians taking cover, to homeless refugees, to victims of flood and earthquake and famine.... She remembered how he had always listened courteously to their stories, asked the right, sensitive questions—not too inquisitive, not too brash—and how he had always looked as if he cared about the people he was talking to...

It was the same face now—but it was thinner and sadder, and more transparent...terribly transparent...so pale that light seemed to flow upwards through the skin.... But no—it was not really sadder—there was a strange calmness and serenity about it.... The grey eyes seemed to see things beyond her.... The voice was slower and quieter...it was almost as if he were listening to some other words than hers...

watching some other event in some other place.... And yet—and yet, she felt she knew him somehow...had always known him...that this meeting was full of recognition and home-coming.... Home-coming? she thought. Could it be? Recognition? Nonsense! It's only because I've seen his face so many times before...and Bill has talked of him so much...

Jake, for his part, when he looked up from his tea-making, saw a tallish, slender woman, with a face like Bill's, only distinctly more attractive, and a smile that lit her up like a lamp and made sparks in her eyes. Hazel eyes, he thought...straight and honest, like Bill's...and friendly without being in the least provoca-tive.... A face he could almost trust...he almost felt he knew it already, somehow...

Then he looked at the boys—who had been hovering rather shyly in the background—and thought at once: they are like their mother—tallish and straight and friendly...the same brownish hair, the same eyes...and the same incandescent smiles. Twins, too, he remem-bered...no wonder they looked so alike.... He wondered what their father had looked like, too...

'I'm a rotten host,' he said. 'Tell you what—while the tea's brewing, would you like to come and help me feed the kestrel?'

'What kestrel?' chorused the boys. And turned to Carol with easy deference: 'Can we?'

'If Jake says so...of course!' she smiled. 'Can I come too?'

They all went round the path to the kestrel's pen. But there, Jake made them stand a little way back in case they frightened the bird. Jake knew Sky hated men. (He had good reason to) and there was no point in frightening him or forcing company upon him. It would only make him retreat more than ever. Even Jake himself was bitterly unwelcome.... Only Bracken's gentle presence seemed to present no threat.

He opened the pen and went inside, laid some meat and one of the mice down on the tree-stump, then went closer to Sky and laid the other mouse near his feet. Sky looked at him stonily.

'Cheer up,' said Jake. 'Your dinner's arrived...and the rain's stopped. Why don't you try those wings?'

As if Sky had heard him, he suddenly flexed his wings and let out his harsh, fierce cry: 'Kee-kee-kee!' and flew straight down the length of the pen and back before settling on the tree-trunk.

'Good!' said Jake approvingly. 'That's wonderful! You're getting stronger every day!'

151

Sky glared at him, and stood on guard over his food like a stiff, angry sentinel.

'All right,' said Jake, smiling. 'I'm going! Bracken will be back tomorrow...you'll feel better then...'

And he slipped out of the pen and closed the gate behind him.

'Who's Bracken?' asked the twins.

Jake took them inside, gave them some tea and some of Bracken's sesame cake, and explained...

They listened, spellbound. So did Carol, watching the tiredness retreat from Jake's face as he talked, hearing the enchantment in his voice as he told them about the marvels he had seen in Bracken's company...

Presently, the boys asked if they could go down to have a look at the lake, and Carol—after glancing at Jake—agreed somewhat wistfully.

'You love this countryside too, don't you?' said Jake gently.

She sighed. 'Yes...we used to come down to this cottage a lot when my husband was alive.... But somehow, since he was killed, I couldn't really face it.... The boys were only six when they came here last...but they still remember it...'

She turned to look at Jake. 'I was wrong,

of course.'

'Wrong? About what?'

'Shutting things out...it isn't any good.'

'No...' said Jake slowly.

'I've come to terms with it now—' she spoke quite naturally and frankly, but Jake knew she was not only talking about herself '—though for a time I was abominably prickly. I wouldn't see anyone—not even Bill—and I wouldn't admit I needed any help.... Even Bill had to fight me to get me to see reason! And he only did it (he says!) for the sake of the boys...'

'They're awfully nice boys, too...'

She smiled. 'I think so...but then I'm prejudiced!'

There was silence between them for a moment, and then Jake said quietly: 'What exactly did Bill ask you to do?'

Carol's hazel eyes were clear and unembarrassed as they regarded him. 'Simply to find out how you were—and if you needed anything...' She paused, and then added: 'And I think he'd dearly love to come down to see you—but he's afraid of bothering you.'

Jake sighed. 'You're very good to be so honest about it!'

Carol laughed. 'Remember, I've been through this too—though in a different way.... I was terrified of pity—I snubbed all my friends!'

153

He grinned at her. 'You're very clever! You've undermined my defences already. I think I ought to keep you here to manage Sky...he won't let *anyone* be nice to him!'

They were both laughing when the boys came back, muddy and dishevelled but very happy.

'It's great down there...' said Matthew. 'So quiet...'

'And everything smells green...' added Mark.

Carol got up to go. But her eyes were on Jake's face. 'You've been very patient with us.... What shall I tell Bill?'

'Tell him...' Jake hesitated, and then went on steadily: 'Tell him I'm managing very well—and I'm happier than I've been for years.... It's important he should know that...my life is richer than it's ever been...'

Carol nodded. 'And—?'

'And—' he drew breath swiftly before he went on: 'And tell him he's a scheming old devil, and I'd love to see him.'

She smiled her relief. 'And Manny?'

He was smiling, too. 'And Manny—of course!'

She went over to him and patted his arm affectionately. 'Well done! You're learning much faster than I did!'

Jake turned to the boys and said: 'I never

used your rods...I don't somehow feel like fishing.... D'you want to take them to Wales?'

'No,' said Matthew, the eldest by five minutes, and therefore the decision maker. 'I don't think so...'

'We can't fish on the back of a pony!' added Mark, dissolving into laughter.

'But that means you've no excuse for coming to see me on the way back!' said Jake.

They all paused to look at him.

'Do you want us to?' asked Matthew, speaking for them all.

'Yes,' said Jake, smiling. 'I do!'

'In that case,' said Carol briskly, 'We'll take the sleeping bags.... Run up and fetch them, boys!'

Bracken did not come the next morning. Jake had just enough food left for Sky's breakfast, but he decided to go to the village and get some more supplies, in case the boy did not turn up...

He told himself that Bracken was probably busy with the horses—and anyway, he had every right to stay away if he liked. But even so, Jake found that he was absurdly disappointed because he did not come.

He had been very exhausted last night after Carol and the boys left.... It was as if the

155

warmth of their visit had been almost too much to bear...and their going had taken some of his strength away with them. He was so tired, in fact, that he could scarcely get up the stairs to bed...but he had made it in the end, and managed to ward off an attack of pain with some of his pills. He had fallen into a heavy sleep in the end, and dreamed wildly. He could remember his dream now—it was full of dark shadows and his feet were sliding helplessly as they tried to climb impossible slopes on shaly mountains...he had reached out his hand to grab at a fragile tree, growing out of the rock.... A real anxiety dream, he told himself, and not to be taken seriously...

This morning he was still tired, but he made himself some tea, went out to feed Sky and walked across the meadow to his car.

It was another pearly morning. He found himself smiling as he thought of Bracken's up-turned face and his voice calling on him from the garden... *'Come on out...it's a pearly old morning...'* Dew lay on every grass blade, winked, diamond-bright on every leaf and flower. His feet made a soft swishing through the wet grass as he walked. Overhead a lark was singing, rising in dizzy spirals, and the cuckoo called to him softly from the distant woods...

A pearly old morning…and yet, somehow, he didn't feel easy. The edge of his dream still clung to his mind…a shadow he could not quite dispel…

In the village, be bought a few things at the store and chatted to Mary Willis, who said she had been so glad to see Mrs Cook back, and weren't those boys of hers growing tall? Then he went on to the butcher's shop, and explained his dilemma about Sky.

The butcher was as round-faced and cheerful as Mrs Willis, and turned out to be her brother, Ted. 'What you need is some rough ends…' he said. 'And I've dressed a couple of rabbits for someone this morning—you can have the remains… The bird'll like those!'

He put his head on one side, consideringly: 'Maybe you should buy a mouse-trap? They've got them at the store…'

Jake shuddered a little. 'Aren't they rather cruel?'

The butcher laughed. 'Life's cruel…especially trying to rear a kestrel. And besides, you don't want mice in your larder, do you? They can do a lot of damage…'

Sighing, Jake agreed, and went back to Mary Willis and bought a mouse-trap.

Suppose Bracken didn't come back? Could he rear the bird alone? How soon would it be ready to fly?

He drove off down the farm lane, parked his car on the grass, and strolled home through the field. Another wave of dizziness caught him half-way across, and he sat down for a few moments on a nearby stone to let it pass...

From here he could hear Bracken's blackbird singing in the pear tree. It sounded as joyous and carefree as ever. But Jake did not feel carefree today...something was wrong...some hawk's wing shadow still hung over his mind...

Back home, he decided to take Sky a morsel of rabbit. His breakfast had been rather skimpy, anyway...

The kestrel was sitting on his tree-trunk in a patch of sun, preening his long flight feathers...

That's a good sign, Jake told himself. If he's beginning to fuss about his appearance, he's feeling better...

He put down a scrappy bit of rabbit's fur and entrails as far away as he could from Sky's perch. Sky turned his head and looked at him. The golden eyes reflected the light, and seemed as wary and full of suspicion as ever.... But he did not flinch when Jake went near.

'That's the way,' said Jake, smiling. 'You're getting used to me...I'm not an enemy, really...'

But Sky was not convinced.

Above him, some swifts were darting about the blue air, swooping and screaming after insects. The kestrel looked up, and there was such anguish, such longing in his lifted head that Jake's heart ached and he wanted to comfort him…. But there was no comfort that Sky would understand…

'Soon…' said Jake softly. 'It'll be soon, I promise. You'll be up there with them—soaring and hovering on those long, beautiful wings. Just get them strong…that's all…'

Sky looked back at him with disbelief and shouted defiantly: 'Kee-kee-kee!' Then he flew down to investigate the bits of rabbit.

Jake retreated to the cottage and sank into a chair to rest.

In the evening, Bracken still had not come, and Jake gave up expecting him and settled down to read.

He was half-dozing in his chair, when there came a quiet knock at the door. Struggling with his now customary waking nausea, he got up and went to see who it was.

A man stood on his doorstep—a brownish, sturdy-looking man, who wore brown corduroys, a cloth cap on his head, and an old-fashioned red kerchief round his neck.

'Sorry to bother you, sir,' said the man

politely—and his voice had a kind of lilting warmth that reminded him of something—'I was wondering...have you seen the boy—?'

Jake's heart seemed to make a sudden stop and then go lurching on too fast. 'The boy—? Do you mean Bracken?'

The man was looking at him keenly with assessing brown eyes. Now, he relaxed a little amd smiled briefly. 'That's what folks like to call him round here—yes.'

Jake saw that brief, non-committal smile, and also the reserve behind it. 'You'd better come in,' he said.

But the man shook his head. 'No, thank you kindly. I'm not much of a one for houses—nor is the boy, come to that.'

'So I'd noticed!' agreed Jake. And then, anxiously: 'I haven't seen him since the day before yesterday—though he left some food for the bird on my step yesterday morning. Why—is he missing?'

The man nodded. 'Hasn't been home since last evening...'

Jake looked at him. 'He's a bit of wanderer, though, isn't he? Hasn't he ever stayed out all night before?'

'No,' said the gypsy. 'Not all night...not without saying...'

'Let's get it straight,' said Jake, trying to be

160

practical. 'Didn't he go with you to the horse fair at Stow?'

'Oh yes...brought the *grais* home for me, too. Put them out to graze, tethered them near the trailers—then slipped off.... Thought he was coming up to see you...but he didn't?'

'No,' said Jake slowly, his mind heavy with dread. 'He didn't...'

He began to think furiously. 'When you were over at Stow—did anything happen...that might've upset him? Did anyone talk about any animals in trouble or anything?'

The man smiled, this time with real friendliness. 'See what you mean...that would set him off! But I can't say as I heard anything special...'

Jake sighed and shook his head. 'You know this country better than I do...he might be anywhere...' He turned back into the cottage to reach for his anorak. 'I'll come with you, if you're going to look for him...'

The gypsy laid a kind, restraining hand on his arm. 'No, don't do that, sir.... We know you've been a bit poorly like...the boy told us. Besides, we can take the *grais* across country... that way, we'll cover more ground.... You'd best stay here...he might turn up here yet, to see after his bird...'

'I suppose he might...' said Jake. But he

looked so anxious and uncertain, standing there in the lamplight, that the gypsy was moved to say: 'Don't worry, sir...he can take care of himself, like all us Romanies.... He'll turn up soon...'

Jake said, suddenly recognising that lilting voice, and the brown, firmly-chiselled face: 'Are you his father?'

'I am that.'

'He's a good boy,' said Jake. 'He's been very kind to me...you must be proud of him...'

A glimmer of a smile passed between them, and the gypsy turned away into the darkening evening. Jake saw then that a shaggy grey pony was tied up at the gate.

'We'll send to let you know when he gets back!' said the gypsy, over his shoulder. He swung himself up on to the furry back of his pony and clopped away up the lane.

It was while Bracken was holding the horses for his father that he heard the farmers talking. He was hidden behind the chestnut flanks of his father's favourite, Gilda, and they didn't realise he was there. But even if they had, they probably wouldn't have bothered to hide what they were saying from a mere gypsy horse-trader's boy.

'Better dig 'em out...' said one. 'Don't feel

inclined to leave 'em—with all my stock involved. Do you?'

'No,' grunted the other. Did you organise anything?'

'Got a few blokes together...'

'When?'

'Tonight would be as good as any...there's a moon...'

'I'll bring the dogs...'

'Yes...mine as well...and the guns.... May take a while, there's several entrances...got to stop them first...'

'I've got some tongs—if one gets stuck...'

They moved off, still talking. And Bracken stood looking after them, cold with the knowledge of what they were planning to do.

It was the far beech-wood sett they would be after, he knew...the one in Hawkswood.... One of those two farmers was the man who owned the rich dairy herd, the one had turned Bracken and his people off his land.... What could he do? he thought. How did you warn a whole colony of badgers that their lives were in danger?

If he got over there first, he would never be able to drive the badgers out of their setts alone...never persuade them to move off down the hill before the farmers and their dogs came to destroy them...

Unless...unless he could smoke them out? Sometimes, he knew, apart from gassing them where they lay in their snug tunnels (and that was supposed to be illegal now)—the farmers would lay smoking rubbish in the entrance and wait for the badgers to emerge...then they would set the dogs on them, or shoot them, or hit them over the head with shovels till they were dead...

He might, if he hurried, be able to get them out first....But there was the horse fair to be got through, and he would be wanted to take any new *grais* home that wouldn't go in the trailer—or the old ones, if his father didn't succeed in selling them...

He would have to wait until he got back to the *hatchintan* and had finished the work before he could set out. He would just have to hope the farmers would be later still...

As he feared, it was late before they got back from Stow. His father had been wanted to examine several horses who might be ailing, and to give his opinion on several more...besides the ones he was buying and selling himself. Dutifully, Bracken led the new string home, watered them and tethered them...and when he saw that the family were comfortably settling down to eat by the open camp-fire, he slipped away into the blue-grey dusk.

He could move fast when he needed to—and he covered a lot of miles that evening, arriving at the ancient beech-roots of the badger sett before moonrise…. There was no-one about yet…though he thought he could hear rather more farm dogs than usual barking in the distance…

Frantically, he cast about for twigs and bits of dried grass and leaves to burn…. He had also remembered to bring a few oily rags from the camp, and he put one of these with every pile of leaves, and placed them inside each entrance to the sett that he could find. Then he brought out a box of matches and carefully lit each little dried-up heap. The smoke curled outwards into the evening air, and the boy struggled desperately to push the burning debris further inside. What if the smoke didn't reach far enough along the interior corridors and only drove the badgers further in? They would wait there, huddled together against the smoke, until disaster fell…

He ran wildly from pile to pile, shoving them further into the holes with a long hazel stick…

At first, nothing happened at all…but then, pushing and grunting, the badgers began to emerge. First came the boars, scenting the air for danger, sneezing and spluttering in the smoke, suspicious and slow to move...and behind them came the sows and their cubs—queuing up at the entrances—waiting to get out when the boars said the coast was clear...

Bracken didn't know what to do. If he ran out, shouting and waving his arms, they would all try to retreat back into the setts. If he stayed still, they would sit about snuffing the breeze and wait for the smoke to subside. Either way, they would be doomed...

He decided to try to work his way round behind them and appear over the top of the bank above the sandy hollow where the tree-roots were. That way, the whole bunch might take fright and run off together...

He moved very silently, keeping down-wind as long as he could—and hoped that when he crossed over behind them the drifting smoke would cover him. Badgers are very short-sighted, he told himself, they won't see me until I want them to.... Wriggling through the beech-mast and bluebells, he arrived at the top of the bank, and suddenly got to his feet and began to shout and wave his arms...

And then—all hell broke loose. From the spinney at the side, came the sudden sharp yelping of eager dogs on the scent—and from beyond the drifting smoke came the furious shouting of men...

'Quick!' yelled one. 'Someone's smoked 'em out for us! Bring up the guns!'

'Put the dogs in!' shouted another.

'I've got a shovel!' bellowed a third. 'Hit 'em over the head! Go on, Boley, after 'em!'

'Let the terriers in!' said another voice. 'Come on, Spot! Get down there! I've got the tongs!

The bewildered badgers looked this way and that, short-sightedly peering out towards the threatening danger—and then, with one accord, they broke out together and dashed away into the woods as hard as they could go. A flurry of shots and shouts broke out, their echoes crashing away through the trees, and one beautiful sow fell in a heap. The rest seemed to vanish into the deepest shadows of the wood...

For a moment, the men and dogs were left in the clearing, not knowing which way to go...and then the foremost dog—the big bull mastiff, Boley, began to give chase...

'Dig out the sett!' ordered a voice. 'Then they can't come back! I'll go after the dogs...we might get another shot...'

But Bracken was ahead of them, driving the blundering creatures on, stamping and shouting, tripping over roots and brambles, zig-zagging along the dim woodland paths, trying to destroy the scent and increase the distance between the badgers and the pursuing dogs.... In any case, he thought, a full-grown badger would be a match for any dog—even Farmer Deacon's Boley—but there were the cubs...

Run! he panted. Run! Slip through the darkest patches of shadow...slide through the darkest undergrowth...hide those tell-tale black and white snouts under the leaves.... Get away—get away—don't let the grasping hands of men and snapping jaws of their dogs reach you.... Run!

He ran himself until he could run no more—and in front of him the silent badgers ran on deep into the receiving woods.... Behind him, the sounds of men and dogs grew fainter...

I believe we've done it! he thought.

But then his foot caught against something soft—and he stooped down and found two of the badger cubs huddled close together, panting, lost and alone...

'You can't stay there!' he said. 'The dogs'll get you....Come on!' and he picked up both the squirming cubs and thrust them inside his anorak and ran on.... Close behind him, the fastest of the dogs—Boley—came crashing through the undergrowth at his heels...

Terrified for the cubs, Bracken ran on blindly—crossed a moonlit clearing, came to a broken wall of stones, a flat verge of scrubby grass, and a dark, unseen edge of sandy soil.... Without a glance, he plunged on...and found himself falling over and over, down and down, bumping and bouncing from boulder to tree-stump, from tussock of grass to scree and shifting shale...down, down the steep sides of the ancient disused quarry where the kestrels came to nest...

Jake could not sit still. He told himself several times over that the gypsy men of Bracken's family would be perfectly capable of finding him—and anyway, he was probably not lost at all, but only helping someone else out, or wandering about looking at things, oblivious of time.... But however much he argued with himself, he could not shake off the feeling of foreboding that had been growing on him all day.... Something was wrong, he felt sure—he could still feel that hawk's-wing shadow pulling him....hawk's-wing? Suddenly, vividly, he remembered his dream...he had been trying to climb the shaly side of a mountain...and every time he took a step forward, the crumbling surface gave way and started a landslide of falling stones and sliding, cascading streams of pebbles and sand. His feet sank into loose gravel and could not be pulled out...he struggled and heaved and took step after heavy step, but the steep, shifting sides mocked him, and the falling yellow sand fell on him, choking him so that he could not breathe...

A mountain? he said. Rubbish! I am in the Cotswolds—gentle, rolling hills, and deep, wooded valleys.... But he remembered the gravelly slopes of the badgers' sett under the beech trees in Frith Wood...they were crumbling enough, where the old tree roots came through...not steep enough to get stuck in, though. Not the ones he knew—that the boy had taken him to...though some of the handholds had been a bit uncertain when he had been climbing up.... No, it would have to be somewhere steeper than that...

And then, from far away, he remembered Bracken's voice saying: *'Over there...an old quarry where the kestrels nest...'* and he remembered, too, the boy's troubled face as he said: *'I think the badgers is threatened...'* And, last of all, he remembered the name *Hawkswood.* Not a hawk's-wing shadow—his mind had been playing tricks all day...it was *Hawkswood...*

He got up, remembering that he had a map of the district in his car. Then, like the old campaigner he was, he coolly assessed the possibilities of going on foot and being slow and tired, or going by car and missing the place altogether. He had always had an exceptionally clear sense of direction—it had stood him in good stead many times in the past out in the field. He tried, with intense concentration, to remember where he and the boy had been sitting that morning...which little hill was it they were on, and which way did Bracken's brown finger point?

Swiftly, he pulled on his anorak and boots, picked up his torch, and went out into the garden. The moon was up, sailing high over the beeches between scudding clouds. Moonlight and shadow chased themselves over the sleeping fields...

Then Jake remembered Sky. He might not be back by morning. The bird would be hungry. He went back into the cottage, seized some of the butcher's 'rough ends' and carried them up to the pen. The kestrel seemed to be asleep, its head hidden in its wing. Silently, Jake tossed the food on to the ground and went away. He hoped Sky would find it before something else did.

The hare's field was quiet and empty. He walked as swiftly as he could over the silver grass—driven now by a fearful sense of urgency.... What if the car won't start? he thought. I've left it out in the lane a long time...

then he recollected that he had been up to the village that day…it should be all right, then…

When he reached the car, he sat with the door open and the roof-light on while he spread out his local map. He shone the torch down on to the intricate mass of fine lines and names. There was the lake—Sedgecombe, it was called —there was Swallowtail Beacon…there was the wedge of beech woods across the valley. Where was the little hill they had been sitting on? Was that it? Whitebeam Hill (British Camp…). No, come to think of it, Bracken had told him about the British Camp and how they would go there one day soon…. It must be that smaller one, then…Ridge Hill….? If so, then the woods Bracken had been pointing at would be over there…to the east of the road…. Yes, there they were—and there was Hawkswood Quarry… about two miles from the top road across the woodlands marked Hawkswood…

Jake laid the map beside him on the seat, snapped off his torch, started the car and turned it on the grass. Then he drove away fast uphill into the deepening shadows of the lane.

He had forgotten to look at his watch, but he guessed it must be about two o'clock in the morning. There was no-one about. The windows of the little houses in the village were curtained and dark…. He drove on, remembering to fork right at the crossroads and keep climbing towards the ridge of the hills.... Hurry, his mind kept saying 'the badgers are in for trouble'. No, I mean Bracken's in trouble... I'm sure he is...

The moonlight poured down out of a clear spring sky. Even the small drifting clouds had disappeared. It was a silvered, black and white world, in which the tall beeches stood out like giants against the flanks of the hills.

He took one wrong turning and nearly landed in a farmyard quagmire...but he turned back and found the right road. He drove on, skirting the woods and following the contours of the hills until he came to the crest of a rise which overlooked the wedge of beeches known as Hawkswood. The quarry, he thought, should be about a couple of miles through the woods, and out on the other side...

He parked the car, picked up his torch, and started the long walk through the woods. Nothing seemed to stir in them as he walked, and he had been too pre-occupied to notice much on the way—though he fancied he had seen a few rabbits whisking away from the glare of his headlamps. Now, he walked in a silent world—except for an owl that hooted sadly far down in the lower slopes of the wood.

All this time he had not stopped to consider

the implications of what he was doing...but now, sudden doubts assailed him.... What had made him so certain he knew where Bracken would be? Why was he following the dictates of a dream? Mightn't he be mistaken? He was a man who was mortally sick—and sick men were prone to fancies.... He could be completely wrong...

But even as he argued with himself, he knew he was not wrong.... Somewhere ahead of him among the shadows and moonlight, Bracken was waiting for him...Bracken in trouble, somewhere alone in the night...

He stumbled once or twice over tree roots in the dark, but his torch picked out the path fairly well, and he did not hesitate. This was the way, he knew.

At last, after walking for what seemed like a very long time, he came out of the trees into bright moonlight and saw that he stood in a clearing near a sandy verge, with a yawning blackness beyond.... I'm here! he thought. This is Hawkswood Quarry...and Bracken is here somewhere...I'm sure he is.

He went to the edge and looked over. It was very dark, but he could discern the broken, shaly sides of the quarry, the few stunted bushes leaning outwards, the tumbled stones and loose shale.... It was just like his dream.

'Bracken?' he called. 'Are you there?'

There was no answer.

But wait a bit, he thought. In my dream I was climbing *upwards*.... If I go over the top here, I shall be climbing down...and I'll bring the whole quarry-side down with me, by the look of it—and he might be underneath.... I'd better go round the edge and look for a way down.

With the torch-beam glimmering ahead of him, he skirted the edge of the quarry—once nearly falling headlong as he missed a deep in-dentation in the rim. When he had gone almost two-thirds round it, he saw a path running alongside it in the grass, which seemed to veer away to the right and circle the quarry's flank until it reached the valley floor. He took the path and followed it down into the darkening shadow, going deeper into pitch-black night with every step.... The moonlight could not reach down here...

At the bottom of the path, he found he was actually standing on the quarry floor, looking up at the sandy flaking sides as he had in his dream.... This is where it was, he said. I must begin climbing *here*.

He called again again: 'Bracken!' but his own voice mocked him with echoes round and round the stones.... Nothing else stirred.

He began to climb. The ground slipped and shifted under his feet, his boots filled with gravel. He had to cling on sometimes with one hand—but he knew where he had to go. There was a small tree growing out of the rock somewhere above him, and if he could hold on to that and pull himself up, he would be there...

The torchlight ahead of him wavered to and fro in his unsteady progress, and then settled firmly on to the little tree. Yes! There it was! Waiting for him.

He was lightheaded with exhaustion by this time but he did not even notice it. Something was driving him now, pushing him on faster with every aching step. His hand reached the tree and pulled.... It was very steep just here, and he inched his way up, clinging hard to the tree's pliant stem. He felt a tight, hard sort of ache in his chest as he heaved, but he disregarded it.... And then—the little tree pulled clean out of the ground and sent him toppling backwards.... He just had the sense to hold on to the torch, when a shower of stones and quarry dust fell on top of him. He slewed sideways, fell a bit further, and landed up in a heap, on top of something warm and soft...

'Bracken?' he said, feeling for him in the dark. 'Is that you?'

He pulled himself into a sitting position and switched on the torch again.... There, spread out before him in a tangle of limbs, was the boy. His eyes were closed. There was a deep gash in his head, and there was blood all over his clothes. For one awful moment, Jake thought he was dead...but then he saw that he was breathing quite naturally, and the blood came from the dead badger cub in his arms...

'Bracken?' he said again, and shook him gently. 'Bracken? Wake up! Can you hear me? I've got to get you home!'

The boy seemed to sigh—and Jake caught the movement of something else, wriggling within his torn jacket. Carefully, he took the small limp body of the dead badger cub away and laid it down on the stones...then he turned back to loosen the boy's coat, and found a second cub, apparently unhurt, cowering in terror against the boy's warm side.

'Wake up!' said Jake again, and cursed himself for not remembering to bring any water with him. An old campaigner like him—he ought to have had more sense!

But then he remembered that Bracken usually carried a flask in his leather bag.... He felt around in the dark and found the pouch underneath the boy's back—the flask inside seemed unharmed. He unscrewed the lid and sniffed the liquid inside. Tea, he thought. Herb tea! Still luke-warm...well, it was better than nothing.

He lifted the boy's heavy head and cradled it against one arm—and then held the plastic cup to his lips. He tipped a little of the liquid into the boy's mouth, and waited for his re-action.... Bracken choked a little, coughed, sneezed once, and tried to sit up.

'Take it easy,' said Jake. 'You've had a bang on the head...rest a while...'

'I knew you'd come...' said Bracken, and sighed again.

Then he started up and said in an anxious voice: 'The cubs? I tried...the others got away...but they shot one of the sows...'

'Never mind,' said Jake. 'You're safe...and one of the cubs is, too...'

'It was my fault—' said Bracken, and suddenly began to weep.

Jake understood then that he was not weeping for himself—but in some way he felt to blame for what had happened...though Jake did not yet know what that was...

'Don't worry about it now,' he said. 'Have a drop more of this magic tea.... We've got to get you out of here somehow!'

Bracken laid a dusty, tear-streaked face against Jake's arm and said: 'Sorry...I was too

178

late, you see...I was just too late...'

'No, you weren't!' said Jake. 'You just told me—the others got away.... And we've got this little fellow here to take care of, see? Come on now, you're the one who knows his way around.... What's the best way to get out?'

'Downward,' said Bracken, still leaning tiredly against Jake's arm. 'We'd never climb up there!'

For a while, they sat still, waiting for Bracken to feel stronger. Jake didn't know whether he himself felt strong or weak...he only knew he had to get the boy home safely somehow. He was trying to remember how steep the actual path was, and wondering whether he could carry the boy and the badger cub, if he found that Bracken could not stand...

But in the end, moving cautiously, step by careful step, he guided the boy down to the bottom, and together they began to climb the circling path. Bracken refused to let Jake carry him, but he allowed him to take the little cub and tuck it inside his anorak.

Often, they stopped to get their breath— often, Bracken swayed and Jake steadied him— but at last they reached the head of the path by the quarry's brink, and sat down to rest in the grass.

'It's two miles to the car...' said Jake. 'D'you

think you can make it?'

Bracken smiled at him with sudden aware-
ness. 'If you can—I can,' he said.

They began the slow walk through the
woods. Jake had his arm round the boy now,
since he was inclined to blunder into the trees
on his own.... Talk about the blind leading the
blind, he thought—and plodded gamely on.
The moonlight seemed to be paling now, and
the east was beginning to lighten in the translucent way of a spring sky before dawn.... He
could even see the trunks of the trees, grey
ghosts standing in rows watching his clumsy
progress down their leafy rides. It's all very well
for you, he said, talking to them in a mad sort
of way—standing there with your roots safely
set in the cool, firm ground.... You haven't got
to go anywhere, you're quite safe where you
are!

'I'm tired...' sighed Bracken suddenly, and
slid down into Jake's arms.

Jake lowered him on to the ground, and sat
down beside him for a moment, trying to think
what to do. I could leave him here and go for
help, he thought.... But I might forget exactly
where he was in these vast dim woodlands. And
anyway, he needs looking after, he's hurt...I've
got to get him back somehow.... *If they wants
to badly enough, they can go on much longer than*

180

you'd think,' said Bracken's voice in his head.

He stooped down, and picked him up in his arms. The boy seemed strangely light and slender in his grasp...small bones, like a bird, he thought...and staggered on.... Even so, the small weight made a sudden, deep ache in his chest.... He was not at all sure whether he would ever each the road, but he had to try.... The trees round him seemed to close in and weave up and down before his eyes...

And then—all at once—there was the sound of voices calling, the clip-clop of hooves, a swinging circle of lights, and willing hands came out to take the boy from his arms.

'Be careful,' he said, very distinctly. 'He's hurt...'—and fell in a heap on the woodland floor.

He came round to find himself lying on a pile of soft quilts beside a bonfire in the open. There were four neat modern trailers drawn up in a circle round him, and to one side, a bunch of horses grazed peacefully, tethered in the long grass. He leant up on one elbow, suddenly anxious about the boy—and found that Bracken was lying fast asleep on another pile of quilts quite near him. Someone had washed the blood off his face and put a neat plaster on his forehead, and his clothes were fresh and clean...

'It's all right,' said a lilting, musical voice close beside him. 'He's not much hurt... nothing a good sleep won't cure.... You brought him back to us—and we thank you.'

Jake turned round and found himself looking into the face of a handsome, dark-haired gypsy woman, who was sitting on the ground nearby, patiently weaving a basket out of thin, pliant withies. She smiled at him and said softly: *'Devlesa avilan....* It is God who brought you...'

'What happened to the cub?' he asked.

'The little one is safe,' she reassured him. 'We put her in a box in the dark.... The men will see after her...'

Jake nodded, satisfied. Then another thought struck him. 'What time is it? I forgot to feed the boy's kestrel...'

The woman smiled again. 'No, you remembered. One of us went up to see to him, and there was still some food on the ground.... The bird is all right, too.'

Jake sighed. So everything was all right... except that he was so deadly tired...

'I have made you some tea...' said the woman, with the shy smile still lighting her face...and Jake, seeing that smile and the brown far-seeing eyes, knew he was talking to

182

Bracken's mother.

'You will feel better soon...' she added, and handed him a china cup full of fragrant, amber-coloured tea...

Jake sipped it gratefully, remembering how Bracken had brought him some one morning when he was feeling particularly low—and how swiftly it had revived him.

'Tell me what happened?' he asked.

'The men found your car on the top road. They were working their way across on the *grais*... so they knew you must be somewhere in Hawkswood.... When they found you, they put you both in your car and drove it down here...' She turned, still rather shyly, and pointed across the grass to the dry-stone wall. 'It's just over yonder...we thought you wouldn't mind...?'

Jake smiled. 'Sounds very sensible to me! And I can drive it home...'

The woman looked at him with a hint of reproof. 'You've got to rest a bit first. Anyways, they've gone up for Dr Martin...he'll come down to look at you, as well as the boy...'

'I don't need—'

She leant forward and laid a brown, slim hand on his arm. 'We don't hold with doctors mostly...we do our own medicine.... But Doctor Martin's different—he's a friend...'

Jake met the brown, quiet gaze with understanding. 'Yes,' he agreed. 'He is.'

It didn't seem necessary to talk, so Jake lay and dreamed, while Bracken's mother sat quietly beside him, weaving her basket.

'The boy's done a lot for me,' murmured Jake after a while, following his own thoughts.

'He does a lot for most creatures as needs it,' said his mother softly.

Jake looked at her out of drowsy eyes and smiled. 'I don't know what you put in this tea! I hope it isn't opium!'

The Romany woman laughed.

Presently, Dr Martin arrived, walking quietly across the grass, with his black bag in his hand.

'Never a dull moment in this village,' he said to Jake. '*Now* what have you been doing?'

He squatted down beside him, seeming quite at home in the gypsy encampment, and took Jake's wrist in a firm, cool hand.

'Hm...' he said, with a glimpse of a smile. 'Might be worse! I thought I told you to take things easy!'

Jake grinned, and pointed to Bracken lying asleep close by. 'There's your casualty...I'm just an also-ran.'

'That's what I'm complaining about,' said Dr Martin severely: 'You walked five miles or so and you *also ran!*'

Beside them, Bracken woke at the sound of laughter and said in a perfectly wide-awake voice: 'He carried me as well.... Is the cub all right?'

'Everyone's all right,' said the doctor. 'Stop worrying. They tell me you need your head examined—and I'm not surprised!'

The laughter flowed round the little encampment—even the dour, sunburned men were laughing with relief.... There had been an emergency—one of their number, a favourite child, had been in danger...and now he was safe, his rescuer was safe, and everyone was happy.... There was suddenly an atmosphere of warmth and friendliness all round them.

Bracken looked up at the soft spring sky and then turned a smiling face to Jake. 'It's going to be a grand old day, after all!' he said.

In the end, on Dr Martin's advice, Jake spent the whole day at the gypsy encampment, idling and resting, drinking endless cups of fragrant tea.

'They can keep an eye on you,' said the doctor, smiling. 'And they need to do something for you today. I don't suppose you realise what you've done! Saving a gypsy's life makes you someone special to them.'

'I didn't save his life. He'd have come round in the end and found his own way home.'

'Maybe—' said Dr Martin, judiciously, 'and maybe not! In any case, they'll want to give you the benefit of the doubt! So let them fuss over you today—it'll do no harm. You're privileged, you know. Not many *Giorgios* get to see the inside of a *hatchintan*—a gypsy encampment— and I expect they'll have a *Patshiv* tonight when the men get home from work...'

'A what?'

'*Patshiv*.... A sort of ceremonial party...in honour of a special guest...' He looked at Jake and grinned. 'I ought to order you home to bed—but I won't!' Then he grew grave for a moment, and laid a hand on Jake's arm. 'All the same, I want to warn you about something —all this activity, and the fall you had, may have set up internal bleeding, you know.... If you start feeling cold or extra faint, you must send someone up for me at once—do you hear?'

Jake nodded.

The doctor hesitated a moment, and then asked: 'How would you feel about going into hospital for a transfusion?'

Jake sighed. 'If it was necessary?'

'It might be...and it might give you a bit of respite from weakness, too.'

Jake looked at him. 'I'm in your hands...I'll

do whatever you say.... But I won't *stay* in—you understand?'

For answer, Dr Martin patted his arm kindly and simply added: 'Rest now, then...and enjoy yourself! I'll see you later.'

So Jake stayed where he was, and the women came and went, bring small gifts of tea and saffron cakes and smiling at him shyly with each new offering.

Bracken took him to see the horses, introducing them one by one, with conscious pride. 'And this one's Gilda...' he said, stroking the velvet nose of a gentle chestnut mare. 'She's my Da's favourite...I like her best, too...'

Gilda pricked up her ears and acknowledged their attentions with a small toss of her head. Then she nuzzled at Bracken's pockets in a reminding sort of way, and whickered softly.

'Yes, all right,' said Bracken. He brought out a piece of carrot and held it for her on his brown palm.

Then he took Jake to see the two yellow ferrets in their cages—and a tame rabbit with an injured leg who hopped peacefully about under the trailers, cropping the grass.... And the two lurcher dogs, Gambol and Streaker, tied up by the leading trailer, grateful for any kind of word and any scrap of food offered. Bracken had something in his pockets for them all.

187

Last of all, they went to look at the badger cub, curled up asleep in a cardboard box in the darkest corner that could be found under one of the trailers. Someone had put an ordinary red rubber hot watter bottle, wrapped in a woollen cloth, in the box close to the little creature's furry side...

And there, in the quiet place behind the trailer, Jake at last asked Bracken what had happened that night...

So Bracken told him—and ended up by saying again: 'I was just too late.... If I'd got there earlier, they'd all have got away...'

Jake shook his head. 'Most of them did. Don't blame yourself any more. Only one sow and one cub lost isn't bad from a whole sett, is it?'

Bracken sighed. 'No. It's pretty good...but I'd rather it was *all* of 'em!'

Jake was thinking about the night's events with some anxiety. 'Did they see you, do you think?'

'No...it was too dark...'

'But they knew someone had got there first...'

'Oh yes...there was all that smoke!'

Jake grinned, and decided to let it go for now... But he thought maybe he ought to have a word with the boy's father.... Frustrated farmers could be pretty angry people...

'What about this cub?' he asked. 'Do you think you can rear it?'

Bracken looked thoughtful. 'Depends if she'll take food.... She must be nearly weaned...she looks big enough, and she's quite heavy.' He grinned at Jake. 'You know that!' Then he grew more serious. 'They don't come out for the first three months usually, so she must be nearly that old.... The trouble is...' he looked round at the *hatchintan* doubtfully, 'I can't really leave her here...it's too noisy.... And the dogs'll worry her. She ought to have a kind of sett of her own—only sort of protected, till she's ready for the wild...'

Jake said, not waiting to be asked: 'We could build one for her up at the cottage.'

The boy's face was suddenly joyous. 'Could we?' But then a faint shadow dimmed his smile. 'It would mean you'd have to do part of the feeding—like Sky...'

'Well, why not? I've nothing better to do...'

So they planned it together, and went back to sit by the fire on their soft *dunhas,* discussing tunnels and underground chambers and old drain pipes...

The women of the camp were busy cooking over their fires by now, and presently Bracken's mother came over with two bowls of steaming, herb-scented hot-pot and two hunks of bread.

'Nothing like a good *jogray!*' said Bracken, dipping his bread in the gravy and munching happily.

'What's a *jogray?*' asked Jake, also munching, and deciding he was quite hungry after all.

'It's...well, it's a kind of stew that gypsies make.... Could have anything in it...rabbit...or pheasant...or pigeon...and mushrooms and potatoes, and any veges we've got...and lots of herbs.... And the gravy's got to be dark and thick, like this—or it's not a good *jogray!*'

'This one certainly is!'

They looked at one another and laughed.

Jake was absurdly happy, though the reaction from his night's exploits was slowly catching up with him. He determined not to let himself feel tired until he got home...today was special.... The gypsies wanted to make it a celebration...he mustn't spoil it...

All that day, he and Bracken lazed by the fire, and no-one bothered them. It seemed that the gypsies had decided among themselves that the two of them needed a day to recover, and the festivities would not begin till the evening when the men came home.... Meanwhile, there was time to rest...

At last, the sun began to sink in a muted blaze of apricot fire. Two lorries came into the clearing, and several men and one or two women got out...and last of all came Bracken's father, on the back of his shaggy grey pony, Ambler.

He came straight across to Jake and Bracken, ruffled the boy's hair with a brown, affectionate hand, and said: 'Well, then? Feeling better?'

Bracken nodded, and before Jake could answer added in a gentle, reproving voice: 'He's overdone it, though...only he won't admit it!'

The gypsy, known as Kazimir Bracsas like his son, turned to Jake gravely: 'We want to have a *patshiv* tonight—for the honoured guest! But you must tell us if you are too tired?'

Jake shook his head, smiling. 'Of course not! I will be truly honoured!'

The gypsy laughed. 'Sit by the fire then, and rest.... It will all happen round you soon!'

And so it did.

During the daytime, the women had worn their dullish working clothes. But now, with a party in the offing, they emerged from their trailers in their brightest and best. Gypsies always loved bright colours, Jake remembered and the grassy clearing suddenly looked as if a flock of brilliant paraqueets had descended on it...scarlet and blue and green—and a flash or two of gold—shone in the firelight. The men, too, wore bright-coloured shirts and most of them also wore a *diklo* a bright knotted kerchief —round their necks. It was not exactly the traditional gypsy costume of long ago—but the vivid colours and suppressed excitement somehow created the same impression of barbaric gaiety.

Jake saw that the *hatchintan* contained not four trailers, but five—for one was parked a little further back near the wall—and there were two lorries as well. Out of these compact dwellings came about twenty adults and a small, cheerful horde of children, also dressed in their best. Each trailer had its own family and its own freshly painted front door—and one or two of them even had painted scenes on the bodywork. From the glimpse Jake got, each interior looked spotless and neat, and filled with brilliant collections of painted china...especially one, in which he recognised some glowing Crown Derby...

The children all came up to look at Jake, a little shyly—and the smallest girls brought him bright posies of spring flowers...

'You've got to take them,' hissed Bracken, smiling at him and whispering sideways. 'It's all part of the *patshiv*—honouring the guest at the fireside!'

So Jake accepted them gravely, along with a

series of other small gifts, including a home-made catapult from one of the boys, a small wicker basket for keeping bait in, and a jar of frog-spawn from one of the smallest freckle-faced boys...

Jake lost count of the number of special dishes the women brought over from their cooking fires for him to try. Each one seemed to taste better—more aromatic and richer—than the last. The air was full of the smell of wood-smoke and roasting meat...

The men had brought out a huge barrel of beer, and they kept filling his mug as fast as he drank it down...

I'm going to feel terrible tomorrow, he thought.... But what the hell—it's worth it...

Bracken never left his side. He kept the other children from bothering him, saw that he had the best space near the fire, and watched him, covertly, in case he began to look too exhausted...

Presently, the boy's father sat down by his side.

'I wanted to ask you—' began Jake, and glanced round to see if Bracken was listening. But he appeared to be ladling a new kind of *jogray* on to his plate from a pot on the fire.

'... Is there likely to be any trouble over the badgers?'

The gypsy's clever, serious face seemed untroubled. 'Shouldn't think so...he says they didn't see him. In any case, I been over there again today—shoeing a horse.... It was kind of convenient, like! I asked around and about...' He grinned at Jake, conspiratorially. 'They told me, Deacon—that's the farmer that threw us off his land—was hopping mad, but there wasn't a lot he could do about it.... Besides, that sett in Hawkswood isn't really on his land at all...'

'Isn't it?' Jake was interested.

'No. Hawkswood belongs to Thornton. He's the biggest *raya* round here...'lord of the manor' they call it in these parts.... The old quarry belongs to him, too...so Deacon can't say too much about digging out badgers there, can he? Let alone boast about letting one of his dogs run the boy over the edge!'

Jake laughed in some relief. 'I wouldn't want to see the boy blamed...'

'Nor wouldn't I,' said the gypsy fiercely. 'He was only doing what he thought was right.... He can't abide animals being hurt for nothing... and I don't hold with badger-digging meself, either...'

'No,' agreed Jake slowly. 'They're attractive creatures. Do they really do much harm?'

'If you ask me, it's a load of old rubbish!'

said the gypsy. 'TB in cows is different...and they have medicines now that cures it, anyways. Badgers were here in this country long before dairy herds was even thought of, I reckon...and no-one's been able to prove that the poor old badgers is to blame...' He leant forward and filled Jake's mug again from the barrel close by. 'No,' he added thoughfully, 'they does a lot of good, badgers does. Them farmers is round the twist, if you ask me!' He looked serious again. 'It could have been a lot worse, you know...running straight off the edge like that. He could have been killed...'

Jake nodded soberly. 'Well,' he said, taking a reckless gulp, 'let me know if anything comes of it—if he needs any help, I mean?'

'I will that!' said the gypsy warmly. 'Drink up! The singing will begin soon!'

'I've brought you a *bokoli*,' said Bracken. 'See if you like it.'

'I'm sure I shall,' said Jake, looking with interest at the thing on his plate. 'What is it?'

'It's a kind of pancake...with meat inside. It's a family thing—my grandmother brought the recipe from Hungary...'

While Jake was eating it, the singing began. Someone brought out a guitar, and someone else had a mouth organ. They sang songs that Jake did not know, sad and fiery, from far away—and the circle of men and women round the fireside clapped and stamped in rhythm...

I can see where the Hungarian influence comes in, thought Jake...these wild, dark, nostalgic songs are full of Magyar yearning and melancholy..and the long, long wanderings of the Travellers...

But suddenly the mood seemed to change, and a couple of the younger men got up and began to dance. The music swung faster now, the hands clapped with mounting excite-ment...heel-tapping, spinning, leaping and finger-snapping, the young men showed off in the firelight.... When the music had pushed them on into a final frenzy, they collapsed in a panting heap and a couple of the older men took over. The dance was graver now—slower, more deliberate. It reminded Jake of Greece, and the slow, careful beginnings of the men's dances in the small island tavernas—slow, quiet, held-back—until the tension suddenly broke into the wild, insistent beat of real abandon.... But here, the music did not break, it stayed serious and restrained, while the men circled gravely, half-remembering the intricate steps of long ago...

Then the guitar quickened its thrum, and it was the turn of the girls. Jake noticed then that the men and girls never danced together—

always separately.... And now the bright skirts swung, the heels clicked, and the gold-coin necklaces clashed as they moved to the mounting beat...

'Do the older ones teach you the dances?' asked Jake, turning to Bracken in the firelight.

The boy nodded. 'If they'll learn! Some of the young ones go off to discos in the town now!' He sounded scornful. 'They say all this is old-fashioned.... I went with my sister once... and the noise hurt my ears something cruel!' He laughed. Then he grew serious again. 'But my Da says the old ways are best...so he tries to keep them going.... A lot of the gypsies have forgotten them, though.... There's not many left who keep up the old songs...or the old dances, come to that...'

'But you like them best?'

Bracken sighed. 'Oh, *I* do! They make me feel excited inside...as if I remember things from long, long ago...' His eyes were filled with smoky dreams.

Watching his face, Jake said no more, but left him dreaming...

After the dancing, the singing began again, and one youngish man with a strong, easy tenor, came out and stood in the firelight, directing his song at Jake.

'It is the *pashtivaki djilia*—the friendship

song...' whispered Bracken. '...specially for you...'

'What do I do?' Jake whispered back.

'Sit still.... When it's over, you offer him a drink...'

So Jake sat still, while the young tenor progressed through many verses of the strange, sad song, singing of undying friendships and long journeys, of partings and meetings and reunions after many days...in the distant times when the Travellers wandered free throughout the world...

The planes of his brown, clear-cut face were lit by the glow from the fire, and there was longing and passion in his voice—and in his sturdy figure—as he stood there conjuring up griefs and despairs and rejoicings from the golden past.... Jake felt stirred by feelings he did not know he possessed...

When it was over, there was a burst of clapping, and the faces round the fire were turned towards the stranger in their midst.

Jake stood up and held out his brimming mug of ale and said—without knowing what prompted him: 'Will you drink with me to friendship?'

Then the young man bowed and accepted the drink, and everyone clapped again. *'tumenge Romale...'* murmured the singer, smiling.

'This song was offered as a gift to worthy men...'

'Was that all right?' whispered Jake, under cover of the sound of clapping.

'Perfect,' answered Bracken, smiling up at him in the flickering firelight.

But Bracken's father had not finished his rejoicing yet. He emerged now, from his trailer, carrying an old, shining viola in his hand. A small cheer went up, and he tucked it under his chin, lifted his bow and began to play.

'I told you Bracsas meant viola-player...' said Bracken. 'But he hardly ever plays it now.... This is really special.... It's a *sumadji*—a family treasure—it belonged to my great-grandfather...'

'Did he bring it with him from Hungary?'

'His father did...so my grandfather used to say.... He played better than my Da.... But he's pretty good at the old tunes, too...'

The man in the firelight played on...deep and lamenting, the voice of the old viola sang out in the night...Jake didn't know what he played. They seemed to be old gypsy tunes, folk songs from the mountains of eastern Europe, slow, quiet dances and sad sweet love songs from the hills and forests of Moravia.... Probably, the man himself didn't know what he was playing— he was playing—he was simply following his father, playing from ear, remembering the ancient songs they used to sing, the dances, the dreaming, sorrowful raptures of a far country and a past long since gone...

When he had finished there was a silence for a moment, and then the clapping broke out again, and the mugs were filled, and laughter and talk spilled over with the home-brewed beer...

Jake had contrived once more to have a brimming mug in his hand to present to the performer. This time, though, he spoke quietly beneath the chatter—since they did not seem to be waiting for him to make a ceremony of it—'Thank you for the music. That is a beautiful instrument you have there!'

Kazimir Bracsas smiled and held it up for Jake to see. 'It is very old...it was given to my grandfather when he was a boy—by a very old Romany *chal* from our family. I don't know how old it is, but it has a good-sounding voice, don't you think? My father taught me to play it...but he was better than I am—'

'You sounded pretty good to me!'

The gypsy was clearly pleased. He looked across the firelight to the face of his son, and then back to Jake. 'I have a reason to sound good tonight!' he said. Then, cradling the voila in his arms, he went back into his trailer to put it away.

Jake was feeling very strange by now. The various bruises from his fall in the quarry were beginning to hurt, he ached all over and he was beginning to notice that he was ominously cold. He wondered how Bracken, who had sustained a much worse fall, was feeling now? He glanced across at him, but the boy was smiling at something one of the men had said, and did not look at all troubled. Jake closed his eyes for a moment, summoning strength to cope with the curious feeling of vagueness and unreality that was creeping up on him...he must not pass out at the party...

'Sit down over here where it's quiet,' said a voice in his ear, and he found himself being propelled firmly but gently by Bracken's mother to a dark patch of grass near one of the trailers away from the noisy rejoicing round the fire.

Sighing with relief, Jake sat down and leant his back against the side of the trailer, looking out at the cheerful ring of faces in the firelight beyond.

'Dr Martin will be here soon...' said Bracken's mother quietly.

Jake turned his head in surprise. 'Will he? Why?'

She smiled at him. 'We asked him to the

patshiv—only he was on duty, he said, till late...but he is coming for a bit, and then he will take you home.'

'I can—' began Jake indignantly, and then stopped. It was silly to protest. He knew he was not fit to drive his car. The world was beginning to look strangely grey and misty, somehow...and this quiet woman with Bracken's gentle smile knew all about him...

'How do the Romanies look on death?' he asked her suddenly.

She did not seem surprised. But after a silence she answered tranquilly: 'It comes to us all...birth and death.... It is natural. We like to die out of doors, with the sky above us, if we can...like Bracken's creatures do.... We believe in honouring the dead. We keep them in our thoughts, and we use special words that remember them...like tonight when the boy's father played his father's viola.... We say: *'Te avel angla tute'*, we do this in your memory... and that keeps them with us...' She turned to smile at Jake as she went on: 'As for ourselves— one day we will know what death is like, so we don't worry about it very much before...God will look after us.'

Jake nodded. It was what he expected... simple and natural...and strangely comforting.

'Have you ever noticed,' she said, with her
202

eyes on Bracken in the firelight, 'when a creature dies, it looks sort of dignified...and—and ready? Bracken had a pet squirrel that died.... We found it curled up all neat and pretty on its side, with its paws over its face. It didn't look at all afraid...' She glanced at Jake, and added softly: 'But then, *you* don't need telling...'

Oh yes, I do, thought Jake. Oh yes, I do!

But then he felt a hand slip into his and Bracken's lilting voice said confidingly: 'I was thinking—we might call the little cub Zoe? My Da says it means "life".'

Dr Martin did not take Jake home. He took him straight to the local hospital, where they put him to bed and gave him a blood transfusion without delay. The bruising from his fall was by now looking ridiculously heavy, and the aches were worse...so was the feeling of hazy unreality. There was nothing to be done but lie still and do as he was told until he felt stronger....then he would get up and go home, whether they liked it or not...

Everyone was very kind to him—he did not ask himself why—and no-one said anything about making him stay in longer than was strictly necessary.... Even Dr Martin, when he came back to have a look at him again, only patted him and said: 'Be patient a little longer, my friend...we'll soon have you out of here...'

Jake had learnt to be patient. He tried very hard to be a good and docile patient, however rebellious he felt inside...he knew they were only doing their best for him. They could not know how he longed for his own quiet cottage and the wide, unspoilt countryside he had come to love...

They did a few more tests and waited to see that he was more or less stable again...and then they let him go. He did not ask about the results of the tests. No doubt Dr Martin would tell him in his own good time—if there was anything to tell.... But he could see already by everyone's exceptional kindness that the results weren't very good. He was not surprised...nor was he very troubled.... His whole mind was set now on willing himself to be strong enough to go home.... The rest would follow when it would...and he would deal with it on his own...

He hadn't had much time to make friends with anyone in the hospital because they had put him in a small side ward and made him lie very quiet...but even so there seemed to be a lot of waving hands and good wishes flying about as he left, and the ward sister wagged a finger at him and said: 'Now be good, Mr Farrant, dear—or you'll land up back in here again—and I'm sure you wouldn't like that, even if we would!' and she gave him a broad wink and a most unprofessional come-hither smile.

He went out laughing, though still rather groggy, and took a local taxi back to his cottage.

When he came somewhat unsteadily down his path, he was touched to find quite a row of small offerings on his doorstep. Everyone seemed to know which day he was coming out of hospital—though he had told no-one himself. There was a home-made game pie from Mary Willis at the shop, together with a small box of groceries and a note saying: 'Hope these will keep you going. Send word if you want anything else. M. Willis.' There was another piece of cheese and an apple turnover from Mrs Bayliss at Wood End Farm...there was a scented packet of herb tea and another slab of sesame cake, and a bunch of bluebells from 'the *hatchintan*'...and two lamb chops and some more 'rough ends for the bird' from Tom, the butcher...and a book about Gloucestershire from Jim Merrett, the postman, who had also left a note which read: 'If you want anything, just leave a list on the step...'

The village had heard about Bracken's rescue. They were fond of their gypsy boy with his gift for healing animals. They were grateful to Jake, and they were determined to show it in their quiet way...not that they would dream of interfering, mind...

Jake carried his presents indoors, smiling a little, and made himself some herb tea from the gypsies' packet. When he had recovered a little from his journey home, he struggled up his garden path to have a look at Sky. He found the young kestrel sitting on his tree-stump, patiently grooming his long flight feathers again... Waiting to go, thought Jake...making sure every feather was in place, ready for the moment when it came...

He had brought a few of the butcher's 'rough ends' up with him, and these he scattered on the ground near the far end of the pen. Sky looked round at him, the intelligent eyes alert and observant...then he flew across to investigate. His wings were clearly stronger.

'Well done,' Jake said aloud. 'You look a lot better...won't be long now...'

Then, mindful of the ward sister's playful warning, he dutifully went back down the path and made himself lie down and rest—telling himself as he did so that he was really much stronger now, and he need not be cautious any longer...

The next morning there were more gifts on the step, and a note from Bracken, written in his careful copybook hand: 'Sky is getting strong...hope you are. The cub is still alive, and eating.' And underneath he had added in a hastier scrawl: 'I brought you a chrysalis. I think it is a hawk moth. B.' Beside the note was a jam-jar full of leaves with a brown, tough-looking casket-shaped chrysalis on the bottom of the glass. Jake carried it indoors and set it down on his table. I wonder when it will hatch out, he thought.

He was still too weak to venture beyond his garden, though he promised himself he would manage it tomorrow...

But tomorrow came, and with it Carol and the boys, returning from their holiday—and still he had not been able to summon enough strength to get beyond his garden gate...

He heard their voices in the lane from the open door, and decided, reluctantly to stay put in his chair rather than appear at the door weaving on his feet...

The twins came down the lane running, but slowed down to wait for Carol as they approached the cottage. Finally, they stood by his door, looking in, their bright faces a little anxious as they saw him in his chair.

'Are you all right?' they chorused. And Matthew added in a breathless voice: 'We heard in the village about you rescuing Bracken!'

'Is it all right for us to come?' put in Mark. 'Or are you still too exhausted?'

'What happened to Sky?' went on Matthew.

'Did you save the badger cub?' asked Mark.

'Wait a bit, boys,' said Carol's voice from behind them. 'Give him a chance…'

She came past the twins and stood just inside the doorway, looking at Jake. Her smile was open and affectionate—and there was the same almost unwilling sense of recognition in her eyes as there was in Jake's. But she was inwardly dismayed to see Jake's frailness and the unmistakable signs of pain and exhaustion in his face.

'Jake—?' she said. 'We should have warned you—but we met Bracken up the lane, and he said you would want us to come—?'

'Of course I want you to come!' said Jake, his face alight with welcome. 'Put the kettle on, boys, and ferret about in my larder…I've been given all sorts of presents…. There's lots to eat!'

Before long, the boys had spread a feast round him, and were munching Mary Willis's game pie and telling him all about pony-trekking in Wales and how Matthew fell into the river. And Jake told them all about Bracken and the badgers…and the gypsy *pashtiv*…. Carol did not say much. She sat peacefully

208

watching the boys and Jake together, and quietly filled up everyone's cup with tea...

But when they had exhausted their news and (she suspected) Jake as well, they asked if they could go and see Sky, and Jake told them to look in the mousetrap and if there was anything caught in it, they could take it up to the kestrel—if they weren't too squeamish, that is...

There was silence for a little while after they had gone. Then Carol said gently: 'How has it been?'

'Full of excitement,' said Jake, wilfully mis-understanding her. 'As you heard...never a dull moment! And since the badger rescue, every-one's been extraordinarily kind!'

'I should think so, too!' said Carol sturdily. Then she shook her head at him with reproach. 'You know I didn't mean—'

'I know what you meant—' interrupted Jake swiftly. 'And I'm fine.'

'Oh yes?' But the words of sarcastic protest which would have sounded like her brother Bill did not come.... Instead, she sat down on a stool close to Jake, where she could look out of the doorway at the garden. 'Jake...while the boys were off on their ponies, I was staying with friends by the sea in Wales. I used to walk along the beach every morning on my own, very early—and I found myself thinking of you a lot...'

'Did you?' He too had his eyes on the garden and did not look at her.

'You see, Jake, I've been living in a kind of—of cold-storage limbo since Bob died.... It's only recently really that I've even been able to let the twins come close.... They felt shut out at first, I know—they've told me so—but we're all fully operational now!' She smiled a little, and glanced at Jake.

He did not speak.

'So...' she went on, 'I wanted to tell you...I know you're happy here—I can see you are—and this countryside has come to mean a lot to you.... But—but, Jake, human affections do matter, too...don't they? Life's awfully... barren without them.... For a long time I've felt like a sort of figure behind glass. I could see other people going about...laughing and talking...but I couldn't reach them...I don't think I even wanted to reach them.... And it was awfully cold in there...awfully silent and lonely...But now—' This time she turned towards him, her candid gaze fixed on his— 'since I met you the other day...the thaw has set in.... The world is suddenly full of warmth and colour and sound again. It's—it's almost like being re-born...and I—I wanted to thank you.'

'Thank *me?*' Jake sounded astonished. Astonished and shaken.

'Yes, you—I don't know quite what you've done...but I'm alive again.... I think its something to do with...'

'Immediate joy...' murmured Jake.

'What?'

He smiled. 'It's what Bracken has taught me. They say the gypsies live in a perpetual "now"...and, in a way, it's true...'

Carol nodded. 'Seeing you here—so delighted with each small thing...'

'Sky isn't a small thing—' said Jake obscurely.

'No.' She did not misunderstand him. 'That's what I'm saying.... Give back life and freedom to another creature isn't small!'

He laughed. 'The boy, Bracken, does it all the time—!'

'Well—so do you, now.... And I'm your first success!'

He looked at her, the laughter dying in his face. 'Carol—'

But she would not let him issue any warnings. She leant forward and laid a hand on his arm. 'This is your gypsy "now", Jake. I'm not talking about the future...I'm not even talking about—about close companionship.... You've

211

chosen the way you want things to be. I respect that—I understand it.... But, Jake, I could walk by the sea and think of you—and feel warm and young again, and full of unexpected joy...I want you to be able to feel the same.... Just an extra source of—of strength?'

Jake was still looking at her, his eyes very bright and strange. 'Now?' he said incredulously. *'Now?...'* Now, when it is so much too late? How can I feel this now?

She smiled at him—that clear, candid gaze so like Bill's, still unclouded. 'Time doesn't come into it, does it?' she said softly.

There was a long, silent pause, and then she went on—sounding almost shy, now, but still determined: 'I've said an awful lot—knowing you'd never admit to human weakness! But—but, dear Jake, *there are many kinds of love...'*

He said, very softly, 'Yes...there are...'

'And we...ought not to refuse to recognise them...?'

'No—' he said, and suddenly threw off doubt and smiled at her with radiant certainty. 'Nor we should!'

And he stooped his head and kissed her very gently.

They looked at each other in wonder—in joyous recognition...but they did not touch again.

Instead, they sat quietly in the falling twilight, talking together of many secrets unsaid things, until the twins came back with Bracken from seeing Sky.

'We found him up there,' they said, laughing. 'So we brought him back.... He wants to see how you are!'

But Carol saw that Jake was tired now—even too much joy was tiring for him these days—and she got up to go, sending the boys on ahead in a scatter of farewells and laughter. And Bracken stayed outside in the twilit garden.

Jake got to his feet then, and gently put his arms round her.

'I—haven't give you an extra burden, have I?' she asked.

'No...an extra dimension, perhaps!'

'You will...be all right now?'

'I will be more than all right—now!'

She laughed, and kissed him gently. 'I won't say goodbye.... Can we come down again at half-term?'

He hesitated. 'Carol, I may—'

'Half-term!' she said firmly.

'All right,' he agreed, sighing a little. 'Yes. Come then, of course...'

'And meanwhile—' said Carol, smiling up at him: 'you can give my love to this valley *every day!* Keeping some for yourself, of course!'

She left him then, rather swiftly, and ran down the path after the boys.

At the gate, they all turned to wave, and went away up the hill together. He heard their voices receding into the distance...and then there was only the quiet night and an owl calling from the trees...

Carol...he thought. Now, when I know I am watching death approach day be day...and yet I feel my life increasing...not diminishing.... Immediate joy...each day.... He put his hands over his face, trying to shut out the longings he must not have and concentrate on present happiness...

Beside him, there was a shadow on the path, and a quiet voice spoke in the night.

'Sky's waiting for you...and so am I. It's going to be fine tomorrow...'

'Bracken?' he said, smiling into the dark.

'Just rest a little longer...' said the voice, fading to the gate. 'The world's still there...'

In the morning, there was another note from Bracken which said: 'There is a present for you in the garden.'

Intrigued, Jake decided to make his shaky legs obey him and went down his garden path to have a look.

When he got to the little strip of grass under

the tree, he saw—placed carefully opposite the best viewpoint—a brand-new wicker-work garden chair with a long sloping back and a footrest. The basket-work still looked fresh and pale—and it was faintly scented like new-mown hay...

'Oh!' he murmured. 'How lovely!' and promptly went to sit in it and admire the view...

Then he heard Sky calling.... 'Kee-kee-kee!' he was shouting. 'Kee-kee! Ki-ki-kik! Kee-kee!' And even from where he was sitting, he could hear the thresh of wings beating against wire mesh...

He got up and went rather unsteadily round the shed till he got to Sky's pen. The young kestrel seemed to have gone berserk. It was flying to and fro, to and fro, screaming and crashing into the wire at the end of every flight.

'You'll kill yourself!' he said, horrified. 'Sky! Stop it! You'll break your neck!'

But Sky would not stop. He went on flying up and down, up and down, fighting his prison at every turn...

And his wings seemed strong and balanced.... He was flying true...

You're ready, then, he thought sadly. The time has come, and you know it.... What shall I do?

215

Behind him a voice spoke softly: 'I told you he'd let us know when he was ready. I'm glad you're here to see him go...'

Jake turned, and found Bracken perched on the tree above the pen, patiently unfastening the staples that held the wire.

'It will be better for him to fly straight up,' he said. 'So I'm going to roll the top wire back...'

'Let me help—' said Jake, forgetting his weakness. And he went round to the other side and began to loosen the wire.

Together they freed it, and furled it slowly back till the top of the pen was open to the free air above.

Then Bracken climbed back on to the branch of the tree and called to Sky, trying to make him stop his frantic horizontal flight and look up...

'Sky...' he called. 'Come on, Sky. The world is yours...look up! Come on, lift your head up and see...you're free now, Sky...you're free!' and he reached down a brown hand and waved it at Sky through the open roof of the pen...

For a moment the desperate bird continued its headlong dash at the wire...then it paused, in mid-flight, as if sensing a change in the air above. The beautiful flight feathers were almost still, the smooth grey head looked up, the

216

golden eyes cleared from their unreasoning panic—and saw not wire, but empty space above. With one swift thrust of those powerful wings, Sky was through the gap, up above the shed, and lifting, lifting, flying straight up into the clear evening light...

'Kee!' he cried, exultantly. 'Kee-kee-kee! I'm free! I'm free!' And he went on, up and up, higher and higher, past the swallows, past the swifts, past the high late-flying geese, until he was only a shadow, a speck, a mote in the wild, free air of heaven...

They stood together looking up until there was nothing left to see but the twilight deepening above the quiet hills, and the first pale star glimmering in the west...

'Goodbye, Sky...' said Bracken softly. 'Fly safe...fly free...'

Jake found that there were tears in his eyes, and he could not speak at all. That's how I should like it to be with me, he thought... sudden and swift—and free...

'That's how it will be—' said Bracken aloud, 'with all of us...'

That evening, after Bracken had gone home, promising to come in the morning and start on the sett for little Zoe, Jake heard a step on the path, and Dr Martin came in through the cottage door.

'How are you getting on?' he asked. 'Do you feel up to a game of chess?'

Jake was delighted. 'Of course! My mind's more-or-less OK. It's only my legs that are woolly!'

They settled down to a tranquil game, and did not talk about anything in particular until they were drinking a final cup of tea beside the living-room fire, which Jake had lit earlier.

Then Dr Martin said quietly: 'The results of your tests came through.... They weren't very good, I'm afraid...'

Jake smiled. 'I didn't expect them to be...it's all right.' He paused for a moment, and then went on: 'I had a talk with Bracken's mother the other evening. The Romany view is very interesting.... And I want to tell you about Sky...'

The old doctor listened gravely, nodding his wise, grizzled head from time to time in agreement. At length he said gently: 'Yes...we have got too far away from the natural world in our lives today.... Out here, it all seems very simple...'

Jake's smile was almost as luminous as Bracken's. 'There are no words to tell you what this place and its people have done for me— but I just wanted you to know that I'm all right

218

now....I know now that there's nothing to be afraid of.... In fact, one way and another, my life is getting richer every day!'

They were both silent for a moment, and then Jake thought of something else. 'By the way, is the boy quite all right now?'

'Oh yes...' Dr Martin's brown face increased into a cheerful grin. 'A few bruises, a mild concussion...and the gash on his head is healing nicely. Tough as old boots, these gypsy boys...!' His grin diminished a little. 'All the same—it's a good thing you got there when you did.'

Jake made no comment on that. But he went on: 'D'you think the farmer—Deacon, was it?—could make trouble?'

Dr Martin looked doubtful. 'I shouldn't think so. He never actually saw the boy, did he? He might put two and two together—but then there's a lot of local people who disapprove of badger-digging...'

'Mm...if you hear anything on your rounds—that might be a nuisance, I mean—will you let me know?'

Dr Martin laughed. 'Companions in crime? Yes, I will.... The gypsies are always being harassed about something, and as far as I can see, they're good sort of people. They only want to be left alone...' He got up to go, putting his portable chess set away in his pocket. Then as an afterthought he took it out again and laid it on the table. 'You might like to play yourself! Or you might get another visitor. In any case, you are the only one round here who can give me a game!'

'Will you come again?'

'Of course!' The old doctor patted his arm. 'Providing you behave yourself and don't go in for any more wild adventures!'

They laughed together, and Jake went with him to the door and stood on the step in the lamplight...

'Goodnight,' called Dr Martin, and strolled away up the stony path.

Jake stood for a while looking out at the darkened valley. There was no moon tonight, but the stars were bright above the hills. Far away in the beechwoods, a fox barked sharply...and the owls were calling to each other behind him in the tall old ash trees at the edge of the field...

The night air was cool and scented with moss and flowers. Down in the pitch-black shadows of the lake below, the old heron stirred in his sleep and called once harshly before settling to more dark dreams of lazy fish in shallow streams...

It was very peaceful...very still...

I am happy here, thought Jake. Profoundly, truly happy...

Quietly, he went inside and shut the door.

In the morning when he came down, he found Bracken already at work by his shed. He had taken down most of Sky's pen, and was busy enlarging the enclosed area by cutting the wire in half and using the dry-stone wall at the end of the garden as an extra barrier.

'She won't need anything too high,' he explained. 'But she'll need to be stopped from going too far. She's not ready to fend for herself yet...though I expect she'll try to dig her way out! I thought we could make the sett over here...'

Jake saw that he had already dug out a squarish hole and two longer trenches in which he had laid some bits of wide, old-fashioned drainpipe...

'Where did you find those?'

Bracken grinned. 'One of us is a scrap dealer...he gets all sorts. That's where I got the wire...'

Jake was feeling better this morning—the betraying weakness seemed to have retreated. He picked up the wire-cutters which Bracken had laid down, and said: 'Show me what you want...'

221

They worked together, absorbed and happy, until Jake said suddenly: 'Is it all right for you to stay so long?' He looked up at the sun which was climbing the eastern sky.

Bracken smiled. 'My Da says I'm to lay off working in the fields this week...and come and help you instead!'

They grinned at one another, and returned to work. Before long they had finished the wire enclosure and laid the drainpipes in the trenches in such a way that they sloped down from the square hole and their open ends came out in two different places in the middle of the grassy cage...

'What will we use for her bedroom?' asked Jake.

Bracken went over to the corner by the shed and came back carrying an old wooden beer barrel. 'I brought this up...' he said. 'If we lay it on its side and line it with grass, it should be nice and snug...' Then he stooped down and picked up his saw. 'But I'm going to saw it in half downwards...' he explained, 'so's we can take the top off to have a look at her at first... She might need dealing with, and she's got to be kept warm. Later on we can fill in the hole and let her get on with it...'

Jake nodded. 'What are you feeding her on?'

The boy sighed. 'We tried bread and milk

at first—but she was sick…. So then we watered the milk down and added some chick feed. She seems to like that. It'll be worms and grubs soon…I can handle that!'

Jake laughed. 'After Sky, that sounds easy!'

Bracken grinned. 'But she'll eat mice and voles and toads and things, too, soon. Da asked the vet about it, when he was doing one of the farmer's horses, and he said puppy meal and raw mince would be all right soon…and some vitamins, he said—like in cod liver oil. Because, you see, in the wild, her mother would still be suckling her a bit, and bringing in lots of small things for her to try…'

He sighed again, a little sadly. 'I'm sorry about the other cub—'

Jake shook his head decisively. 'No, Bracken. I've been thinking about it. That second cub was injured by more than the fall… it was covered in blood. I think one of the shots must have caught it as it ran…' He looked at the boy's troubled face and added gently: 'It was probably dying anyway…before you fell.'

For a while Bracken was silent, looking down at the newly-turned earth round the artificial sett.

'I expect you're right,' he said at last, still a little sad. And then, with a mercurial change of mood, he looked up, smiling, and added:

'Well—at least we've got Zoe to deal with. We mustn't let her feel lonely...I'll bring her up this evening—if it's all right?'

'Of course,' agreed Jake. 'I'm looking forward to it. Does she mind people much?'

'Not now—when she's so small. So it's just as well to get her used to us now.... And she'll need brushing and combing at first, the vet said, because her mother would have done it for her...I expect she'll let you do it—she doesn't mind me. But we oughtn't to handle her too much. I s'pose, or she'll never go back to the wild.... Just like Sky...I never dared to get too friendly!'

Jake smiled, thinking privately that it would be almost impossible for Bracken *not* to be friendly—with everything! 'Come and have some tea,' he said. 'I'm going to sit in my brand new chair and admire the view...'

Presently, they sat side by side, with Bracken perched on the wall, and looked out over the sunlit valley...

'Next week...' said Bracken dreamily, 'we might start going out again.... My Da says we can borrow the two *grais,* if we like...'

Jake looked at him. 'Really?' He knew that was a signal honour from a gypsy horse-dealer.

'The quietest two!' said Bracken, brimming with sudden laughter.

'They'd better be!' Jake was laughing, too. 'No more sudden descents down quarries, please!'

'Look!' said Bracken, pointing across the valley. 'There's a kestrel hovering...I wonder if it's Sky?'

'Would he come back?'

'No.' The boy shook his head firmly. 'Not he! But he might stay in the area...I suppose it might smell like home to him...' He looked out again at the steady, hovering shadow. 'Still, there are lots of kestrels round here. He'll find his way about, I'm sure...he's about old enough to be looking for a mate soon, I should think...' He looked at Jake, half-smiling. 'They're like swans, you know...they mate for life...'

'Do they?'

The boy got up from the wall and stood looking gravely at Jake. 'Will you rest a bit? I'll be back this evening...'

'I will...' Jake was smiling at him. 'I'll sit in this beautiful chair and dream. Will you thank them for it?'

'We all helped to make it,' said Bracken. 'My father cut the withies. My mother boiled them and stripped them—the sun dried them!—and I made the frame, and the others wove the basket-work round it...' He patted the pliant canes with his hand. 'We were afraid it wouldn't dry in time. You have to work with the withies damp, you see...but luckily it was sunny!' He paused, with his hand on the chair still. 'In the old days, my Da says, the Romanies used to put a blessing on everything they made...even clothes pegs!' He looked at Jake, half-serious and half-full of mischief. 'I hope it still works!'

'I'm sure it does!' said Jake.

He must have been dozing in his chair—more deeply asleep than he knew—for he didn't hear the voices and footsteps in the lane. But he felt someone's shadow fall across him, and he opened his eyes to see Bill and Manny standing beside him on the grass, both of them looking at him with anxious but friendly solicitude.

He could see that the two of them were shy—something he found hard to believe about either of them—especially Manny. But he covered their awkwardness and silence with smiling affection.

'Well I'm damned!' he said, feeling a rush of warmth at the sight of his old friends. 'You took me at my word! Come on in and have a beer!

He led them both inside and went on talking easily until he had them both sitting down in his living-room with a glass of beer in their hands.

Bill was looking at Jake with disbelief—almost with awe, he seemed so changed. He was much thinner now, and the planes of his face had sharpened. Like Carol, his sister, Bill saw the fragility of the bones and the way light seemed to flow outward from the luminous, transparent skin. It was clearly the face of a man who was mortally sick...but it was also a man who was entirely tranquil—entirely happy.

Manny, too, saw all these things, and behind it all a certain grim humour lurking in Jake's too-observant gaze.

'Well—?' said Jake grinning. 'What do you think of me?'

'I think you're fantastic!' said Bill, lifting his glass. 'Isn't he, Manny?'

'Oh, I am, I am!' agreed Jake. And then, quite deliberately, he put them at their ease. 'You don't have to worry about me, you know...I've found a good life down here—an amazing life, really. I couldn't be happier...so drink up. I've got lots to tell you...and you can bring me up to date on all the office gossip...'

Filled with a strange mixture of relief and sadness, the two men relaxed—and the three of them began to talk and exchange news as old friends will. They talked for a long time

227

in the quiet cottage—and Jake told them about his adventures with Bracken and the saving of Sky...

'And then there's Zoe,' he said.

'Who's Zoe?' asked Manny, with a wild hope in his eye.

'If you stay long enough, you'll meet her,' said Jake, eyes dancing with mischief. 'She's coming tonight.'

Bill was not deceived by the mischief. 'Another lame duck?' he asked.

Jake grinned. 'A badger cub, actually...' and he began to relate the dark happenings of Hawkswood Quarry.

At length, it all seemed said on either side, but Bill still looked at Jake with a troubled, tentative gaze, and still did not seem to be able to get out what was on his mind.

'You got on well with Carol, didn't you?' he asked.

Jake's smile was full of warmth—and something more which Bill did not quite understand. 'Got on well? She simply took me by storm! I shall never be the same again!' And that was true, he reflected soberly. Then he went on, more sedately: 'I liked the boys, too... They're all coming back to see me at half-term, all being well, that is.'

Bill was surprised, and pleased. 'She didn't

tell me that!' But he was pursuing another line of thought. 'So...you aren't entirely averse to visitors?'

'No, of course not. I sent a message to you two, didn't I?'

'Yes, but—' Bill grinned in a self-dismissing manner. 'We don't count—'

'Oh, yes you do!'

'I mean...how would you feel...about other people?'

'What other people?'

Bill was silent for a moment, and then—greatly daring—he said: 'Your daughter, for instance?'

Jake was staggered. 'Beth? You must be joking!'

'No,' said Manny seriously, backing up Bill. 'He's not joking, Jake...she wants to see you.'

Jake shook his head slowly—a heavy reluctance growing within him. 'Why? All these years...she's not shown much interest in what happened to me.'

'Have you shown much interest in what happened to her?' countered Manny, bluntly.

Jake winced a little. 'That's not fair! You know I kept as far away as possible, with intent...I didn't want their lives torn apart by warring parents.'

'I know,' said Bill, glaring at Manny.

229

'She understands that, now,' agreed Manny, glaring back at Bill.

Jake sighed, looking from one to the other in affectionate disapproval. 'Hadn't you better stop glaring at each other, and tell me what's going on?'

'Nothing's going on,' growled Bill.

'Nothing,' echoed Manny. 'Except that the child has suddenly developed an urge to see you...call it conscience, if you like—or even curiosity. She *is* your daughter...' he added, to Jake's sceptical look.

Bill said, speaking slowly and painfully: 'My instinct was to say no—they've been grasping and self-centred long enough, God knows! But then, I thought—maybe it matters to her—and maybe it matters to you? She's the future generation. Perhaps she shouldn't be left with this to live with—never having made the effort —never knowing if you'd have liked to see her or not....?'

Jake said, equally painfully: 'Bill, I don't like farewells...wouldn't it be better left as it is...?

'I don't know...' said Bill, sounding anxious and uncertain. 'I thought so myself...but Manny said I was wrong...'

Manny, who during this time had been silent, suddenly said: 'Damn it all, Jake, you know me! As far as I am concerned, *any spark you can kindle on this benighted earth is worthwhile...'*

Jake looked at him in surprise. His face softened. 'You sound like Bracken grown up,' he said. And, after a pause, he added: 'Very well...if she wants to come, she can. But for God's sake come with her, and don't let her stay long!'

All the same, he kept looking at Manny, as if seeing something in his old friend that he hadn't known was there...

While they were still wondering quite what to say next, there was a light tap on the door, and Bracken's voice said: 'I've brought Zoe up. Come and see!'

He did not show any surprise when three men, not one, came out of the door. He just smiled at Jake and said gently: 'Better go softly...she's still a bit scared of loud noises...'

They followed him out to the wire enclosure, and there, in a cardboard box on the ground, was the tiny badger cub. Bracken had taken off the lid of the box so that they could see inside. She was curled up asleep, surrounded by wisps of hay and pieces of woollen cloth to keep her warm. The small black and white face was perfectly marked, but the fur on her back was brindled and scrappy, and stuck up like tangled wire.... Jake's fingers instantly itched

231

to have a brush between them and to start smoothing the rumpled fur down...

'How old is she, do you think?' asked Bill, in an awe-struck voice.

'Nearly four months, the vet thinks...' said Bracken. 'She's weaned, you see...and one tooth is growing...'

'Will you be able to rear her?' asked Manny, also stricken by the sight of the cub's smallness and weakness.

Bracken looked at Manny, and then up at Jake. 'I dunno...but we're going to try...'

He busied himself then, measuring out some food—a handful of chick-feed, a moistener of milk and water, a drop of fish-oil, and half a chopped-up worm...

'You'd better watch me...' he said to Jake. 'So's you can manage if I can't come...'

'Don't you dare not come!' said Jake. 'I'd be terrified!'

They laughed, but Bracken went on, unperturbed. 'She's got to get used to you, too.... You'd better have a go at feeding her...' and he handed Jake a small metal spoon. 'By the way,' he added cheerfully, 'I've deloused her.... No fleas at the moment!'

'I'm delighted to hear it,' said Jake, grinning.

'She'll wake up in a minute,' went on the boy. 'It's getting near dusk...'

Sure enough, the small body uncurled and stretched, the questing snout with its clean white blaze, came up to sniff the air, and the little short-sighted eyes opened and looked round with distrust.

'There now,' said Bracken, crooning to the cub in his softest, most caressing voice: 'See, Zoe, we've made you a new house all of your own. It's a big bad world, I know, but you'll be safe up here...come on out now, and have a look round.... It's your dinner time as well...'

Talking all the time, he lifted the little cub out of her box and set her on the ground. She sat still for a few moments, quivering all over—but then her curiosity got the better of her, and she began to look about her, and then to snuff along the ground. She came up against the bowl of food with a bump, and sat down again on her haunches to look at it, and smell it...

'Now!' said Bracken. 'Hold some up in the spoon!'

Jake scooped some up and held it towards the twitching nose. The little cub stared at the approaching spoon with deep apprehension, and then butted it violently with her snout.

'Try again...' said Bracken, totally unperturbed. 'She often does that at first...'

Jake tried again. This time, the cub let the spoon approach and then snuffed forward and knocked all the food off the metal bowl of the spoon onto the ground...

Patiently, not even waiting for Bracken to tell him, Jake began again.... Zoe inched forward and took the food off the spoon almost before he got there.

Absurdly pleased, Jake produced some more. Again, the little cub came forward and sought for the food with her sensitive nose...

'Now,' said Bracken softly, 'try holding the spoon near the dish...'

Before very long, Zoe had discovered for herself that a dish held more than a spoon. The neat little head pressed forward, eating tranquilly from the bowl...

'Wonderful!' breathed Jake.

'You're doing fine!' said Bracken.

The two others stood watching Jake, so absorbed and happy, and did not say a word.

Zoe ate all her food, and then began to explore her new home in earnest. Bracken had left Sky's tree-trunk for her to climb over—but now he also arranged a few bigger stones, and an extra log or two as climbing obstacles in her playground. She tried to clamber over these, fell over backwards, and waved her feet in the air...then scrambled up and darted round in circles, playing with a leaf or a twig or a pebble—pouncing like a kitten, and backing away in mock terror...gambolling cheerfully, quite unafraid in her new-found freedom.

Last of all, Bracken tossed a furry baby's ball, quartered in brown and black, into Zoe's path.... She was delighted with it, rolling it, jumping on it, chasing it, and finally settling down with it pressed close to her furry side in a corner of the pen...

'I thought she might like it,' said Bracken. 'She misses her brothers and sisters, you see.... We'd better put it in the box with her when she goes to sleep...'

'Will she be all right there?' asked Jake. 'Won't she get cold?'

'Not yet...' Bracken looked at her judiciously. 'She's at her most active just after dark. When she gets tired, she'll go back to her box. We won't put her in the big barrel yet...not till she gets used to all this...' He looked up at the blue evening sky. 'It's a warmish night...she'll come to no harm...'

As he spoke, the little cub began to prance about again, rolling and playing, lying on her back, and chasing shadows and her own imaginary tail...

Fascinated, the watchers found themselves unable to tear themselves away. They stayed there, admiring Zoe's kittenish antics, until she began to tire, and Bracken stepped in and gently restored her to her box, complete with her woolly ball. Seeming perfectly content, the small cub curled herself into a second woolly ball and went to sleep.

'She'll come out again later on,' whispered Bracken. 'She knows her way about this time.... We can leave her now...'

He laid an extra bit of blanket over her in the box, and tiptoed away.

Manny and Bill stood on the path, and looked at Jake in the falling dusk.... They neither of them knew how to say goodbye.

But Jake took a step forward and grasped them each by an arm. 'I'm glad you came down,' he said. 'So you could see for yourselves I'm all right! Come again when you can!'

They both went on looking at him for a moment, unsure if he really meant it. Then they seemed to see something reassuring in his face, and Manny—speaking for them both—said stoutly: 'With marvels like Zoe to look at, you bet your sweet life we will!'

Jake thought perhaps Bracken had slipped away unnoticed, but he reappeared at this moment, carrying a swinging storm lantern, and said in his gentle, lilting voice: 'It's a dark old night...shall I light you up the lane?'

They followed him gratefully, turning to wave at Jake from the gate—and made their way up the dark stony track to their car at the top of the lane.

When he left them, Bracken lifted the lantern a little to look into their faces and said, very softly: 'I'll look after him, you know…while I can…' and before they could answer, he had gone into the shadows, the lantern swinging in his hand.

Jake was extremely exhausted after Bill's and Manny's visit. He didn't like admitting it himself, but it was clear that the effort of conversation and keeping a cheerful countenance in front of his friends was becoming too much for him. He was entirely right to have come away…

Here, in Bracken's quiet company, and among the wild creatures and this enchanted countryside, he could be himself…

He sighed as he thought this, because he had been very glad to see his old friends—however tired it made him…but now he was paying the price of too much exertion. It was his own fault, he told himself, and he'd better lie down and make the best of it…

All the same, he was anxious about the badger cub. Supposing she came out of her box and couldn't find her way back? Suppose she got cold? Had they made the wire secure enough underneath? Suppose a fox or a dog got in? Wasn't she still a bit young to be out alone—even in a protected pen?

Tired out with all his own arguments, and groaning a little at his own idiocy, Jake dragged himself out of bed, put on his dressing-gown and went out into the garden to see if little Zoe was all right.

He came up to the pen quietly, and saw the small black and white mask gleaming at him in the dark through the netting. She was out and about, wandering and sniffing, seeming quite well and undisturbed by her new home.... He went round to the other side of the pen to make sure the cardboard box was intact and the opening in the end of it was clear for the cub to go in and out...

'It's all right...' said Bracken's voice in the dark. 'She's been out several times...and I've put a bit more food out for her, in case she gets peckish...'

'Why aren't you in bed?' said Jake sternly to the shadow by the pen.

'Why aren't you?' retorted Bracken—but there was a smile in his voice. 'You need your sleep more than me,' he added, as if stating an irrefutable fact.

Jake laughed softly and turned once more to watch the little badger exploring her new territory.

Then, by common consent, the two of them crept away and left her alone in the dark.

They sat together drinking tea on the step, as usual, and Bracken looked at Jake's tell-tale pallor in the light from the doorway and said reproachfully: 'You let them tire you...'

'Yes,' agreed Jake, sighing. 'But friends are important, aren't they? And I can rest tomorrow...'

'I'll come up a bit later then,' said Bracken. 'The cub will sleep in the day-time anyway. Look what I found on your path!' And he held out his palm, on which lay a tiny thread of light, glowing in the dark.

Considering Jake's thoughts about Manny and sparks, this seemed a littly uncanny of Bracken.... But then, Jake reflected, a lot of things about Bracken were a little uncanny...

But Bracken looked from Jake's face to the quiet night beyond the garden and said obscurely: 'Even glow-worms needs rest before they can shine...'

A day or two after their visit to Jake, Bill and Manny decided they had better ring Beth and tell her what had happened.

The girl was silent while they described Jake's condition and his reaction to her request.

Then she said, in a voice that sounded jerky and abrupt: 'I see. Then, please will you come to Oxford with me and tell Charles?'

Sighing, the two men agreed.

They arrived in Oxford on a golden summer day—and found Charles in his rooms, surrounded by coffee cups and friends.

His eyebrows went up—reminding them of Jake's—when he saw Beth and the two men standing in the doorway, but he did not get up from his chair, or stop what he was saying to one of his friends.

He isn't very like Jake, thought Manny, except for the eyebrows. Those fair, slightly arrogant good looks are more like his mother's. But I don't think those eyes are quite so glacial...

Bill thought, with a flick of anger—that supercilious mouth, like Margaret's—a spoilt brat with too much money and too little sense!

'Charles...' said Beth, speaking abruptly because she was a bit nervous, 'we need to talk to you—'

'...this evening,' Charles was saying, 'if you can escape from Simpson—'

'Not Simpson,' murmured one of the young men, 'royal command...sherry with the Dean...'

Charles waved a hand. 'Well—escaping from the Dean is easier than Simpson.... More

240

absent-minded. So, we're meeting at the boathouse, as soon as you can get away...and we're going on to the Trout...'

'*Charles—!*' repeated Beth, and when Bill heard the note of rising panic in her voice, he spoke himself, in the clipped, hard tones he used for difficult interviews in the field...

'Forgive us for interrupting—we haven't long. I think you'd better hear what we have to say—'

Charles heard the note of authority in Bill's voice. He got up with rather deliberate slowness and said to his friends: 'Sounds a bit heavy...I hate to be uncouth, but I think you'd better melt...'

The three others got up then, apparently not at all dismayed, and drifted out of the room, trailing scarves, books and squash racquets, and one rather battered guitar...

'All right,' said Charles, a glint of anger in his eyes as he looked at his sister, 'since you've ordered my friends out of my rooms—what have you to say?'

So Bill told him. He stood there listening, his eyes dark with shock, while Bill said, in no uncertain terms, that his father was dying, had probably no more than a few weeks left, had deliberately cut himself off from his friends, from all help and comfort—and what was

Charles going to do about it?

'What *can* I do?' he asked at last, with the faintest shrug of his shoulders.

'You could show some concern for a start!' snapped Bill.

Manny laid a hand on his arm, and turned to look at the boy. 'He's understandably upset,' he explained. 'And so am I. We're fond of Jake, you see.'

There was a silence, while the imputation behind those words sank in.

A faint flush seemed to touch Charles's face, and receded, leaving it as pale and handsome as before. 'The trouble is...' he said, by way of excuse, 'he never gave us much chance to be fond of him...'

'No,' said Manny. 'That was deliberate policy. He believes kids should be left alone to make up their own minds...'

Charles glanced across at his sister. 'Oh? But he's agreed to see Beth? Did he *ask* for me?'

'No,' said Bill, his voice still hard and angry. 'he didn't ask for anyone. In fact, he tried to put us off.... He said he didn't like farewells, and wouldn't it be better left as it is...'

'Well...?' said Charles, after looking from one to the other, 'Wouldn't it?'

'That's up to you—' murmured Manny softly.

'Think, Charles...' began Beth.

'I *am* thinking!' said Charles in a driven voice. 'And I don't much like what I'm thinking!'

'It may be your only chance—' she said.

'But—does he really *want* it?' asked Charles. 'After all—what can I say to him?'

'You don't have to say anything,' said Beth, sounding suddenly young and near to tears. 'Just *come!*'

The others waited.

Charles shook his head uncertainly. 'I don't know...I'm not sure it would do any good...'

'You're his *son*, dammit!' said Manny, all at once sounding as firm and authoritative as Bill. 'There's no other future a man can have. Would you deny him that?'

Charles looked as if Manny had struck him in the face. At last he said in a shaken voice: 'If you put it like that...I have no choice...'

Jake was ill again in the night. A wave of nausea hit him, and when he had staggered back from the bathroom, his legs buckled under him and he could not reach his bed. After a while, though, he struggled up and found his pills.... A bout of pain was beginning, and it took longer each time for the drugs to work...

He crawled back into bed, feeling weak and

exhausted.... But then Bracken's unexpected remark about the glow-worm came into his mind, and he began to laugh. A fine sort of glow-worm I am! he said, giggling weakly. Can't even get out of bed to light the lamp! But somehow, the warmth of Bracken's voice stayed with him.... He saw, behind his closed eyes, a clear picture of the boy's hand, holding a small glowing creature in his palm. Sighing, freed from pain and terror, his mind stilled... the glow-worm shone in his mind...and he fell asleep.

In the morning, he did not wake till late. He knew it was late because the sun was high, half-hidden behind slow-moving clouds, and the early chorus of birds was over. The blackbird was still singing though in the pear tree outside his window...

When he went outside, he found Bracken up by Zoe's pen, tinkering about with some further additions.

'She's fast asleep,' he said, by way of greeting. 'And all the food is gone.... We'll try showing her the proper sett tonight, shall we?'

Jake looked down while Bracken lifted the lid of the box for him to see the little cub. She looked small and lonely, curled up with her neat, striped head turned in against her flank.

The woolly ball was close beside her, and Bracken had made sure she had enough bedding carefully tucked round her to keep her warm. She was breathing evenly and calmly—far out in the quiet world of sleep—and did not seem at all like a deprived and frightened orphan...

'She's doing fine...' said Bracken softly. 'But she'll likely need a bit of company when she wakes up...'

'Her fur needs brushing—when ought I to do it?'

Bracken considered. 'I tried it when she was eating. She didn't seem to mind too much....I think she might even come to like it...'

He put back the lid on the box, covered the whole thing with an armload of old cut bracken, and left the little cub to her day-long sleep.

'I brought some tea up today,' he said, glancing at Jake's transparent face, and he led the way purposefully to the bright new chair on the strip of grass...

They sat peacefully looking out at the awakening valley. Jake found that it was not so very late after all. He had forgotten that it was well into summer now, and the sun got high in the sky very early...

'My blackbird's got five mouths to feed,' said Bracken, 'They're both busy all day long...'

'How d'you know?'

Bracken grinned. 'I climbed up to see...when she wasn't looking!'

Jake glanced round at the fork of the old ash tree behind the shed. 'Up there? What were you doing?'

'There was a jay about. I remembered about you and the magpie...I wanted to see they were all right...'

He looked at Jake's face in the early sunlight, assessing its tiredness—and caught the longing in his eye.

'We could go just a little way...?' he said to that saddened gaze.

Jake stirred and laughed. 'I must be very transparent!'

'Yes,' agreed the boy, smiling too. 'You are!'

So they wandered out into the cool morning, and by common consent drifted slowly down the sloping valley to the lake where the wild swans lived.

The dog-roses were out in the hedgerows now, and meadowsweet and cow parsley grew tall along the edges of the fields...

'We mayn't see anything special—' said Bracken, looking up to watch a cuckoo fly, still calling unevenly, across the valley to the woods beyond. 'Not every time—'

'Everything's special to me,' murmured

Jake, also watching the cuckoo, seeing the sunlight glint on its wing as it passed...

Bracken nodded, smiling. 'Me, too,' he said.

They arrived by the reedy fringe of the lake and settled down to watch the ordinary everyday life of that small enclosed world. The swifts were darting low over the water after insects, their high, thin voices echoing in the still morning air. The little coots and moorhens still chugged fussily in and out of the bulrushes. There were muted quacks and sudden watery flourishes from the mallards hidden in the thick eyots of reeds.... A fish plopped suddenly, making rings on the surface, disturbing the reflections of the purple loosestrife nodding to themselves at the water's edge...

'Oh, the ducklings are hatched!' breathed Bracken, 'Look!'

And from behind a tussock of tall rushes came the neat brown mother, with seven golden, fluffy ducklings swimming in a straight disciplined line behind her. The drake was there too, brilliant in his smart spring plumage, his beautiful neck feathers iridescent in the sun. He swam purposefully round his little family, circling them with a watchful, protective eye...

'Watch out!' said Bracken suddenly, aloud. 'Look behind you! Take care!'

But he needn't have bothered. A fine vee of

ripples was spreading behind the swimming head of a big, powerful stoat who was gaining fast on the last of the swimming ducklings.... The drake saw the moving water and went into action. Squawking and flapping, scooting along the water, trailing his feet and splashing furiously, it drove the marauding stoat away and chased it all across the lake. The mother duck and her trim little fleet went sailing on, unperturbed...

It's like a war, thought Jake sadly—a ceaseless war with endless skirmishes...and the weakest ones always lose...

'They mostly survive,' said Bracken comfortingly. 'Got to lose a few, though—we'd be swarming with creatures, else!' He smiled at Jake. 'Look!' he added, softly: 'There's the old heron fishing...I bet he keeps the fish down!'

The tall grey bird was far out across the lake, standing on his long stilted legs in the shallows, his elegant crested head looking down, beak poised in readiness. He was utterly still, utterly silent, a statue of a bird.... Then, like lethal lightning, he struck with his fierce, pointed bill. The head dipped, then rose—something silver flashed in the sun and was gone in a single gulp...

'Doesn't waste any time, does he?' said the boy, grinning. 'How about us having breakfast now?' and be brought out his flask and a couple of flat oatmeal scones...

'I've got some cheese,' said Jake. 'And some apples...'

'There's a dragon-fly!' said Bracken, while they were eating. 'Look, there he goes! Doesn't he look new!'

The darting, transparent wings flashed in the sun, the long, delicate body seemed to gleam with fresh paint, the speckled browns and greens were so bright. Jake watched it, breathless, and presently it skimmed quite near to them and settled on a lily leaf to dry its gauzy wings.... So beautiful, so fragile...thought Jake...gone in a day.... He could see every marking on its body quite clearly—the fine veins on its wings—even the two jewelled eyes reflecting the sheen of the brown water beneath it. At last it grew tired of sunning itself on the lily pad and darted away with a thrum of wings —swift and ethereal in the bright morning...

'I don't think the swans are coming today...' said Bracken, with his mouth full. 'They're usually earlier than this...'

But even as he spoke, two of the great white birds came pulsing overhead, the music of their flight throbbing in Jake's head like fire—so stirring and so strange. They landed far down the lake in a skidding stop, sending up a sparkle of spray, and sat there, quietly floating, their snowy, graceful outlines meeting their two reflections in perfect symmetry.

'Only two?' said Bracken, sounding a little anxious. 'Where are the others?'

And then Jake pointed, too enchanted to speak. For out from the willow shadows came their two mates, proudly gliding like ships in full sail, and with them came six small grey cygnets, swimming gallantly, small legs cleaving the water in their efforts to keep up with their two noble mothers. The four adult swans met in mid-water—each cob greeting his mate with grave courtesy, dipping his long neck, touching beak to beak, and then turning to swim beside her, his pearl-grey downy offspring following behind...

'Aren't they handsome?' Bracken's eyes were warm with admiration. 'They'll stay together always now...'

'But there were five,' said Jake, 'the first time. What happened to the other one?'

'I expect his mate had begun nesting somewhere further off already...' Bracken waved a hand towards the farthest reaches of the lake. 'Even on another lake. They've probably got a family too by now...'

They dreamed and idled a while longer. The dragon-fly came skimming back, passing them with a shimmer of translucent wing.... Once more Jake heard the fine whirr of its flight, it passed so close. The ducks talked quietly among themselves, dibbling in the water and diving for food. The tranquil swans sailed on...

High above the lake, a solitary kestrel swung and hovered, its wings outspread, leaning on the summer wind...

'It might be Sky...' murmured Bracken, lying back on the grass and gazing up into the clear blue air...

Sky...thought Jake. I believe I miss him, I miss his fierce, angry independence...the tameless golden eyes and arrogant head. But I'm glad he's up there somewhere in those wide spaces, flying free...

'We must look very small to him from up there,' went on Bracken in a dreaming voice, 'with all the wide world to play in...'

'Yes...' Jake's voice was as dream-laced as the boy's. 'We must...'

'Motes...' drowsed the gentle voice, 'just bits of the pattern...'

A small summer breeze stirred the willow leaves, sent pollen drifting from the flowers, and lifted a thistledown head into the air.... It sailed close over Jake's head...Bracken reached out a lazy hand and caught it. He held it in his brown palm and offered it to Jake.

'Next year's flowers...' he said, smiling his strange, tender smile.

Jake looked down at the perfect shape, the intricate filigree stars and miniscule feathery haloes round each tiny seedhead, the fine, hair-thin threads of stalk.... So beautiful, so fragile (like the dragon-fly), with a world of summers in its keeping...

'When I die...' Bracken's voice was as soft and light as the thistledown, 'Just think! I'll be part of a dandelion clock...or a dragon-fly's wing...or a worm!' His smile grew luminous with unexplained joy. 'I'll be part of Sky!'

Jake did not answer. He knew what Bracken was telling him. There were tears in his eyes—but he wasn't sure if they were grief or some of Bracken's immediate joy...

He lifted his hand and let the thistledown blow away on the wind.... It hung for a moment in the air above his head, shimmer-ing in the sun—and then it drifted upwards on the merest breath and sailed away across the valley...

They lay still for a while, silent and content in the quiet morning... And then Bracken said, without turning his head! 'If we go through the bottom meadow, it won't be so steep going back...'

In the afternoon when Jake was alone, he had a visitor.

The man who stood at his door was solid and friendly, with a bluff, weather-worn face and the quiet blue eyes of a countryman. He wore an old pair of cords tucked into large wellington boots, and an ancient jacket of good but battered tweed. His grey curly hair stuck up in a ring round his head, and his smile was calm and kind.

'Sorry to disturb you, Mr Farrant, I'm Bayliss of Wood End Farm. I wonder...could I have a word?'

'Of course,' said Jake, meeting his smile with one of his own. 'Come in.'

The farmer looked down at his boots doubtfully. 'D'you mind if I shed these here? They're not fit for company!'

He followed Jake into the cottage in his stocking feet.

'Have a chair...' said Jake. 'A glass of beer? Or tea?'

'A cup of tea would be more than welcome!' said Stan Bayliss, settling into his chair.

He noticed, in his quiet, observant way, how frail and transparent Jake Farrant looked these days. Like a good many other people, he had seen this man on his television screen many times in the past—sending back reports from scenes of drama and carnage. He had looked brown and hard and keen then, and full of a kind of driving energy and anger about the things he had to relate. There had been pity, too, in his eyes and in his voice as he spoke to the victims and survivors of yet another disaster.... A good man, Stan Bayliss had thought then—who did his job well and cared about people...

Stan Bayliss cared about people, too, in an inarticulate sort of way. And he was sorry to see this man so near the brink of disaster himself...though he looked steady enough still.... Quite easy and friendly, he seemed, with no hint that he was in dire trouble. In fact, come to think of it, he looked like a remarkably happy man—content with his lot...

'Now,' said Jake, bringing him a mug of tea. 'What's on your mind?'

Stan Bayliss took a gulp of tea, and decided to come straight to the point. Jake Farrant was not a man who needed silly preliminaries.

'It's about the gypsies...' he began.

Jake's heart gave a lurch of fear. 'What about them?'

'I thought, maybe, a word of warning from you might come less amiss than one from me—'

'Warning? About what?'

The farmer shifted in his chair uneasily. 'It's

the dogs.... At least, I don't rightly think it's these dogs at all—but I'm having pressure put on me by Ralph Deacon...'

'*Deacon?*' said Jake—and paused. He must not admit it to this kindly farmer that he had any prior knowledge of Ralph Deacon's exploits.

'He's always had it in for those poor gypsies,' said Bayliss slowly. 'Fair *badgered* them, he did!'

Jake looked at him. The farmer looked back, and one eyelid drooped in a slow wink.

'Yes,' said Jake calmly. 'The boy told me that Mr Deacon threw them off his farm. But what's the trouble now?'

'Sheep worrying,' said Bayliss. 'Something's attacked some of Deacon's lambs. He says it's not a fox, and he's seen something running the sheep. But he was too far off to recognise it...'

'I see,' said Jake.

'Now, I'm a peaceable man meself, Mr Farrant. The gypsies never did me any harm—and they're good workers. They've been useful on my land, and I've no reason to turn them off—' He stopped and looked at Jake hard. 'But Deacon's a powerful man. If there's any chance of proving that one of their dogs was a wrong 'un, he'd have 'em off and out.... D'you see what I mean?'

'Yes.' Jake sounded troubled. 'But I think they keep them tied up at the camp...'

'So do I,' agreed Bayliss. 'But—if it came to the crunch, could they prove it? People aren't that good about taking a gypsy's word...'

'I see what you mean,' said Jake. Then, slowly, he went on: 'What do you suggest I do?'

'Just warn 'em. I've got sheep myself...I don't want any trouble.... And if you could see your way to having the dogs up here for a day or two—till the varmint's caught, I mean—it wouldn't do no harm...'

Jake nodded.

Then he said deliberately: 'You know we've got a badger cub up here?'

Stan Bayliss smiled. 'I did hear tell of something...I like badgers meself...'

'You...wouldn't have any objection...when the time comes to let her go?'

'No, I wouldn't. So long as the vet's given her a clean bill of health. God's creatures have as much right to live as we have, I suppose. It's like the gypsies...they may not live quite like us...but they never did me no harm....Nor did the badgers—far as I know!'

'D'you have a dairy herd, Mr Bayliss?'

'Yes, I do...and I've had badgers in my beech woods as long as I can remember.... And we never had a sign of TB in our herds. The Ministry never proved it, did they?' He grinned. 'I've had a lot of experience of Ministry men. They mostly do nothing but talk and try to interfere with things they know nothing about. We've been farming this land for generations—my family, I mean—and the kind of knowledge you get from years and years of watching things grow doesn't come out of books. What do these little jumped up clerks with their half-baked theories and printed forms know about the land? There's a whole plan of action out there, Mr Farrant,' he went on, sweeping a brown hand round towards the view from Jake's open door, 'a whole long history of life and birth and death as the seasons come round...a whole cycle, as you might say. Nature's a wonderful thing, Mr Farrant—and who are we to interfere with it?'

He suddenly paused, and looked at Jake apologetically. 'Got on my hobby-horse—sorry!'

'I'm not!' said Jake, smiling. 'My views exactly! Only I don't have your experience!'

Stan Bayliss laughed. 'Oh well...I get my living from good old Mother Nature. I see the seasons come and go...and the more I see, the more I realise there's a lot more to the land than just sowing and reaping.... Live and let live,

I say!'

Jake was still smiling. 'You're a man after my own heart, Mr Bayliss!'

'Stan. Call me Stan. Everyone does round here!'

'Well then Stan—I wish there were more like you!'

The farmer got up to go, shaking his head a little at the ways of the world he lived in. 'I don't know…. It's all money these days…bigger farms, bigger acreage, bigger fields, no hedges, burn off the crops…. We'll have a dust bowl like America soon, I shouldn't wonder. Mind you—I'm not in farming just for daisy-dancing, either!'

Jake laughed.

'But—' said Stan Bayliss, getting back into his boots by the door, 'there's more to life than a bank balance!'

Jake went with him to the gate. 'I'll do what I can about the dogs.'

The farmer nodded. 'Knew you would…. I'll let you know if I hear anything more…' He stopped suddenly and looked at Jake over the gate. 'It's good country this, you know. Gives you more than you can put back…'

'Yes,' said Jake, smiling. 'I know.'

In the early evening, well before it was dark,

the little cub came out. Jake was up there alone, since Bracken had not yet returned from 'seeing to the *grais*' for his father...

The cub wandered about her grassy pen, sniffing and rooting among the leaves and the gnarled claws of the old apple tree. Jake noticed, too, that she musked a couple of times round the edges of her territory as if to declare her ownership.... She was already beginning to grow up...

Jake mixed her up some food and put it down in the bowl. Then he put some on the spoon and introduced her to it. Little Zoe clearly remembered this pattern.... She ate what was in the spoon and then lowered her beautiful, clever little head to look for the food in the bowl...

'That's right,' said Jake. 'You're a fast learner, aren't you? I hope you like your food, that's all...'

The little cub seemed to be very pleased with it, and when Jake found a worm and chopped that up, she ate it too. Her roughened fur bothered Jake still, though, so he went down to the cottage and fetched an old clothes brush with a long handle and began to brush Zoe's back while she was still polishing off the worm. At first she shied a little, but then she seemed to get used to the feeling, and even to rub herself against the soft bristles of the brush as if she liked it...

'Good...' said Jake. 'We'll soon have you looking like a beauty queen...'

He stood back to look at her, and she promptly rolled over on her back and waved her legs in the air like a playful kitten.

'All right,' he said. 'I get the message...you scratch my back and I'll scratch yours!'

He brushed the soft underfur as gently as he could—and if Zoe could have purred like a cat, she would have done so. Before Jake could finish, though, she began to play with the brush in his hand, wriggling and kicking and rolling over, in a kind of ecstasy of playful abandon.... He did not persist. That was enough for the first day. At least she had made it clear that she liked being groomed!

He put his hand in his pocket and brought out various titbits for her to try.... Some of them were grown by him in his own garden, and he was absurdly proud of them...

She approved of a small, new carrot...and a radish went down very well. She liked a sultana or two...and a small piece of apple did not come amiss.... But a bit of bread smeared with some of Bracken's honey was obviously best of all...

'That's enough now,' said Jake severely, 'you'll get too fat to climb over your logs....

Go and take some exercise!'

Zoe didn't need telling. She scrambled up and down her climbing frames, and ran in and out of the shadows investigating corners and bushes and even the bottom layer of the dry-stone wall...

Jake watched her and thought to himself, she's not a bit afraid. It won't be long before she's over that wall! Or under it!'

He decided to tell Bracken about it when he came.... Then he thought he ought to introduce her to the home-made sett. Would she discover how to crawl out of the drainpipes into the grassy enclosure?

She had begun collecting small stones and carrying them back to her cardboard box...so when she was busily engrossed in arranging these Jake picked up the box with her inside it, and set it down with the opening leading directly into the warm interior of the wooden barrel which they had lined with grass and dried fern...

After a moment's pause at the sensation of being lifted, Zoe's inquisitive nature got the better of her. The pointed, questing black and white snout came forward. She came out of her box and went unhesitatingly into the mouth of the barrel...

Jake waited, breathless...

For a while she rooted about inside, turning round and round and scratching up her bedding into what she considered a more suitable position...then she turned round—and found herself facing another dark hole leading into one of the pipes.... She stopped to sniff at it, lifted her nose in the air, peered vaguely round with her short-sighted eyes, and then disappeared down the pipe...

Jake went silently over to the exit in the grass, and carefully laid another small morsel of bread and honey by the end of the drainpipe. Sure enough, the little black and white head came through...the nose twitched, alert for danger...then the whole, agile little furry body came through—and the bread and honey rapidly disappeared...

'Well done!' said Jake, really pleased. 'But can you find your way back?'

He went over to the mouth of the barrel again, and put yet another small item of food inside it...

For a while the cub played round the edge of the drainpipe, but then she found yet another small treasure—a shiny piece of bark— and took it with her into the pipe and back to her bedding in the barrel...

There was still one more opening to explore...and this drainpipe led further down the enclosure, coming out near the wall. Bracken had done this with a purpose—though he had not explained it to Jake.... But now, looking at this exit, Jake understood. When she was ready, the way over the wall would be cleared and made easy.... She would be away down the long hedge by the field and into the woods beyond...

Not yet, though, he thought. She's not ready yet...she hasn't begun to find herself any food yet...not enough to live on, anyway...

'Put this by the pipe...' said Bracken, close by his ear. 'Let's see what she makes of a frog...' and he handed Jake a very small limp bundle of legs and bright green skin.

Jake repressed a shudder, and laid it down by the wall. Zoe went through the same process...scrabbling with her bedding, turning round, investigating the new way out...working her way along it, and emerging into the garden, her nose a-twitch with excitement. She found the frog, and sat down to consider it. Presently, she got up and stood on it, beating it to pulp with her feet.... Then she swallowed it whole...

'Ugh!' said Jake, laughing. 'Rather you than me!'

He straightened up, clinging for a moment to the apple tree as a sudden wave of dizziness assailed him…. Then the world righted itself, and he looked at Bracken and smiled.

'Can we leave her out here on her own?'

'Oh yes. We'll come back in a bit and see how she's managing with the barrel. She seems to know already what to do. I should think we could almost cover it in…she'll probably feel much safer if we do…'

'Come on then,' said Jake. 'Something to tell you…'

He took Bracken back to the cottage, made the usual tea, and sat on the step with him to look at the settling twilight. 'Stan Bayliss came to see me today…' he began.

When he had finished, Bracken was silent for a few moments. Then he sighed and said: 'It's always the same, isn't it? We think we're safe, in a nice friendly place—and then…trouble starts…'

'It hasn't started, Bracken. That's the point. Stan Bayliss wants you to stay on his land…but he wants you warned…. Shall I have the dogs up here for a bit?'

Bracken looked doubtful. 'I don't know…I'll have to ask my Da. He likes them there to protect the *hatchintan*…'

'Tell him from me, it makes sense,' said Jake. 'Then if anything goes wrong with the sheep, I can swear blue that they were here…'

Bracken nodded, with a glimmer of a smile. Then he grew serious again. 'They wouldn't touch a lamb...or run the sheep, our *jukels*. I'm sure they wouldn't...'

'No,' agreed Jake. 'Even Stan Baylis didn't think they would, either...' He was silent for a moment, and then went on: 'But *something* has...and Deacon says it wasn't a fox...'

'How does he know?'

Jake shook his head. 'Probably doesn't...but he's spreading tales about dogs...and tales are hard to kill...'

Bracken thought for a bit. 'They might frighten the cub...?'

'We'll have to take that risk,' said Jake firmly. 'I can tie them up down here, by the front of the house...and you can come up and feed them. It'll only be for a few days, I expect....'

'All right...' The boy seemed to make up his mind at last. 'I'll talk to my Da...and bring them up tomorrow—'

'No, Bracken,' said Jake. 'Not tomorrow. Now! A fox—or anything else—could get at those sheep tonight.'

Bracken turned to look at Jake in surprise. Then he gave a seraphic smile. 'I've never heard you sound so fierce before! All right, I'll go down there now!'

He turned to run out of the gate, and then swung back and put a brown hand on Jake's arm. 'Thanks!' he said—and went swiftly away into the dark.

Jake sat on in the gloaming and dreamed.... He was tired again tonight, ridiculously tired, but he did not mind it now.... As long as he had enough strength to look after little Zoe— he could always idle the day away tomorrow...

While he was sitting in his chair by the wall, he began to hear an extraordinary banging and scraping and rooting noise down on his path. He got up to investigate, and found Bracken's hedgehog, whom he had been feeding regularly each night but had never seen till now, busily lifting up his saucer with his snout and letting it fall again with a clang on to the stone of the path.

'I do believe you're telling me I forgot!' said Jake, smiling. 'I didn't know you *hotchi-witchis* were so clever! Wait a bit, then...I'll fetch you your supper—since you insist!'

He went back into the cottage and mixed up a little bread and milk, and took it out to the hedgehog in the garden. When he put it down on the path, the little spiny creature moved with speed towards it, and put his nose down into the saucer of food at once—without show- ing any fear of Jake's tall shadow on the ground...

'I'm sorry I forgot!' said Jake, moving away into the darkening garden. 'I'll try to remember tomorrow!' and he went back to the badger's pen to see how little Zoe was doing. When he went into the enclosure, she was snuffling about in one of the corners, but she came galloping towards him and rolled over at his feet, as if welcoming a familiar playmate.

'Well, hello!' said Jake. 'This is so sudden! Shall we play hide-and-seek?'

But he was absurdly pleased at her welcome, and spent a long time just sitting here, rolling stones for her, and letting her gambol round him...

At length he heard a step on the path, and Bracken's voice came to him quietly from the shadows. 'I've brought the dogs...and my Da is here to see you.'

Jake extricated himself from the frolicking Zoe's games, and came down his path to meet the quiet dark man at the gate.

'This is good of you, Mr Farrant, sir,' said the gypsy.

'That's all right.' Jake smiled at him in the dark. 'It was Stan Bayliss who thought of it. You've a got a good, fair-minded boss there!'

The man nodded. 'Yes. We're lucky there, I know...not too many of 'em about.'

'It won't be for long, I expect,' said Jake. Let's hope they catch the dog or whatever it is.'

'If there *is* a dog—' murmured the gypsy.

Jake looked at him. The thought had occurred to him, too. 'You think it could be a put-up job? Out of spite?'

The gypsy shrugged fluid shoulders. 'Could be...I've known people do worse, where us gypsies were concerned.'

'We'll just have to sit it out, then,' said Jake, and something in his voice suggested to the gypsy that this man liked a fight now and then —and was a very good ally to have.

'I was going to say—before this happened— you could have Ambler tomorrow, and Sheba, too...I shan't be using the *grais*. I'm going in the lorry with the men. Would you like a ride?'

'I would,' said Jake, smiling. 'That's very kind...'

'You can go further that way,' said the gypsy, also smiling. 'And it'll take a weight off your feet!'

They grinned at one another.

'Right then,' said Kazimir Bracsas to his son. 'I'll leave you to settle 'em.... And choose a good ride tomorrow for the *grais!*'

He lifted his hand in a friendly gesture of farewell to Jake, and melted into the shadows as quietly and swiftly as Bracken had before.

Beside him, Jake found the boy stooping over the two dogs, fiddling with the chains on their collars. 'There now,' he said to them. 'You'll have to be good up here, mind—no barking about nothing—or you'll frighten Zoe.'

One of the dogs whined—Jake thought it was Streaker, the greyer of the two lurchers. The other one—Gamboll, who was a pale amber colour—sat down and thumped his tail.

'If I chain them to these rings by the gate,' said Bracken, 'they'll not get away. I've brought them a couple of bones to chew.... If I could just fill their water bowl...?'

'Why don't we set up a zoo while we're about it?' said Jake. 'D'you know what your *hotchi-witchi* did?'

And he sat down again with Bracken and told him all about it—and about Zoe's welcome. The dogs, seeing them there so peaceful and content, lay down on the path and went to sleep.

'Listen!' said Bracken suddenly. 'I thought I heard...? Yes, there it is! In that tallest tree by the edge of the field.... Can you hear it?'

Jake listened. And the night was all at once filled with throbbing song.... Trill after trill—cascade after cascade of pulsing notes poured out into the still, scented air...

'A nightingale!' Jake whispered.

269

'Yes!' Bracken clutched his arm with excitement. 'Never heard one so far up the valley as this before…they usually keep to the lower woods…. Listen! I think he's coming nearer…isn't he lovely? Sounds like moonlight turned into notes…' He was silent, listening entranced, and Jake was silent, too, while the liquid silver song poured out of the sky, quite close above them now from the topmost branches of the pear tree…

They sat there, spellbound, until the tireless bird caught the echo of a silver-throated answer from the woods below, and flew off to meet it…

The two listeners stirred, as if out of a dream, and Bracken said practically: 'We'd better have a look at Zoe. I meant to fill in the sett, but I'll have to do it tomorrow now…'

They went up the path to the enclosure to see what the little cub was doing. She was still snuffing about in the grass. alternately rooting and playing…rolling about in the moonlight and pouncing on dead leaves in the shadows…

Carefully, Bracken laid an armful of cut hay over the cardboard box and the wooden barrel, and covered the whole with an old tarpaulin he had found in the shed. 'That'll keep her warm and dry till tomorrow—' he said, speaking softly so that Zoe would not be scared of his voice.

Jake emptied his pockets of their various tit-bits and laid them down in the grass for Zoe to find...

Then the two of them left her playing, and went away down the moonlit path.

'I'll be up in the morning with Amber and Sheba,' said Bracken. 'I hope the dogs don't keep you awake!' He paused by the gate and added, with a faint jerk of his head: 'He's still singing out there somewhere.... If you listen, you might just hear him!' and he disappeared quietly into the dark.

That night, Jake could not sleep. He supposed he was overtired, and did his best to make himself relax with all the usual aids. He made himself a hot drink. He took some of his pills. He even went into his larder, meaning to make himself an extra snack. But the thought of food repelled him, and he gave up the idea.... In the end, he wandered out into the garden again, too restless to keep still.

He went first to the dogs, in case they began to bark. They were both lying down, noses on paws, but their ears were pricked and alert. He laid a hand on each silken head and whispered: 'It's all right...go to sleep...you'll see him in the morning...'

Then he went on to see what the little cub

was doing. At first he thought she had gone to bed—there was no movement at all in the pen.... But when he got closer, he saw the cub sitting quite still in the middle of the grass, her neat white head with its two black bars pointed towards the distant fields beyond the wall, as if she was listening for something.... She looked very small and lonely all by herself in the dark night, and Jake wondered if she consciously missed her mother and the other cubs...or was she simply caught by the scents and sounds of the night, longing for freedom...? Something about that tense, listening head reminded him of Sky...

He had not intended to go into the enclosure this time, but the little cub must have heard him, for she came right up to the wire and tried to reach him through it. Silently, Jake let himself in and went to talk to her.... He wondered if she had got hungry again, as young animals will, and how often she would have eaten when out with her mother in the wild. In the end, he fetched her another lot of food—rather less this time—and put it down for her on the ground....She ate it ravenously, and played round his feet for a little while afterwards...then, when she grew tired, she went off quite sensibly to one of her drainpipe entrances and disappeared inside to have a sleep in her new bed.

Jake roused himself from his observation post on Zoe's log, and went back to the cottage to get some rest. But still he could not sleep...and a bout of pain seemed to be coming that he could not avoid.... For a time he paced about the room, but at last he wrapped himself in his thickest coat and went out to sit in his wicker chair and look out at the night. The moon had set now, but it was still only half-dark.... He could see the stars glinting above the valley in a sky already paling towards morning...and the shapes of the beech trees against the skyline were black and strong.... He could not hear the nightingale any longer...at least, he didn't think he could, but there were faint stirrings and sounds all round him in the night. An owl called once, and something roused a few sleepy ducks down on the lake. He could hear the high, thin squeak of the bats and the thrum of their wings as they darted by...

Sighing, he settled back in his chair. It was better out here, he could breathe again, and the panic fear was gone.... Out here in the calm, receiving night, he forgot to be afraid.... Presently, as the first faint glimmer of dawn grew in the east, he fell asleep.

Bracken found him there in the morning, fast

asleep in his chair. He wouldn't have woken him, but the dogs, when they saw him, set up a chorus of welcome, and the two ponies, which he had tied up in the lane, whinnied their answer to the dogs—their familir friends.

Jake opened his eyes, and found Bracken beside him, and two inquisitive ponies' heads looking at him over the gate.

'Morning!' he said, confused. 'Must have overslept!' And then, looking at his view of the valley he added: 'A grand morning, too! Wait while I put my kettle on!' and he struggled indoors to shave off his midnight beard while the kettle sang on his calor-gas stove.

Bracken, meanwhile, walked the dogs in the lane, knowing that Jake would not let him take them with them today—not with that threat hanging over them.... Once let them get away after a rabbit, and the damage would be done. He would never be able to prove they hadn't gone after someone else's sheep...

When he had run them up and down as much as he could manage, he returned them to their post by the gate and went to have a quick look at Zoe's pen. She was not to be seen, so he assumed she was asleep in her new sett.

'Tea!' called Jake from the door way. 'And yesterday's currant buns,' he added, grinning. 'Mary Willis sent them!'

Bracken was looking at him a little anxiously. 'Did you stay out there all night?'

'Well—er—not exactly,' said Jake, looking guilty. 'I started off indoors...but I couldn't sleep, so I went to play with Zoe...and then I sat in my chair and sort of drifted off!'

Bracken laughed. But he was not fooled. His friend Jake looked desperately pale this morning.... He'd better not take him too far—in spite of the *grais*...

Jake, on the other hand, had taken one of the doctor's pills and was saying sternly to himself: I'm not going to spoil this morning by being weak! And I'm not going to put the boy at risk either, by passing out! He came out into the garden, looking fragile but determined.

'I've been to look at Zoe,' said Bracken cheerfully. 'She's asleep, I think.... Now, be good *jukels* till we come back.... Guard the cottage for us...' And he led Jake out of the gate to the two ponies.

'You'd better have Ambler,' he said. 'He takes my Da everywhere—Sheba's all right, too, but she's a bit lazy. You have to kick her a bit...'

Jake climbed on the grey pony's broad back and felt instantly at home. Ambler turned his head and had a look at this new man on his back, and then decided he was all right.

275

Bracken leapt up on to Sheba and gave her a dig with his heels, and the two of them moved off slowly and peacefully up the steep, sun-dappled lane.

‘Where are we going?’ asked Jake, pleased to find he could look over hedges and see the morning hills from a different angle.

‘I thought we’d go up to The Camp...’ said Bracken, waving an arm towards the ridge of hills ahead of them. ‘You can see for miles from the top...feels almost like being up above the world, like Sky...’

They did not hurry. The ponies clip-clopped along the road and then turned off up a long grassy track skirting the edge of the beech woods. The grass was bright with dew and starred with flowers. A few adventurous young rabbits were still about in the early morning and leapt away into the hedges at their approach...

Presently, the track led into the woods, and they went on climbing steadily but gently through the soft brown carpet of last year’s leaves under the new young green of the beech trees. The woods seemed full of bird song...full of golden sunlight and shadow...marvellously lit by the early rays of the sun...

Eventually, they came out of the trees on to the curving brow of the hill and went on up-wards, across the short springy turf till they reached the first circle of the British Camp.

'There were soldiers here once..' said Bracken, in a dreaming voice, 'fighting off the Romans. They used to light beacons on the tops of all the hills to tell each other when the enemy was coming...' He pointed on upwards to where the ground rose into the next grassy ridge. 'And when things got bad, they went on up to the next level...and then to the top...and the Romans came on up after them...and circled all round them, until they knew they were done for and had to give in.... But some say they never gave in at all, and they all died fighting...'

'Where did you learn all that?'

Bracken smiled. 'They told us a bit of it at school once when I was there...and afterwards, the school lady gave me the book. It tells you all about this place...and where the burial chamber was...underneath that mound over there...'

The ponies had been continuing to climb up the separate ridges and levels of turf all this time, but now they had reached the smooth crown of the hill—and Bracken slid off Sheba's back and waited for Jake to do the same with old Ambler...

They tethered the two ponies to the only tree nearby—a stunted hawthorn—and sat down on the grass to look at the view...

Before them lay the wide, rich plain of Gloucester, with the silver Severn threading its way down towards Bristol and the sea. Beyond that lay the far blue mountains of Wales—and to the right of them stood the dramatic ride of the Malvern Hills...

'I often think of them up here...' said Bracken dreamily, 'fighting on and on until they died. They must have loved this land...it was theirs, and they didn't want it taken away from them. There's probably swords and things buried underneath...and gold as well, I shouldn't wonder...'

'Didn't you ever want to look for it?'

'Oh no!' said Bracken, shocked. 'Let it lie—if it's there...it belongs to *them!*'

He had picked up a small stone and was turning it round in his fingers. 'Look!' he said. 'Long before all that, this land was all covered in sea...' and he held out the small fossil of a perfect shell for Jake to see. 'The earth is awfully old...' he said, still dreaming.

Jake held the small curved shell in his hand and marvelled at the fluted indentations, still visible in the stone. Awfully old, he thought... millions of years old, like this shell in my hand...and here I am worrying about a few short weeks...

He looked out at the 'coloured counties' of the plain, and then turned to watch the sunlight gleaming on the Severn as it turned in a shining loop below the Cotswold edge...

'So wide...' he murmured. 'So much space. It makes the sky look huge...'

'Mm...' drowsed Bracken. 'And there's a kestrel up there. I do believe Sky's keeping an eye on us!'

Jake smiled. He would like to think so, too. Up there, he thought...sailing in airy freedom... with all high heaven to play in.... It won't be long now...I shall be with you soon...

But something was troubling him, and he wondered how to say it to this cheerful, watchful boy beside him, who resolutely never let him think more then one day ahead.... How much did he know—or guess? Ought he to warn him? Had he the right to go on enjoying these marvellous expeditions with his own hawk's wing shadow hanging over him?

'If I was one of them soldiers...' said Bracken, still apparently dreaming, 'and I saw the enemy coming, creeping up the hill...'

'Yes?' said Jake, strangely. 'What would you do?'

Bracken did not look at him. His eyes were fixed on the sky, and that faint, hovering wing-shadow. 'I'd say to myself: if I can't beat 'em,

I'll go down fighting.... But if this is my very last day, I'm going to enjoy it first! And I'd turn my back on them creeping up, and look at the view!'

Jake was silent—his breathing curiously uneven. Then he said, steadily enough: 'But supposing...you were looking at the view...and an arrow struck you...and your comrades had to come out into danger after you?'

Bracken did look at him then—with incredulity, almost with contempt, though there was a kind of loving warmth behind it. 'Don't be daft,' he said. 'What are comrades for?'

When they got home, Bracken tied up the *grais*, and Jake went—a little shakily—to rustle up some bread and cheese and tea. He came out carrying a tray, and went to set it down on the wall by his willow chair. Then he straightened up—smiling a little as he remembered Bracken's words—and stopped to look at the view.

But something about the distant green hillside opposite made him pause.... There was a movement over there, a flicker...and the white dots of the sheep suddenly seemed to bunch together and then run, scattering across the grass...

'Bracken!' he called sharply. 'Come here a minute!'

Hearing the note of urgency in his voice, Bracken came running. 'What is it?'

'Look over there! Do you see what I see...?'

Bracken looked. Then he turned back to Jake swiftly. 'Something's after them.... What shall we do?'

'Whose sheep are they?'

'Farmer Bayliss's...that's his top pasture...'

'Then go for Stan Bayliss—*quickly*. I'll stay here with the dogs.... Run, Bracken!'

'I'll take Sheba,' said Bracken, running. 'It'll be quicker...I can go over the fields...' He sprang on to the shaggy pony's back, brought her through Jake's garden, put her into a rising canter on the grass, leapt the dry-stone wall and cantered off across the hares' field towards the farm lane beyond.

Jake watched them go, and then turned back to look at the top pasture hillside. The sheep were still running crazily in circles...something dark was running with them. And there were one or two ominiously still white blobs on the grass...

It seemed an age before anything happened, and by that time Jake had made up his mind that he might be needed too. It was pointless to take the car—it would not cross those grassy slopes—so he got up on to Ambler's stolid back, and plodded up the lane again and across the ridge of hillside towards that bright green slope he had seen from his garden...

Meanwhile, Bracken had arrived in Stan Bayliss's yard in a scatter of mud and hens, flung himself off Sheba's back and run to the farmhouse back door. Stan himself was just sitting down to breakfast after the milking, when the panting boy arrived.

'Quick!' he said. 'The top pasture...there's something after the sheep!'

Without wasting any time, Stan Bayliss seized his gun and ran for his landrover. 'Coming?' he asked, over his shoulder.

'Can I leave Sheba here?'

'Yes. Tie her up. Come on...'

They drove out of the yard and roared up the hill, scattering the hens once more as they went...

When they arrived at the head of the sloping hill, Stan parked his landrover on the grass verge, climbed the wall and went running down hill, with Bracken close beside him.... And there, below them, a sight of awful carnage met their eyes. Two or three of the lambs lay dead, their throats torn out, their furry little bodies lying in a helpless tangle of limbs. One sheep lay upside down in the ditch, feet feebly waving, and another was caught in the brambles of the hedge.... The rest were still milling and weaving in frantic terror, and a dark, brindled body was circling round them, closing in with every stride...

Bracken, with a cry of outrage, out-distanced Stan Bayliss and ran swiftly over the grass to get between the nearest terrified lambs and the snapping jaws of the dog...

'No, boy!' shouted Stan. 'How can I shoot? I'll hit you! Look out, he's gone wild—he'll bite!'

But Bracken did not heed him.... He went on running, and scooped up the first two frightened stragglers in his arms. The snapping jaws came furiously close and met in his arm.... A shot rang out, and another...and the big, heavy dog stopped in mid stride and fell in a heap on the grass...

Stan came running, his gun still unfired in his hands. 'Are you all right? You might've got yourself killed!'

'I'm not hurt...' said Bracken, untruthfully. 'You shot him!'

'Not I!' said Stan grimly. 'It came from over yonder! D'you know whose dog it is?'

Bracken looked down at the dark, brindled shape of the bull mastiff at his feet. His eyes went wide. 'Yes,' he said. 'It's Boley...It's Deacon's.'

From across the field, a man came out of the

shadows, carrying a gun. He walked down the field towards them, and stopped when he saw the dog, his face grim.

'Well, Deacon,' said Stan Bayliss, sounding as grim as the other man looked. 'D'you recognise this dog?'

Deacon nodded. He had been fond of his old hunting companion, Boley. The big, powerful dog had been with him through many a season.... It was a shock to see any dog go wrong like this, let alone one of his own. He knelt down and turned the dog over sadly. It was quite dead. Then his eye fell on the destruction in the field.

'I'm sorry about this—' he began.

'It's a bad business...' said Stan, shaking his head. 'Looks like I've lost several lambs...'

Bracken, meanwhile, had put the unhurt lambs down on the grass, and had one hand tightly clasped round his bitten arm. 'Hadn't we better pick up those poor sheep?' he said.

Deacon glanced at him sharply. 'I might've known you'd be here!'

From behind him, Jake's voice spoke very crisply and clearly. 'If he hadn't been, Mr Deacon, there would have been much more damage done. And for your information, I have the gypsy dogs tied up at my house...just in case there should be any misunderstanding...'

Deacon stared.

'And while we're about it,' added Jake. 'We'd better get that arm seen to.... A dog bite can be nasty. You were quite lucky not to get shot as well!'

He laid an arm round Bracken's shoulders and added, as he turned away:. 'Shouldn't we tell the police? There'll be compensation to see to...?'

Stan Bayliss was staring at him, too, with respect in his eye. 'How are you proposing to get back?'

'On Ambler,' said Jake, with a brief smile. 'I daresay he'll manage the two of us...'

'No,' said Stan. 'You take the landrover and see to the boy...and tell Sergeant Daly.... I'll stay here and clear up with Deacon. I can bring Ambler back down later...'

Jake nodded. 'All right. Come on, my young friend. You've done all you need to here—' For Bracken was gazing down at the dead lambs and the strong sturdy body of the dog with tears in his eyes...

'What a waste...' he murmured, as Jake led him away up the hill. 'What a stupid waste...'

Jake patted his good arm, and said no more.

Behind him, the two farmers went across to the hedge and began to work together to rescue the frightened sheep...

In the end, Jake asked them all to come back to his cottage, and sent for Bracken's father as well. He decided that this stupid feud had got to end before more damage was done...

He had managed to get a large fruitcake from Mary Willis—and he handed out beer and cake all round in his front garden, making sure that Bracken could reach his with his undamaged left hand...

Then he addressed himself to Farmer Deacon.

'As you probably know, I came down here for a rest!'

The others laughed, but Jake went on. 'I've seen too much of wars and disasters one way and another, Mr Deacon.... It seems to me that life's too short for needless disputes...there's trouble enough in it already!' He grinned. 'It's not my business, of course—but this young fellow here saved you a lot of extra expense today...things could have been a lot worse.... Shouldn't we all let bygones be bygones, and call it a day?'

It was a longish speech for Jake these days. It sounded a bit pompous too...but he thought he was probably the only one who could say it...

'I could keep my eyes open for a new dog—?' said Bracken's father, speaking quietly, but with intent. 'I see a lot on my travels...'

For a moment it looked as if Deacon was going to utter a sharp refusal. But he caught the gleam in Jake's eye—and something about this man's transparent pallor, and obvious frailty made him ashamed. 'Good idea-' he said gruffly, and managed an awkward smile. 'I'd be obliged if you would—'

Bracken let out a sigh of relief, and Stan Bayliss gave Jake a hint of a wink.

'That's good,' said Jake, and lifted his glass. 'I'm going to drink to this marvellous country-side—and everyone in it who's been so kind to me!'

Solemnly, as if it was a most important toast, they all lifted their glasses in response.

Bracken wanted to say: Don't forget the creatures. They live here, too. But he thought Jake probably meant them as well.... In any case, with Deacon here, it was better not to mention them—especially not badgers...

He also thought, looking at Jake's face, it would be better to get everyone away as soon as possible—so he went over to his father and said, like a dutiful son: 'Shall I fetch the *grais*, then?'

'You'll do no such thing!' growled his father.

'You stay here and rest that arm. I'll fetch the *grais*—and you can ride Sheba home.... We'll take the dogs when we go...if that's all right with Mr Farrant?'

'If we're talking of *rest*—' said Dr Martin's voice from beside the gate, 'we'd better let Mr Farrant have the one he's always talking about! We don't give him much of a chance!'

There was a general laugh, and the little party broke up. But as Deacon passed, still a bit red-faced and awkward, Bracken touched his arm shyly:

'I'm sorry about Boley, Mr Deacon. He was a good dog once...'

The tough farmer looked at the boy and nodded slowly. There was an unaccustomed lump in his throat which confused him. 'Yes...' he said at last, with sudden grief in his voice: 'He was a good dog once.'

When they had gone, Dr Martin put a firm hand on Jake's arm and said: 'You'd better keep quiet for the rest of the day! Doctor's orders! Positively no gallivanting—at least till tomorrow! And as for you, young man, I want you to rest that arm...give that injection a chance to work, see? And come and see me in a week without fail—d'you hear me?'

'Yes, Dr Martin,' said Bracken meekly, and smiled his most seraphic smile.

'Talk about the quiet countryside!' grumbled the doctor, answering Bracken's smile with a mischievous one of his own. 'Never a moment's peace!'

He left another packet of pills for Jake, without comment, and refrained from giving Bracken any painkillers, knowing he would not take them. 'Be good now, the two of you!' he said, and stumped off up the lane to his car.

Bracken looked at Jake, half-full of mischief and half-serious. 'I told you looking at views was worth while!' he said.

The next few days passed in a haze of weariness for Jake. He knew he had overdone it, and he was bound to feel the consequences. But pain and weakness took over to such a degree that he was scarcely aware of what he was doing. He was ashamed of this, and did his best to disguise it when Bracken came. By day, he spent a lot of his time lying back in his wicker chair...

Each evening, Bracken came up to see to Zoe, telling Jake firmly that he could manage alone. But Jake had got mysteriously attached to the little badger cub, and he could not resist coming up to have a look at her...even though it seemed to take him a long time to get up his garden path...

She was as welcoming and as playful as ever—and each time Bracken had brought her a slightly more varied diet to choose from. She tried everything—and seemed particularly fond of slugs and last year's hazel nuts...

A couple of days later, Bracken began to fill in the new sett with earth and stones—leaving the top of the barrel just clear so that it could be lifted off if necessary. When Jake protested about him using his bitten arm, he grinned and said: 'I can do it with one hand if you like—but it'll take longer!'

They often sat watching Zoe play until quite late, and then Bracken would go home, saying cheerfully: 'I'll be up tomorrow—but we'd better not go out again yet, or Dr Martin'll be after me!'

One night just before Jake went up to bed, there was a sound of scrabbling in his chimney and a lot of soot fell down into the grate.

It's those wretched jackdaws! thought Jake. Bracken said they were nesting up there...I suppose the young ones are getting obstreperous!

He fetched a dustpan and brush and swept up the soot, and carried it out to the garden. Then he thought he'd better protect his living-room from yet more dust, so he put a few sheets of newspaper over the chimney opening and wedged it in position with the old brass fire-screen...I can clear up the rest tomorrow, he thought, and went rather exhaustedly to bed.

The next morning when he came down, there were more scrabbling noises in his chimney, and when he looked at the grate for signs of another fall of soot, he thought he saw the newspaper move.

He took the firescreen away and pushed back the paper, prepared for yet another dusty cascade. But there was something else in his grate. In the midst of a new pile of soot and twigs, stood a bewildered young jackdaw. It gazed at Jake out of bright, astonished eyes— as if to say: where on earth am I? There I was one minute, asleep in my warm nest, and the next I was falling down a hole, and now look at me!

Jake couldn't help laughing at the poor bird's indignant expression. It was a trim, glossy creature, young and slender and strong-looking —and it had its head on one side, looking at Jake enquiringly and without any sign of fear. Clearly, it expected him to do something and was waiting to see what would happen next.

'You stupid bird!' scolded Jake, smiling as he leant forward with both hands poised to grip it tightly before it could flap its wings. 'Fancy falling down a chimney! You ought to look where you're going!'

The bird tilted its head the other way, and let out a tentative 'Krak!'

'Now, hold on...' said Jake. 'Don't move! And no pecking, either. I'll soon have you out of there!'

As he talked, his hands crept nearer, and suddenly they pounced and clamped themselves round the jackdaw's slim young body. The bird quivered a little, but it sat quite still in Jake's hands and did not try to struggle.

'Hold still now!' said Jake. 'I hope you can fly. Are your wings all clogged up with soot, I wonder?'

He carried the shiny black bird out of the cottage and into the garden. There, he lifted his two hands above his head and threw the bird into the air. The poor creature let out a startled 'Krak!' and fell like a stone into a clump of daisies.

You fool! Jake told himself. The poor thing can't fly! It might've broken its neck. But there was something so comical about it that he could not help smiling. The bird looked slightly more bewildered, but it did not seem to be hurt.

Once more he picked it up in his hands, and this time he took it over to his garden wall. There was quite a drop the other side which might help it to take off. Above him, he became aware of a cacophony of kraks and squawks from the parent birds, and one of them flew over his head, dive-bombing him in furious agitation.

'All right!' he said. 'I'm only trying to help! Give me a chance!'

And he stood close to the wall, and lifted his hands, and once more threw the young jackdaw up into the air. For a moment it looked as if it was going to crash to the ground again, but it righted itself, levelled off like a plane coming out of a spin—and sailed off to the nearest tree, with a sharp 'Krak!' of relief.... Jake was relieved, too.

The parent birds clacked anxiously and flew round a couple of times before deciding that their offspring was not only safe but well and truly launched.

Jake stood and watched them arguing and flapping to and fro in the sun. 'No need to make such a fuss!' he said. 'Nestlings fly every day! Though not too often down chimneys, I suppose!'

Chuckling to himself a little at the noisy, flustered birds, he went indoors again to make some tea.... I must tell Bracken when he comes, he said...

After five days of this 'malingering'—as Jake privately called it—he announced that he was better again, and Bracken joyfully arrived the next morning with Ambler and Sheba, their coats neatly brushed and shining in the early morning light.

It had been raining overnight, but the sky was clearing now, and tattered clouds were drifting away to the east...

'One of your pearly mornings,' said Jake, smiling, and climbed on to Ambler's patient back.

They went gently this time, through the beech woods and along the lower slopes of the hills. But even so, Jake knew that he would have to forgo his morning rides very soon.... Even this gently jogging seemed to start deep, strange aches in his bones...and he had a frightening feeling of disintegration—as if bits of him inside were falling apart.

I shall have to go back to walking, he thought —and even then I won't be able to go far.... But he said nothing to Bracken, and fell to admiring the sunlight on the beech leaves, and how the light flashed on a bird's wing as it darted by.... When a grey squirrel suddenly ran up a tree in front of him, he stopped and gazed, and almost forgot to go on...

They were just turning back to go down the lane, when Jim Merrett, the postman, caught them up.

'Letter for you, Mr Farrant...I was just going to bring it down...'

Jake thanked him and, after glancing at the handwriting, put it in his pocket to read back at the cottage. It was from Bill—and he guessed what it would say.

Bracken tied up the ponies and went to inspect Zoe's sett—tactfully leaving Jake to read his letter.

'Dear Jake,' it said 'As you (reluctantly) agreed, I have contacted Beth. The upshot of it is she is coming down with Manny and me next weekend (Saturday), and we are picking up Charles in Oxford on the way. We'll all have a meal at the Farmers' Arms and come to see you in the latish evening. Then your little Zoe will be up and can break the ice...? Hope you approve. If not, and you simply can't face it, leave word at the office somehow and I'll cancel the whole thing. I know we're a nuisance, Jake —but Manny's sparks simply won't lie down. Sorry! Bill.'

Jake smiled a little at Bill's obvious doubts about the plan—and then fell to wondering about Beth and Charles and what the meeting would be like. Could he face it? What on earth would they have to say to one another? All the same, he thought, I suppose I've got to try...

A sudden picture of Carol Franklyn came

into his mind—and he heard her voice saying: *'Well done...! You're learning faster than I did!'* Was he? He didn't know...but he still felt a kind of reluctance and dread about this meeting.... How absurd...to be afraid to meet your own children...but it was just one more shackle—one more weight to shed before he was free...like Sky.... Only, Carol said: *'There are many kinds of love'*...and then he felt ashamed of his own reluctance...

He came out of his anxious thoughts to find Bracken perched beside him on the step, and his own kettle singing on the stove.

'Bracken!' he said, amazed. 'You went inside!'

Bracken looked a trifle confused. 'Well...you needed your tea...and you seemed kind of...bothered.'

Jake smiled. 'I've got some visitors coming...and I don't know what to do with them...'

'When?' said Bracken, practically.

'Let me see...' Jake consulted the postmark of his letter. 'Is it Saturday? Tomorrow night!'

'Late?'

Jake nodded. 'When Zoe's up, they said.'

'That'll help, won't it? But they mustn't scare her.... She's got used to you and me...but badgers is very shy creatures...they don't like a lot of noise...'

'They're not the only ones!' said Jake. And Bracken laughed.

Jake was nervous and strung up all day...but when he heard all the voices in the lane, a sudden fatalistic calm came over him.... They were here now, there was nothing he could do about it...better make the best of it and try to keep everyone happy.

He was experienced in handling difficult situations and awkward interviews, and suddenly his old skills seemed to return—and all his long training in the field seemed to concentrate into one focal point.... He felt a curious surge of power flow through him. He was not tired any more—or apprehensive.... He was just a well-schooled, compassionate professional trying to put a lot of worried people at their ease.

His old charm and ease of manner came back to him. He felt—as had happened sometimes before in his working life—that this particular assignment was going to be one of those golden moments when everything came together and he couldn't put a foot wrong.... He was sure it was going to work...

He met them at the door of the cottage and took them all inside. He was friendly and courteous, and gave them to understand from the start that this was a cheerful reunion—and not something fraught with emotional tensions or unspoken farewells...

'It's been a long time,' he said to Beth. 'More my fault than yours, I'm afraid.... But no-one told me you'd turned into a beauty, or I might've come home sooner!'

While they were laughing, and Beth was tossing the blonde hair out of her eyes and thinking how distinguished and how frail her father looked these days, Jake turned to Charles and added wickedly: 'I can't say you've turned into a beauty exactly, can I? But you seem very couth to me!'

And since this was a word that Charles and his friends were cultivating at the moment, he could not disguise either his surprise or his (somewhat grudging) pleasure at Jake's remark.

Jake saw then with his assessing eye, that Charles had inherited his mother's fair good looks, but his eyes were different.... In fact—and here Jake met them suddenly with a faint shock of recognition—they were rather like his own.... And as for Beth, so young and blonde...he wasn't sure whom she took after...? Maybe, though there was something about her that reminded him of himself when young...?

'Bill,' he said carelessly, 'you and Manny can do the honours.... There's only beer, I'm afraid, or home-made scrumpy from Wood End Farm, which—I can tell you—is powerful strong! You know where everything is...I want to talk to these two...'

And he sat down astride a chair between them and by skilful questioning got them talking about their own lives and hopes and future careers.

'...a travel agency...' said Beth.

'In London?'

She hesitated. 'Yes...at first.... But I'm hoping to be a courier.... It will mean a lot of travelling—like you!' She smiled at her father a little shyly.

'And dealing with lots of people,' added Jake.

'I like people,' said Beth, 'also like you!' And there was no reproach in her glance.

Jake turned to Charles. 'And you? After Oxford...?'

Charles looked faintly embarrassed. 'Don't laugh, will you? I'm going to the BBC—to train as a foreign correspondent!'

Jake gazed at them both in astonishment. 'But this is absurd!'

'Well, you see,' said Charles, 'you may not believe this—maybe it's because you were always so far away, we never saw through you! But, to us, you were always rather a hero—'

'Was I?' He sounded genuinely surprised. 'You amaze me! Though I suppose far-flung outposts do conceal feet of clay!'

They grinned at him, suddenly finding they rather liked their father...

'Go on,' he said to Charles. 'Tell me more.'

Maybe it was Stan Bayliss's scrumpy, or the scented summer night and the lamplit cottage, but the evening suddenly seemed to take on a special glow... They were all dazzled by Jake's brilliant gaiety and courage, and could not resist the challenge of his laughter. Both his old friends knew that he was more fragile and more transparent than when they came down before, but they found themselves laughing with him while he told them of his exploits with Bracken, and could not help responding when he led them on to talk even more of themselves.... Even Bill and Manny got drawn into regaling him with bits of office gossip and talk of work...

'And incidentally,' said Jake, looking severely at Bill, 'why are you two still kicking your heels on the home front?'

Bill's eyes went wide with innocence. 'Oh— you know Bob.... He usually makes us toe the line when we come home...good for us to go back to the old routine—!' He glanced at Manny. He'll be sending us off again soon...'

'Hm—' said Jake, not a bit taken in by that

innocent gaze. 'So it's Bob doing, is it? Well, you tell him from me—'

'Yes?' said Manny, and there was a gleam in his eye that Jake could not miss.

'He's the best boss I ever had,' said Jake, smiling, 'but editors shouldn't have hearts!'

He got up then to fill their glasses, since Bill and Manny seemed unaccountably confused. Then he said gently, still smiling: 'Shall we go and look at little Zoe?' He glanced round at his visitors and added warningly: 'But you'll have to be very quiet...she'll go back into her sett if she gets scared...'

They all came out on to the path and tiptoed up the garden. Beth even took off her expensive high-heeled sandals and walked across the springy turf in bare feet...

It was late dusk by now, and the first stars were just beginning to appear in the primrose sky...but it was high summer, and the nights never got very dark. The shapes of the trees were still visible, and the white moon daisies in the field seemed to be filled with light...

They reached the wire enclosure, and Jake left them there while he went round to the other side to let himself in. Zoe was rooting about in a corner, and she came galloping across to meet him, grunting and squealing with pleasure...

301

'All right,' said Jake, 'I've got your dinner... I know I'm a bit late...'

He set the bowl of food, which he had mixed earlier, down on the grass. Zoe needed no prompting now, and her long striped snout was into the dish before he could turn round. He fetched the long-handled clothes brush and gave her a brisk grooming while she was eating. She wriggled her back a little with delight, and went on concentrating on her food until the bowl was empty.... Then she began to play...

Jake had found the woolly ball lying in the grass near one of the drain-pipe exits—she must have brought it out from her bed—and he began to roll it for her and watch her pounce on it and shake it, worrying it like a small dog with a rat.... But presently she seemed to grow tired of playing, and went up close to the wall where the hedge began and the first tall ash tree beckoned and whispered in the night about wild woods and secret paths and old tree-roots and hidden sandy banks...

Zoe's small face was lifted to the night air, and her sensitive nose was wrinkling and twitching with the heady scents of summer.

'What is it?' said Jake softly. 'Do you want to go already...? You're a bit small yet, you know, to manage on your own...'

But the little cub still sat there, listening and

scenting the night air, her whole small body filled with yearning...to be free...to be wandering those silent, leafy paths...to be searching for grubs all on her own in last year's beech mast...to be gambolling in the moonlight with the rest of her kind...

Jake wondered, then, if she would actually find another group of badgers and be allowed to join them.... He must ask Bracken about this, and soon, now—for it was clear to him that Zoe was beginning to pine for her freedom, and he must not keep her much longer.

'It won't be long now—' he said, as he had said to Sky, and his voice was gentle and comforting. 'Soon—' he said softly. 'Soon...we will be able to let you go...'

As if the little cub had caught some of the comfort in his voice, she turned her head to look at him in the glimmering twilight, and came across and thrust her small snout into his hand...

'You might like this...' he said, 'as a special treat...' And he brought out a small piece of treacle tart that Mary Willis had sent him.

Zoe decided that treacle tart was exactly the right food for badgers. But when she had eaten it, and given a little display of delight on the grass, finishing up with another playful butt against Jake's arm, she returned to her silent vigil by the wall.... It was as if she could not resist the pull of all that lay beyond in the darkening woods...

'She'll be all right...' said Bracken's voice close to Jake's shoulder. 'It won't do her any harm to yearn a bit.... It'll make it easier to find her way out when the time comes.'

Jake nodded at him gratefully in the dark, unsurprised that Bracken always seemed to arrive just when he was most needed.... He got up from his log, where he had been perching to watch Zoe, and went out of the pen to join his enchanted guests.

They each thought privately that they would never forget the sight of Jake kneeling there, comforting the small badger cub in the quiet summer night.

'Isn't she simply *lovely!*' said Beth, in a whisper.

Charles was silent—but his face was as lit with wonder as the rest...

Wonder, thought Jake. That's it.... That's what I've found here, with Bracken to guide me—a sense of wonder....And of all the gifts in the world, it is this one I would want to bequeath to them most...

'Did you bring—?' he whispered to Bracken, and he saw the brown head nod, and the boy held up one closed hand for him to see.

When they got down the path near to the cottage, Bracken turned unerringly to Manny and held out his hand.

'This is for you—' he said. And, with a faint smile in Jake's direction he added: 'He said... you were keen on sparks...'

And he opened his hand and offered Manny his glow-worm.

Manny looked down at the small, glowing creature in the boy's hand. The greenish light from its tail seemed to flow outward, making Bracken's fingers seem almost translucent...

'It's beautiful!' he breathed. Then he looked up at Jake, and at Bill, and Jake's two children standing in puzzled silence beside him...and he found he could not say one word more.... Silently, he put the tiny glow-worm on his own palm and held it out for the others to see...then he turned back to Bracken and carefully transferred it again to the boy's warm brown hand.

'I've never seen one before...' he said, sounding strangely shaken by something. 'You'd better keep it for me, though...it wouldn't survive long in London...'

Bracken nodded, looking at Manny steadily in the half-dark.

But Bill, seeing Manny turn away somewhat blindly, took his cue then and grasped Jake by the arm. 'We must go now...I promised to get

305

Charles back to Oxford tonight.... Hope we haven't worn you out?'

'No,' said Jake, smiling. 'I've enjoyed it very much...' He gave Bill's hand a cheerful squeeze while it was still grasping his arm and added softly: 'I'm glad you all came...you were right!'

To Manny, who still seemed curiously silent, he said on a breath of affectionate laughter: 'Old glow-worm Manny! Satisfied?' and grasped him, too, by the arm, for a moment.

Then he looked at Beth and Charles, standing almost shyly now in the lamplight from his door—and knew he must make it easy for them.... I don't like partings, he said, especially this one. But these two are going to be all right...they're going to be fine.... Only, they don't quite know what to say to me...

'Thanks for coming down,' he said, and put an arm round each and hugged them cheerfully. 'It's good to discover I've got such nice offspring!'

'Shall—shall we come again?' asked Beth, her eyes a little too bright and too anxious.

'I'd like that,' agreed Jake, with perfect equanimity. 'But get in touch with Bill or Manny first—' He did not look in their direction now. His farewells had already been said.

'Good night!' they called, as they left, and Jake stood watching them go, his hand lifted to them in the dark.

But as Manny went through the gate, Bracken—with the glow-worm still in his hand—said very softly: 'I'll keep it safe for you....It'll go on shining for quite a bit yet...'

Manny touched his glowing hand briefly with one finger, and followed the others away up the lane.

Jake waited till they had gone, standing very still and straight—and then fell in a quiet heap on the grass...

He came round dizzily to find himself lying back in his wicker chair, and Bracken coming towards him, carefully carrying a mug of tea.

'Sorry...' he murmured, and smiled a bit lopsidedly. 'Overdid it again!'

Bracken grinned. 'It's all that talk...very tiring, too much talk is!' He held out the mug, and made sure Jake's hands were firmly round it before he let go. 'It's a lovely night,' he said, perching beside him on the wall. 'Soft as milk...you won't come to no harm out here.... No need to go anywhere. ..'

Jake sipped his tea, saying nothing, waiting for the stars above the pear tree to stop spinning.... In a little while, they did—and he reached for one of his pills in his pocket...

'Shouldn't you...be home by now? It must be quite late...'

'Doesn't matter,' said Bracken, gazing out at the sleeping valley. 'They knows where I am...'

'What did you do with the glow-worm?' Jake asked suddenly.

Bracken smiled. 'Put her back in the grass.... She'll light up your path for a few days yet!'

'That's good...' murmured Jake, growing drowsy.

Bracken sat there for a long time in the scented dark, waiting for Jake to fall asleep...

Presently, he did.

Jake woke next morning to find himself warmly wrapped in the rug from his kitchen, and his wicker chair turned a little sideways to catch the morning sun.... He felt strangely rested and at peace out here in the summer morning...

The sun was warm on his face, and the air smelled of flowers and moss, and fresh-cut hay from the meadows...

Memories of last night returned to him slowly. He was left with a picture of Beth's too-bright eyes as she said: 'Shall we come again?', and his son, Charles, looking at him quite straight as he left and saying nothing at all.... Bill grasping his arm and putting on his old campaigner's no-nonsense face...and Manny— tough, sentimental old Manny—looking from

308

the glow-worm to Jake with tears in his eyes...

And then there was Zoe—little Zoe sitting up straight in the darkening garden, her questing head lifted to sniff the cool night wind...the longing for freedom clear in every line of her body—just as it had been with Sky.... He would have to do something about it soon—before she began to know her loss and beat herself against the wire as poor, desperate Sky had done...

'I brought some tea today,' said Bracken, standing beside him in the sunlight... 'And I thought we might be able to make Zoe's cage bigger....so's she could try a bit of the wild hedge at the end, before she goes...'

Jake had almost ceased to be amazed at Bracken's way of knowing his thoughts. Now he said slowly: 'I think we should let the vet have a look at her...before she goes.... Then we'll be sure she'll be all right and we aren't doing the farmers any harm.'

Bracken nodded. 'I'll ask my Da. He sees him most days...'

'Better be soon,' said Jake sadly. 'She's getting restless already...'

Soon...he thought, and resolved to make sure somehow that he did not collapse on Bracken's hands again. I must take more care, he thought...and ration myself, so that I don't risk getting too tired.... And I hate being cautious! But soon I must say to him that I can't go on any more morning jaunts...

'I think when we first let her go, she'll want to come back to sleep here...' said Bracken thoughtfully, 'and she'll probably want you to go a little way with her...just to make sure she knows the way back...'

'Do you think so?'

'Mm...she'll find the world a big old place... a bit frightening, I shouldn't wonder...' He smiled with sudden radiance at Jake's pale morning face. 'So it'll be night wanderings, not mornings! Only short ones, mind!'

Jake gazed at him, speechless, while he poured him out some more tea from his flask and gave him a bit of the gypsies' sesame cake to go with it...

'All the same,' said Bracken, rightly judging the expression in Jake's eyes, 'I think we could do a couple more mornings before she gets too restless!'

The vet came up that evening, and pronounced Zoe to be strong and healthy as far as he could judge without handling her too much and frightening her to death.... He also took away some droppings for analysis from the neat pile at the side of the sett.... Beyond that, he said, he could only wish her well and hope she would find her way around in the wild...

Zoe did not seem to mind him handling her, though she did scuttle back to her sett for some privacy and a rest after he'd gone.

Jake took him back to the cottage with Bracken for a cup of tea, and they all sat in the garden looking out at the dusk-filled valley and the dark hills beyond...

The vet—Alan Johnson—was youngish and squarish and kind.... He knew Bracken's father well, and had a great respect for the gypsies and their ancient knowledge of herbs and healing. Several times in the last few years Kazimir Bracsas had managed to save a horse when he had given it up as a lost cause.... And this brown, tangle-headed boy beside him had the same strange gift, he knew. He could charm the birds off the trees, and mend the sickest creature...and Alan Johnson was much too wise and fair-minded to write off such a power as unimportant. He wished, though, that there was something either of them could do for the man beside them...

He sighed, and waved a blunt, competent hand at the view beyond the garden wall. 'There's nothing to beat this country, is there?'

Jake smiled, and nodded agreement.

'You must have seen a good many different

ones though?'

'Yes...' He spoke slowly, almost absently. 'Yes, I have...and you're right—nothing can touch this one!' He turned to Bracken, smiling. 'You've seen a good few places, too...what do you think?'

Bracken's answering smile was as luminous as the night. 'I like most places...as long as it's out of doors! But this one's special...'

Alan Johnson looked at the boy thoughtfully. 'Have you ever thought of being a vet, Bracken?'

He laughed and shook his head. 'They asked me that at school once...I told them I could never stay under a roof long enough to do all that studying..!' His face suddenly grew serious, and he turned to Johnson earnestly, almost apologetically. He respected this man, and he wanted him to understand. 'I've thought about it sometimes...I'd like to know all you know about helping creatures.... My Da says you mustn't leave out the new learning just because you believe in the old...but it's true what I said....I can't really stand school for more than a day! If they'd let me study out of doors, maybe I could do it...but if I had to go to college, it would kill me!'

Both men were silent, both seeing the logic of what the boy had said. Jake thought of him

312

cooped up in a town, shut in cramped little rooms and crowded lecture halls, surrounded by people and noisy traffic—and he shuddered. His Bracken, who would scarcely set foot in his cottage except in dire emergency—who spent his life running free in this smiling countryside? No, it would never do!

'I'm best left as I am,' said Bracken softly, trying to reassure these two good men whom he admired. 'I like wild things best...I understand 'em...and I'll go on doing what I can for 'em...in my own kind of way...until I grow up. I expect I'll be like my Da...though I'm not so good with the *grais* as he is.'

'Will you always travel, do you think?' Alan Johnson still sounded a little saddened. He hated to waste good material!

'I expect so...' His voice was tranquil. 'We gets restless after a while...' He glanced at Jake swiftly, and his smile was suddenly gentle. 'Like little Zoe.... When the time comes to move on, she'll know...'

Yes, thought Jake painfully. She'll know... and I shall know, too.... And I suppose Bracken will accept it without fuss, like he does everything...

'We might have a look at those closest beech woods tomorrow,' said Bracken, 'and see where she's likely to go first.... What do

313

you think?'

'Sounds like a good idea.' Jake smiled at him.

'It's not far,' said Bracken softly. 'So I won't come too early...'

Alan Johnson rose to his feet. 'I mustn't sit idling here any longer—nice though it is!' He stood looking down at Jake very kindly. 'Don't get up. You look very peaceful sitting there.... Let me know if there's anything else I can do.'

'Thanks,' said Jake, smiling up at him. 'I will...'

'Bracken tells me you've got a nightingale in your garden—d'you know you're very lucky?'

'He came back late last night,' said Bracken, and looked at Jake as if offering a gift of secret comfort and reassurance. 'If you wait awhile— he'll come!'

Jake sat on alone in the quiet garden, waiting for his nightingale.... And presently, he came...and the night was once more filled with silver song.

The next day, they explored the nearest beech woods, marking the high, sandy banks and hidden hollows under the ancient tree roots where Zoe might want to make another sett. Bracken also looked for signs of other badgers, and found one sett near the far end of the woods which was clearly occupied. There were piles of scraped earth and old tufts of bedding outside, and in one corner was a tidy dung-heap among the brown covering of beech mast and last year's leaves.

'She might make friends here...' said Bracken cheerfully. 'At least she won't be all alone in the woods...'

'They wouldn't attack her, would they—being a stranger, I mean?'

'Oh, no,' said Bracken, shocked 'Badgers is friendly creatures—even to each other! I expect they'll adopt her...'

That evening they introduced Zoe to her larger domain. She went rooting in the wild hedgerow, and seemed very busy and happy. Jake thought she seemed to be finding quite a few earthworms and grubs on her own—but he still put out her food in her usual bowl, and she came back to eat it eagerly.

Again she played and rolled and scampered about the grass—and often came back to Jake to nudge at his hand or tug at his boots. But in between, she still went and sat by the wall, scenting the night, her head tilted wistfully towards the distant woods—clearly longing to clamber over the stones of the wall and explore the green world beyond...

The next day, Bracken brought up another

piece of old drainpipe, and dug a way out through the garden between the end wall and the hedge. For the moment, he stopped the end which came out into the hedge—using a piece of wire netting. 'We can take it off when we're there to see what she does,' he said, and added with a hint of mischief: 'I'd better bring a few extra titbits tonight, and so had you—then we can bribe her to come back!'

So when Zoe came out that night to sit by the wall and yearn for freedom, she found a piece of delectable bread and honey by a new hole close to the stones…. She sniffed at the food, and decided to eat it there and then…who knew where the next meal might come from? Then her inquisitive nose led her on into the hole…

Jake held his breath…she was going then. Little Zoe was almost free, though she didn't yet know it…

The dark-striped head came through the other end…. It halted, while she sniffed the wind for danger. Nothing seemed to threaten… so she came out of the drainpipe into the open field by the hedge…. For a few moments she sat there, seeming almost puzzled by all that space around her…then she began to forage in the hedge—not hurrying, but searching peace-fully among the docks and nettles for food….

She ventured a little further...and a little further...and then turned round and came back again...

'Put another piece of food down,' whispered Bracken, 'so she can find her way back...'

Jake laid it by the hole in the garden, and stood there, waiting. The questing nose came closer...and she plunged into the hole again and came out in the garden.... Once again, she ate the proferred food, and then came galloping up to Jake with every sign of welcome. 'Oh, there you are! Where've you been!' she seemed to say.

'There!' said Bracken, comfortingly. 'She's glad to be back. I told you she'd find that old world outside very big!'

Jake gave a sigh of relief. He had to confess that he had been a little afraid the cub would gallop off, never to return—only to find herself lost in an alien world with not nearly so much easy food to find!

Now, it looked as though her emancipation would come slowly. She could go and come as she pleased...but she would probably not venture too far afield at first. It was very clever of Bracken, he reflected, to know exactly how to make the transition so gradual and so safe...

This pattern was repeated for several evenings, and each time Zoe went a little further, but always returned of her own accord. Jake still put food down for her—not sure how much else she was getting—but Bracken said he ought to cut it down soon, so that she would have to forage for herself...

They went into the woods after her on her first wanderings...keeping track of her whereabouts, but not staying too close. She would often come gambolling back to them, as if pleased to see them—and never seemed to resent them being there...

'She will go soon...' said Bracken one evening. 'She's getting much more independent now. She's even begun to dig out a new sett in one of those old ones in the wood...'

'Yes,' agreed Jake, a little sadly. He knew he would miss the little cub, just as he missed Sky. But he knew he must not say so.

And then it was half-term, and Carol and the boys returned.

They all came up the path together this time, and all flung their arms round Jake and hugged him, laughing and chattering and exclaiming over the change he and Bracken had wrought in the overgrown garden...

It was like a home-coming, thought Jake—and they are like my family...far more like my own family, somehow, than those two wary strangers, my own children. Though even they got less unreachable in the end...

Then he saw Carol looking at him searchingly, and he smiled and tucked her arm through his and said: 'Come on in. We'd better visit Zoe before she goes out on her rambles.... You've only come just in time, you know—' Then he saw the look of shock on Carol's face, and went on hastily: 'She'll be gone very soon now, Bracken thinks...'

They all went up to the grass enclosure. Zoe was already out in the summer dusk, rooting about at the bottom of the hedge. When she saw Jake coming, she stopped whatever she was engaged in, and came galloping across the grass to meet him, Jake sat down on the tree stump to talk to her, and she actually stood on her hind legs and reached up to put her front paws on his knee while her clever, thrusting little head burrowed in his pocket for titbits.

'All right, all right,' he said. 'Your dinner's over there.... You're extra hungry tonight, aren't you? Been a long way, have you?'

Zoe grunted. She had found a very interesting collection in Jake's pocket—a piece of cheese, a walnut, a few crumbs of sesame cake and a radish.... All these went down very well...

But Bracken had laid out a little cache for

her near the exit to the field—and this was even more exciting, for it contained two worms, a small dead shrew and a large black slug...

After demolishing these, she tackled her dishful of dinner, which this evening included some honey-coated wheat kernels from Jake's breakfast cereal. He had to admit to himself that he was spoiling her—against Bracken's advice—in the secret hope that she would stay with him a little longer. But he knew that he must be stern with himself in future. It would be better for Zoe if she learned to find all her own food before she set out entirely on her own...

'Oh!' murmured the twins. 'Isn't she beautiful!'

And Carol whispered 'Hush!' in a voice as enchanted as theirs...

Zoe had decided to play that evening before she went off exploring—and for a time she tumbled and rolled and lay on her back, kicking her feet in the air, or chased her own tail, or pounced on Jake's foot in the grass...

But at last she tired of all her games, and the sensitive nose went up as the heady scents of the summer night began to remind her of distant places waiting for her in the sweet damp woods beyond the garden wall...

She sat for a while by the opening, and then

slid swiftly into the tunnel and came out on the other side—a black and white shadow in the deepening twilight.

'Oh!' sighed the twins. 'She's going out.... Can we follow her?'

Jake looked round for Bracken. He was probably up here somewhere, though he had a marvellous capacity for disappearing tactfully when Jake had visitors. But now, he felt, someone ought to go with the twins if they went after Zoe, in case they frightened her with their too-eager trampling...

'I'll go with them—' said Bracken, appearing out of nowhere. 'I won't let them get too close...' and he showed the twins where to climb the wall, and went with them into the shadowy field beyond...

Carol and Jake turned back and walked slowly arm in arm down through the garden to where Jake's chair stood under the ancient pear tree. There they stopped and stood side by side looking out at the valley.

'How have things been?' asked Carol.

'Pretty good,' said Jake. 'In fact—marvellous.'

'I'm glad you let Bill and his party come down.... Were you very exhausted afterwards?'

'A bit. But it didn't matter. It was worth it.'

'Truly?'

'Yes. You were entirely right.'

She grinned. 'I'm not often told that! As a matter of fact, I had awful doubts after I left you last time.'

'About what?'

'About whether I said too much?'

'You did not!' He turned a smiling face in her direction.

Carol sighed, and feeling his increasing exhaustion as he stood beside her, she said gently: 'Won't you sit in Bracken's chair? I want to picture you there when I'm snowed under with teaching in London!'

Jake submitted gracefully, not admitting that it was because he was tired, and Carol sat on the wall beside him, gazing out at the deepening night. She wondered if she could ask him if he needed anything, or whether there were things he wanted done...but she supposed she must not. It would only remind him of things which he seemed resolutely determined not to talk about.... Better let it alone. He was happiest with nothing said.

'Carol?' began Jake, sounding tentative but determined.

'Yes?'

'I want to tell you something...but I'm not sure how...'

She had turned to look at him now, serious

and attentive. 'Go on...'

'It's about—how things are for me down here. I mean, Bracken and his simple acceptance of the natural world around him have well and truly put me in my place.... So that, even before you came, I had plenty to rejoice about.... You and Bill and Manny got it all wrong, really! There was no need to be concerned about me...and now—I think I'm a bit delirious, one way and another!'

Carol tried vainly to match his smile.

'What I'm trying to say is—Bracken told me he'd be part of a dragon-fly's wing...or a worm...or part of Sky.... And I feel the same. It's the continuity that counts...the marvellous, ceaseless teeming life-cycle of the earth.... Do you follow me?'

'Yes, Jake.'

'So you see, everything is perfectly all right...' He reached out a hand and touched her quietly. 'Especially now—'

She nodded, keeping her eyes very wide in case the tears should spill over.

But Jake knew they were there. His fingers reached up and brushed them off her eyelashes. 'No,' he said softly. 'That's why I'm telling you all this...I want you to feel as I do...enriched and secure in love.'

She blinked, as if his words had struck her

like an arrow. *'Enriched and secure in love?'* she repeated, in a voice of wonder. 'That's beautiful!'

'I'm anxious about you,' he said, his voice suddenly deep with compassion. 'I know how it was for you before...and I'm trying to say, it's all right...your Bob is still part of all this—' and he waved an arm at the dusk-filled valley, 'just as I will be.... It was you, after all, who said there are many kinds of love—remember?'

She nodded, silently.

Jake smiled at her in the falling twilight and murmured: 'Now maybe I'm the one who's said too much!'

'No!' she said, in swift protest. 'You haven't.'

'You will be happy?'

She drew a long breath of resolve. 'Yes. I will.'

'I'd like to think you'll come back to the cottage now and then? Not run away from it any more?'

She looked at him, confused. 'Yes...I'll come.'

His smile was now almost as luminous and full of mischief as Bracken's. 'I shall be here—in every leaf! You'd better watch out!'

He had brought her safely out of tears towards laughter, he thought.... He was silent for a while, waiting for her to grow calm again.

Presently he said, with the half-smile still in his voice: 'Do you still feel...as if everything is new?'

'Yes,' agreed Carol, half-smiling too. 'I do.'

'So do I.' He spoke softly, almost too himself. 'New wonders at every turn...'

Then he grew serious for a moment. 'Those boys of yours—so friendly and affectionate.... They won't—?'

'Jake!' protested Carol indignantly. 'Have you forgotten what I said? We can't live for ever on ice for fear of getting hurt! I'd rather they felt things—at least they're alive!'

'Oh, they're alive all right!' said Jake, laughing. 'No need to worry about that!' Then, catching something he was not supposed to see in Carol's face, he leant forward, framing it with his hands and added softly: 'As for me—I feel more alive every minute—especially now!' and he kissed her quietly, still smiling a little in the summer night.

Above their heads, Jake's nightingale suddenly let out a crystalline trill of sound...and as they looked up into the branches of the pear tree, they saw the golden, smoky summer moon come up behind the hill...

They sat there a long time, listening to the tireless bird, hands clasped in perfect accord, until they heard the voices of the twins returning with Bracken from the woods.

It was the boys this time who made the tea and carried it out to them on the grass—for Jake and Carol seemed a little dazed and unable to free themselves from the spell of the nightingale...

The twins chattered on about Zoe and where she went, and the exciting sounds in the woods at night.... But Bracken, sitting alone in the shadows, was very silent...

At last, Carol got up to go. The parting was hard this time...very hard, in view of the knowledge she saw in Jake's transparent face.... No need to say 'He has outsoared the darkness of our night' to that face! she thought. And he's done it already...he doesn't need us now...

But she did her best to sound cheerful and normal—especially as the twins were standing beside her, still full of bubbling excitement at the night's adventures.

'Goodnight, dear Jake,' she murmured, 'go on feeling new!' and she put her arms round his neck and kissed him once more...

Jake's arms tightened round her for a moment and then let her go. I must not hold on, he thought. I must let her go. Now. It will be easier so...

The boys reached up and hugged him, too—and then they all went down the path together, leaving Jake alone by his chair in the moonlit garden.

I hate partings, said Jake. I don't want to watch them go. I'd rather remember the boys clambering over the wall with Bracken, and Carol looking up at the nightingale in my pear tree...

So he did not turn to see them wave. And they, looking back, saw only a tall, quite figure gazing out at his darkening valley, with the moonlight clear on his face.... But then, all at once, he remembered Manny with his glow-worm—so he turned round and lifted his hand to them in the dark, and called out: 'Good night! God bless!'

Bracken did not go with them, or offer to light them on their way. He sat still in the shadows, watching Jake, until he saw him sway a little with weariness and put a tired hand up to his eyes...

Then Bracken came forward, and gently led him indoors, saying nothing at all, and saw him settled in his chair before he closed the cottage door and went away by himself into the night...

Jake was very tired the next morning, and too weak for a while to get up, so he came down late. He had not recovered his strength very fast after his last collapse, and he knew now that each time it took him longer to get over it…and each day that passed left him a little weaker. He had not spoken of it, and Bracken, had not shown by any sign that he was anxious, but he had been very careful not to suggest doing anything very strenuous. This morning, Jake knew, the meeting with Carol had taken its toll…. But he would be all right after a bit of a rest…

When he went out to look at the morning, he found Bracken already in the garden, waiting for him. 'I was thinking—' the gold-flecked eyes were alight with welcome, 'little Zoe's not going to need us up there much longer…she can manage on her own…' And then, as if instantly recognising Jake's sudden sense of loss, he went on: 'So we can go out again mornings—after you've rested a bit!'

Jake grinned. 'Is that an order?'

Bracken nodded, smiling. 'You had a long day yesterday…. Anyway, I've brought you some tea this morning, and I'll stay and do a bit in the garden, shall I? We can go out tomorrow…'

'Yes,' said Jake, his eyes on the golden summer morning. 'Tomorrow…' But then, some moth's wing shadow seemed to touch him—the faintest nudge, almost as if…. 'No,' he said, suddenly, with a glimpse of rebellion in his smile, 'let's go today...'

Bracken, who had been weeding between a row of lettuces, looked up at him swiftly. Then—seeing his face—he straightened up and said tranquilly: 'All right...today...'

Jake reached out a hand and tugged at one of Bracken's wildly tangled curls. 'Don't look so disapproving! It's a lovely day!'

The boy laughed.

When Jake went inside to get his boots, he heard a curious, muffled thumping and whirring sound coming from upstairs in his bedroom. Puzzled, he climbed the stairs to have a look, noticing with inward dismay that it took him longer to do this each time. Nothing seemed to be stirring anywhere...could another bird have got in? Or a bat?

Then his eye fell on the table by his bed, and the glass jam-jar with the chrysalis inside that Bracken had given him.... Only it wasn't a chrysallis any more. It was a big, beautiful, new-painted moth, trying desperately to escape from its glass-walled prison.

'Oh!' he said, enchanted. 'Aren't you handsome!' And he carried the jam-jar downstairs in his hands, feeling the pulse of those frantic wing-beats through the glass. Life, he thought... new, marvellous, urgent life...beating through my hands...

'Bracken!' he called. 'Look what I've got! Come and help me let him go!'

Bracken came running up, his face once more luminous with instant joy. 'I forgot all about him! Isn't he *bright*...all new and polished...'

Together they looked at the vivid velvet-bloom colours of the new-hatched moth.... The front of his wings were a glowing cinnamon brown, shading from pink to buff, with intricate darker waves and delicate markings. His back wings began with an even brighter pink close to his body, and shaded towards the outer tips into pale, finely-striped gold...but on the lower edge of his wings were two perfect eyes... blue circled with black...

'An Eyed Hawk Moth,' said Bracken, awestruck. 'I thought it might be...isn't he beautiful!'

'How shall I let him go?'

'Just open the lid—and hold him up to the air...he'll go.... He'll soon smell the morning...'

Jake did as he was told and held the jar up to the sun. For a moment the beating wings went on fighting...then they were still, the sensitive antennae weaving to and fro to pick up any scent or sound wave.... Then the wings folded close, and the delicate feet began to move as the moth crawled upwards.

'Tilt it sideways now!' said Bracken.

The moth continued to climb, warily, and then came out of the jar, and perched for a moment on Jake's encircling fingers. He felt the thin pressure of those thread-like feet cling to his hand. He could see the fine veins on his wings and the velvety hairs on his thick body... then the great moth seemed to feel the sun on his wings. He stretched them wide, flexed them once or twice, and suddenly lifted into a swift thrum of flight into the morning air.... Once, twice, he circled the garden, planing and gliding in the sunshine, and then he flew over the wall into the fields beyond...

'There he goes...' said Bracken, smiling. 'Over the hills and far away...'

'Let's do the same!' said Jake.

They did not go as far as the lake that day. They wandered through the summer fields until Bracken led him out on to a grassy ridge, looking down at the long brown stretch of water below...

'I call this my listening post...' he said, smiling at Jake in the sun.

'Why?'

'You'll see. It's something about the shape of the valley...the way the hills stand round it in rings.... All the sounds seem to come up

331

here...extra clear...'

'Magnified?'

'Mm...like a loud-speaker, almost.... Listen!'

Jake listened. He could hear a lark singing somewhere up above his head, spiralling and soaring, singing as it went. Below him, the voices of the ducks on the lake came up clear and crisp, talking busily among themselves. There were the coots and moorhens, too— calling sharply to one another. He could hear the thresh of wings on water...even the plop of a fish as it jumped at a passing may fly.... And the swifts, darting over the water, to and fro, screaming in high thin voices as they searched the air for the dancing gnats...

The old cuckoo was silent now, his voice changed and broken and gone. But there was a thrush still singing loud and clear in the beech woods, and closer by in the tall ash-tree there was a blackbird who sounded like Bracken's in the pear tree at the cottage—only he hadn't got quite so many different notes...

There were the white sheep on the hillside, the lambs grown big and woolly now, but still calling to their mothers in plaintive voices... And down at the bottom of the valley there was a farm dog barking, and the unhurried deep voices of the cows he was rounding up in the water-meadows below the lake.

Jake saw how the great wedges of green beech woods sloped down the hillside. That was where the badgers were...that was where little Zoe would go looking for her friends. Somewhere, in one of those cool, dark woodland rides, she would find another sett to live in and start again on her own. Somewhere, too, in those deep woods, was the old sett that Deacon had destroyed, and the quarry where Bracken fell...

'I went back there to look...' said Bracken softly. 'Just to make sure they hadn't tried to come back...'

'Did you?' Jake shuddered slightly. 'Not to the quarry?'

Bracken grinned. 'I did just...sort of look over the edge, like...' He shook his head at Jake, smiling. 'It's a wonder we weren't all killed!'

'Was it all quiet by the sett?'

'Oh yes... I don't think they'll go back.... It probably smells too much of dogs and men...' He glanced at Jake's anxious face. 'She'll find somewhere safe—don't you fret!'

Jake sighed. He knew he was a fool to worry —but still.... She was awfully small and young to manage on her own...

'Creatures has to go their own way—' said Bracken. 'You can't protect them for ever.

They've got to learn to cope—same as the rest of us!'

'Yes,' Jake agreed. But his voice was still a little sad.

'Look!' said Bracken, pointing. 'The swans are still there...'

Down on the brown lake, four white stately forms sailed out across the water, gliding smoothly over the surface with scarcely a ripple round them.... And just behind them came the six cygnets—bigger now, but just as grey and fluffy, keeping in a close flotilla near to their parents' calm protection...

Jake watched their quiet progress across the lake until they were hidden by the reeds. Soon after them came the ducks, swimming more busily—and one or two got up off the water and skimmed down the lake in a flashing arc of spray and glinting wings...

'I can't see the heron' murmured Jake.

It was like a plan laid out before him, he thought.... The lake, full of busy growing life, the secret woods above, the scented stretches of grassy turf leading the eye up to the horizon...the wide, strong shoulders of the hills and the steep rings of the British Camp beyond.... The whole of it set before him in a perfect arc...

A sudden picture of Carol's boys came into

his mind. He could see those cheerful, energetic limbs hurtling down those grassy slopes. *'Let's go and look at the lake...'* they said in his mind...and Carol, her eyes on his face, saying shyly: *'An extra source of strength...?'* Yes, he thought, smiling, it is! Of course it is!

'We will if we wait...' said Bracken, answering Jake's remark a long while after. 'He'll come out fishing, I expect. But I don't think we'll ever see the little old otter again...they're shy creatures, otters...'

'It doesn't matter,' drowsed Jake. 'It's perfect as it is...'

Bracken agreed, but he thought a little breakfast might make it even more perfect. He brought out his usual flask of tea, and a couple of pastry rolls that looked like Cornish pasties.

'Try one of these...' he said.

Jake remembered his duty and patted his pockets, producing some cheese and apples, a bar of chocolate and two thick wedges of apple pie...

'Mm...' he said, munching. 'What is it?'

'Don't ask!' said Bracken, laughing. 'Minced up *jogray!* Probably rabbit...or pigeon...or even pheasant...'

'Whatever it is,' said Jake, still munching, 'it tastes very good!'

They stayed there a long time, dreaming in

the sun. And presently, as Bracken had predicted, the old grey heron flapped out on slow, lazy wings and settled down to fish in a corner of the lake.

'The lilies are out...' murmured Bracken. 'The water's white with 'em that end. Can you see them?'

'Mm...'

'The dragon-flies will be pleased...'

As in answer, two thin blades of light shot past them, dancing on the wind, and darted down in zig-zag flight to the water's edge below...

'Bracken...' said Jake slowly, gazing up at the sky. 'When I first came...'

'Well?'

'You were there, waiting for me.... How did you know?'

Bracken turned on him his slow, sweet, luminous smile. 'Sometimes,' he said, 'things tell us when we're needed. No sense in asking why.'

Jake nodded. Bracken, as usual, was right... no sense in asking why.... 'It's been the happiest spring and summer of my life,' he said softly. 'Did you know?'

Bracken did not answer at once. Then he said slowly, his eyes on the green and growing world around him, 'All days is happy...if you let them be...'

Yes, thought Jake. How simple! All days are happy...what am I worrying about?

'Sky's up there somewhere—' said Bracken, in the same gentle voice. 'I expect he's happy, too...'

A small blue butterfly came and settled on a flower near his hand. He did not move—just lay and watched it with his calm, gold-flecked eyes, until it lifted its wings on a breath of air and sailed away...

I'll be part of a dragon's-fly's wing...a worm...I'll be part of Sky'...sang Bracken's voice, joyously, in Jake's mind.

'Have you ever got lost?' Jake asked suddenly.

Bracken looked at him in surprise.

'I mean—I know you can usually tell where you are by the sun.... But what if it's cloudy? Or dark?'

Bracken began to smile. 'I mostly knows where I am...' But there was something about Jake's voice that made him pause and look at him oddly. 'Once or twice, though, in the night I've gone too far, and it's been a bit hard to find my way back. Why?'

Jake was fumbling in his pocket for something. Now he drew it out to show the boy beside him. 'This is my old pocket compass. I've had it years...through all sort of adventures

337

when I was working.... It's got my initials on—see? And oddly enough, it's got a kestrel stamped on the leather case...or it may be a hawk.... I think it's because kestrels always know where they are!'

Bracken laughed and bent to examine it.

'It's luminous in the dark,' said Jake. 'It always got me home...' He laid it in Bracken's hands.

After a moment, since the boy did nothing but gaze down at it with his head bent, Jake added softly: 'There's a magnifying glass in the middle. Look, it swivels out like this.... I think it's for reading maps really, but you can use it to look at fine things...like a moth's wing or a feather.... And there's a barometer on the back...not that you need telling what the weather's going to do...'

'Me?' said Bracken, with incredulity.

'Yes, you,' said Jake, still speaking softly. 'I want you to have it.'

Bracken stayed still a moment longer—still as stone. Then he raised his head and said in a fierce, strange voice that Jake scarcely recognised: 'I don't need nothing to remember you by! I'll remember anyway! But I'll keep it till I die!'

He sat there, clasping it in his hands, staring at Jake. Then the fierce light died in his eyes and he began to smile again—the old, joyous upspringing of light that Jake had come to know...and love.

'Better get home—before I burst!' he said, laughing, and pulled Jake to his feet. 'I told you all days was happy—if you let them be!'

He carefully hid the old, battered leather case in his pocket, and skipped before Jake over the sun-dappled grass.

'We'll go up to see our Zoe once more tonight,' he said. 'Shall we? And then we must leave her be...'

'Yes,' agreed Jake.

'But first you better rest—all right?'

'All right,' said Jake. He turned to look once more at the lake and the sailing swans, the beech woods standing tall, and the hills beyond.

'I don't trust you much!' said Bracken. 'You sound a bit too meek and mild to me!'

And he laughed at Jake in the sun and led him home.

That evening, when they got to Zoe's enclosure, there was no-one inside it.... They searched the corners and lifted the top off the barrel to have a look inside the sett.... But they knew in their hearts that she had gone.

Presently, without consulting each other, they climbed over the wall, went down the length of the hedge by the field, and on into the woods. Maybe they could catch a glimpse of her somewhere ahead of them in the shadows.... They walked softly over the golden carpet of last year's beech leaves, trod gently where the tall stalks of the bluebells had been...and hoped that their footsteps would not be too noisy and scare her away altogether...

Jake had not tried calling her yet—though he often used to in the safety of her pen, and she would come galloping up, her hopeful nose a-twitch for some titbit or other. Now, he suddenly thought he might try—though it seemed a bit foolish out here in the dark beech woods.

'Zoe?' he called softly. 'Zoe? Are you there?'

He stood listening. There were all sorts of small noises around him among the trees—rustlings and scamperings, creaking tree branches and sleeping owls beginning to wake and whicker among themselves.... But no sturdy young badger, galloping towards him along the woodland rides.

'Try again,' said Bracken, close beside him. 'She might hear you...'

He called again, just a little louder, and waited—and called once more. Then, absurdly disappointed, he began to walk on through the much-too-empty woodlands.... She had gone then, little Zoe...gone for good.

Bracken kept close beside him, saying nothing.

But all at once, a black and silver shadow detached itself from the surrounding darkness and came confidently towards them along the path. The compact, shapely body moved smoothly through the undergrowth, the firm strong legs in their neat black fur kept up a steady mile-consuming trot...and the striped intelligent head was held low, thrusting forward in eager anticipation as she came toward them...

'It's Zoe!' breathed Jake. 'She's come back to see us!'

'I told you she might hear you!' said Bracken, sounding as pleased as Jake was.

The cub came straight up to them, and rubbed up against their legs with every sign of affectionate recognition. Jake's hand went to his pocket. Then he hesitated and looked at Bracken.

'Should I—?'

'Don't see why not—' said Bracken, hearing the note of longing in Jake's voice. 'It won't do no harm for her to know she can come back for a titbit now and then...'

Jake produced her favourite—a sticky honey sandwich—and a few nuts. Zoe reached into his hand with her long, striped nose, and took them happily...

For a while, she played round the two of them, prancing and pouncing in her old playful manner.... But then she sat up with her head pointing westwards into the heart of the wood and seemed to be listening or scenting something a long way off. At last, she got up, circled them once, and trotted off into the shadows. Just before she disappeared from sight down into a leafy hollow among the trees, she paused and looked back at them.... They saw the neat striped head turned towards them, and then a faint flash of white as she turned back and moved further away...then she was gone, and they were left staring at nothing but the dark boles of the trees...

Well then, she's gone, thought Jake—the brave, affectionate, funny little badger cub he had come to love—gone out into the wild summer woods to join the rest of her kind...

'Goodbye, little Zoe,' he said aloud. 'God speed!'

It seemed a bit strange to be saying it to the tall listening trees—but Bracken did not seem to think so...

'She'll be all right now,' he said, his voice full of warmth and certainty. 'We've done right to let her go...she's where she belongs—out there in the dark!'

Jake was silent. He knew Bracken was right.

But something irrational inside him grieved for the little cub he would not see again...

'Come on,' said Bracken, touching his arm in the darkness beneath the trees, 'your nightingale will be singing to nobody if you don't get back soon!'

Together, they wandered back through the woods, and came out into a clear blue summer dusk in the field where the hares used to play. In fact, they were out then, leaping and frolicking in the corner of the field, but the grass and moon-daisies had grown so high that Jake only caught a glimpse of some ears and a flashing tail and a wave of moving grass as they passed...

They came back to the garden and climbed the wall, and Jake went to put his kettle on, while Bracken perched on his wall under the pear tree and waited for the moon to rise behind the black curve of the hill. It was almost the last of the big summer moon...tomorrow it would be waning, and rising late...and Bracken fancied the weather might be going to change. But now, the sky was clear and pure—still golden in the west, but deepening into true azure as the night came down.... A beautiful night to sit out in.... He hoped the nightingale would sing...

They sat together, drinking tea and admiring the night, and not talking very much...and presently the small brown bird came back to the pear tree and poured out his silver song...

This evening, Jake had felt a change within him...something had seemed to give and settle, as if one more strand of the rope that held him tethered to earth had broken. He had not understood it then...only he had felt cold... cold...and the leaden weakness seemed to grow heavier and drag at his heels...

But now, strangely, out here with Bracken, listening to the nightingale and watching the smoky orange moon climbing up behind the trees, he had felt all this weariness fall away... leaving him curiously light and untroubled in the beguiling summer night. There was nothing now but this searing beauty of moonlight and silver song all round him...and Bracken's quiet silhouette against the blue night sky...

At last, the bird ceased singing and Bracken stirred and leapt lightly down from the wall.

'Time you was resting...' he said, smiling a little. And then, looking at him half-shyly, he added: 'I said all days is happy—but this one's been special!'

'Yes,' agreed Jake. 'It has.'

Bracken was still looking at him, head a little on one side, with a questioning air that reminded him somehow of the badger cub. 'Why did you say "God speed" to Zoe?'

Jake smiled. 'Yes...I suppose we do say it too lightly, without thinking what it means.... But I should think a kindly God would care about animals, too?'

'Oh yes!' said Bracken, full of certainty.

'Well then?' Jake prompted him gently.

'I just wondered...if you could say it about people, too?'

Jake was silent for a moment, drawing a deep, unsteady breath. Then he said quietly: 'Yes, Bracken. Of course you can.'

The boy's voice in the darkness was reflective and slow. 'We say. *Te avel Devlesa*, go with God...'

'That's almost better.' Jake was smiling again. 'You wouldn't feel lonely then!'

'Oh, you wouldn't be *lonely*,' said Bracken, almost indignantly. 'Not lonely at all!'

There was another small silence between them.

Finally, Jake stirred and murmured, half to himself: 'No. You're right...'

'I like your word "speed" though,' the voice was full of quiet dreams, 'it reminds me of Sky...'

Jake nodded, 'In any case...they mean the same thing really...'

Bracken smiled at him in the darkness. Light seemed to spring in his face and flow upwards

345

till Jake was dazzled.

'That's all right, then,' he said softly. 'So I can say "God speed" to you!'

After Bracken had gone, Jake could not sleep. He did not attempt to go upstairs, knowing he would only lie awake—if he ever got so far as climbing the stairs at all.... He tried to settle down to read, and could not concentrate.... He even tried to sit at his typewriter and work—but he could not keep still...

The summer moon burned on in the sky, luring him out, and he could not resist it.... Sighing, he reached for his jacket, picked up his torch, and went out again into his garden...

He stood for a moment looking out at his valley, and then—almost automatically—his feet took him towards the old wire enclosure near his shed. There was no-one there, of course—the silvered grass lay empty and silent—but as he turned away, something caught his eye... a shape—a shadow—a more dense patch of darkness.... Something was sitting motionless on top of Sky's tree-trunk perch...something strong and slender, with furled wings, and a smooth, unmoving head...

'Sky?' said Jake incredulously. 'Sky? Is that you?'

For answer, the dark shadow unfurled its

wings and launched itself upwards, circling over Jake's head. He could hear the fine, quivering thrum of its wings above him... 'Kee!' it called urgently. 'Kee!' and then let out the kestrel's brittle alarm call: 'Kikikik! Kikikik! Kee!'

'It *is* you!' said Jake, sure in his mind now that he heard that fierce, harsh voice. 'What's the matter?'

'Kee!' shouted Sky—circling overhead, dropping and lifting, almost touching Jake's upturned face with his long flight feathers.

Jake suddenly remembered Bracken's blackbirds and the marauding magpie...the way they had screamed and circled overhead, crying for help. 'What is it?' he said. 'Can't you tell me? What can I do?'

For answer, Sky called once again, imperiously, and began to fly away from Jake in widening circles, but always returning to hover overhead.

'I see...' said Jake, quite sure now what Sky wanted. 'All right...I'm coming...lead the way..'

He had been very tired all day, and consciously ignoring it—and then there had been that curious sensation earlier of something finally giving way.... He had been cold, too...very cold...and the hampering weakness had made his feet like lead.... But now, he followed Sky without hesitation, putting aside his weariness and the strange, increasing cold in all his limbs...knowing within his mind that this perilous night journey might well be his last...

It's absurd, he said, to be following a kestrel across a field in the middle of the night! But I'm sure that's what he wants...and since it is Sky, I can't refuse. Maybe, he thought strangely, he knows it is time for me...

Above him, Sky circled on impatient wings, trying to persuade this clumsy human to hurry. 'Kee!' he called. 'Kikikik! Be quick! Be quick!'

And Jake followed his urgent, stooping flight, stumbling a little on the tussocks of moonlit grass...

He did not know how far he walked in the dark, with the kestrel's shadowy wings just ahead, leading him on.... They went across the fields, through small copses and spinneys and clumps of elder and willow, skirting the edge of the great beech woods, up one hill and down another. Jake's legs scarcely knew they were moving, or whether they would hold him up for another step. But he was past being tired, now.... He walked in a white trance, moving from moonlight to shadow, from shadow to moonlight..until he came to a steep sloping field on the edge of yet another wood.... And here, Sky uttered one more fierce 'Kee!' and sank down on to the grass. Jake stumbled forward, hearing a wild threshing of desperate wings that seemed to grow louder and louder in his ears as he approached...seeing a strange-shaped thing on the grass that glinted like dull metal in the moonlight...

When he got near, he saw that it was indeed metal...and in its wicked, gleaming jaws was another kestrel like Sky—only he fancied her head was brown not grey—and she was struggling desperately, trapped in those dreadful teeth of sharpened steel...

Sky called 'Kee!' again, but more softly now, and flew up and hovered, flew down and settled, flew up again and circled, and then came down and stood anxiously beside his terrified mate.

'So you brought me to her...' said Jake looking in pity at the torn and wounded bird by the light of his torch and the waning moon. 'I'll try, Sky...I'll do my best...but she's badly hurt, I'm afraid.... I may not be able to save her...'

He bent over the trap to see what he could do. The female kestrel had stopped struggling now, and looked at him out of despairing, fear-crazed eyes....

'Gently...'he said. 'Try to keep still. I don't

349

know if I'm strong enough to shift it...'

He heaved and pulled at the steel jaws of the trap, but he could not muster enough strength to open them. If I could get a solid piece of wood to lever it up, he thought...and cast round for a bit of broken branch.... At last he found one, wedged against a stone wall at the edge of the field, and carried it back to the trap...

Sky was standing patiently on a stone beside his mate...and he spread out his wings and called 'Kee!' as Jake approached. But he did not fly away.... The female bird gave another convulsive heave and threshed with her wings, and then lay still again.... There was agony in her eye...

Riven by her suffering, Jake struggled with the trap again.... Pulling with his arms made him dizzy and faint, and set up a sudden deep ache in his chest.... His heart began to thump wildly...but he fought on, forcing the jaws of the trap apart and inserting the tree branch inch by inch, until he had enough solid wood inside to act as a lever... Then he leaned on it with all his weight, and wrenched the deadly clamping teeth apart...

But the wounded kestrel was too feeble to move, and did not seem to know that the trap was sprung...

Groaning with frustration, Jake gripped the piece of branch under one arm, and leant down to grab the bird. He seized her by her feet and flung her aside, just as the branch snapped under his arm, unable to sustain the crushing weight of the spring. The steel jaws clashed together with a snap, trapping Jake's hand, the end of the branch rammed itself into Jake's side with a sickening blow, and he fell forward on to the bloodstained grass...

A great wave of pain came over him then for a moment and then receded, leaving him in a floating mist of weakness.... So it is now, he thought.... Well, I'm glad I'm alone...I didn't want Bracken to have to face this with me.... This is how it should be...

He thought he heard wings then, beating about his head...a great strong rush of wings all round him...circling and soaring... He thought he heard a kestrel's cry, growing fainter on the wind...

His body felt light now...not heavy at all... and it was not cold any more. He lay on the dewy, moonlit grass and did not feel cold at all.... An enormous sense of peace and tranquillity came over him. It was entirely right, and he was ready...this calm, serene acceptance of rest was all that was required of him.... He was safe now...

The wings still seemed to soar all round him. Swans' wings and kestrels' wings...swift and strong and free.... Their music seemed to pulse right through him.... He was part of their lifting, soaring flight...

Sky? he said...though no words came...are you safe? Is your wounded mate flying free?

He thought he heard Carol's voice then, quite close to him, full of warmth and comfort, saying: '...*rich and secure in love...*'

And then Bracken seemed to come, all luminous with welcome, and take him by the hand, saying: *'God speed!'*

Smiling, Jake laid down his burden on the grass, and went out to join those soaring, swift strong wings...

It was Bracken who found him the next evening —Bracken, who had been searching for him through the woods and fields all the long day from very early in the morning when he found him missing.... And it was Bracken who went running for Dr Martin and Farmer Stan Bayliss —though Jake was more than fifteen miles away beyond Wood End Farm.... So it was those two good friends of his that brought him home...

He was still smiling when Bracken came to him...serene and at peace in the summer grass.

The two kestrels were gone but there was blood on the ground and in the trap where Jake's hand was still caught, and a scatter of long wing feathers on the grass...

No-one could understand how Jake could have got so far—more than fifteen miles from home, over very rough country—or why he had gone out like that, alone in the night...

But Bracken knew.... He looked at those torn wing feathers and up into the wide summer sky, and thought: Yes. He came here to help something. His last act on earth was to set something free.... To Bracken, standing alone in the tumbled grass, this seemed entirely right.

Jake's friend Bill was the one who knew what to do next. He made all the arrangements, and he took charge of Jake's typewriter and a certain pile of manuscript he had been writing which had a note on top of it saying: 'For Bill and Carol...'

He saw everyone in turn who had been concerned with Jake—even Bracken's father—and last of all he asked to see Bracken himself.... Then he remembered that the boy didn't like houses, so he went outside to sit with him beside Jake's empty chair. He explained, very gently, that Jake had left him some money to use for his animals and birds...

'You could use it now, Bracken, if you wanted to…. But your father agreed with me that maybe it would be better kept in trust for you till you're ready for it? What do you think?'

Bracken shook his head fiercely. 'I don't want his money!'

'Not now,' said Bill, understanding his fierceness all too well. 'But one day—you might want to set up some kind of sanctuary for your birds and animals…like the one you made for Sky and Zoe, only bigger…? Mightn't you? I know money isn't important to you, Bracken—and I know it can't bring Jake back—but he wanted you to have it. He thought you might find a use for it later on…. You mustn't refuse him, must you?'

Bracken turned to him then, the gold-flecked eyes dark with grief. 'All right…if he wanted it…. But I'd rather have him back than all the money in the world!'

'I know,' said Bill sadly. 'I know, Bracken…. So would we all…'

Bracken got up from the wall, and stood staring out at the valley. Then he looked down at Jake's chair, standing empty on the grass.

'It's a good thing he was a *Gorgio*…'

'Why?'

'If he was a Romany, we'd have to burn that

chair—and everything else...' He sighed. 'I've never understood why we have to...I'd rather be reminded...' He glanced down at the chair again. 'Can we leave it here? I'd like to think...he could find it if he wanted to...'

Bill nodded.

'Besides, the nightingale needs someone to sing to...' he said obscurely, and walked away from the cottage, and Bill, without looking back.

There was a surprising number of people at the funeral in the little village church. Some quite famous people came down from London. Bill and Manny were there, and with them a tall blonde girl, and a young man with eyes that reminded people of Jake.... And Carol Cook and her boys came, looking somehow both sad and proud at once.... And there was someone called Bob, who they said was editor of foreign news on a famous newspaper...and there was an even more famous doctor called Andrew Lawson...

But besides these strangers from London, almost the whole village seemed to be there. Mary Willis from the shop, and her brother Tom, the butcher...and postman Jim Merrett, and, of course, Dr Martin and Farmer Stan Bayliss, and not far behind them in one of the pews was that dour man Ralph Deacon.... And Bracken's own father, twisting his best cloth cap in his hands, sitting alone at the back...

Bracken did not go into the church. He sat outside on a tombstone and listened to the singing. The gypsies had their own ceremonies when an old friend died.... His father would arrange it, he knew.... There would be speeches made, they would praise famous men and Jake in particular, and say: *'Te avel angle tute'*...and then there would be singing and drinking in the firelight. But Bracken would not feel part of it...any more than he felt part of this ceremony in the church...

In any case, the gypsies were moving on after today.... His father—perhaps thinking it would be best for the boy now—had decreed that they should go.... The whole *hatchintan* was packing up to move down Hereford way for the hop-picking. By tomorrow, there would be nothing left in the clearing but the trampled grass where the *grais* had been and a few rings of blackened stones...

But the thought of moving on did not comfort Bracken. He had lost a friend who could never be replaced, and he had to find his own way out of this grief he did not understand. He knew he had done all he could for his friend, Jake.... He had shown him all the

356

wonders he knew...and cared for him when he was tired, as best he could. Hadn't Jake said it was the happiest spring and summer of his life? Well then, it ought to be all right...he ought not to feel this aching sense of loss, here in the bright summer sunshine when every leaf and flower shone with life...

But he did.... Brightness was gone from the day—because there was no longer a loved companion beside him to gaze and admire when he pointed to something new and said: 'Look! There's a dagonfly!'

Then he began to remember the conversation about thistledown.... He had been intent on comforting his friend then...and he had known, quite clearly, what to say to him... *I'll be a leaf, a piece of a dragon-fly's wing...a worm...I'll be part of Sky'*, he had said...telling Jake what he knew to be true.... So why was he letting this sadness dim the bright sky? Jake was there —as he had said he would be—in every leaf and flower, in every blade of grass, and every singing bird...

The people were coming out now, and walking round to the new grave in the grass. Bracken waited till everyone had gone. Only four of them stopped—Dr Martin, Manny and Bill, and Carol Cook. And Bill, speaking for all of them, put a hand on his shoulder and squeezed it tight and whispered: 'Thank you!'

Thank you? he thought. For what? My friend is dead. But he is alive all round us, if you'd only look—only I don't know how to tell you so...

When they had gone, he went over to the graveside and looked at the flowers. There were a lot of them—all expensive and stiff from the shops in the town...

But Bracken stooped and laid his own offerings down among the pile—a handful of kestrel feathers, a shell fossil—millions of years old—from the high hills, and a small bunch of white moon-daisies from the field where the hares used to play...

Then he walked away alone, and climbed the highest hill, and stood on the topmost point, looking out at the wide valleys and rolling hills beyond...

He looked up into the summer sky, and thought he saw a faint speck hovering there....
Far and clear, there came to him on the wind, the cry of a bird...the call of a swift, wild kestrel...flying free...

Magna Print Books hope you have enjoyed this Large Print book. All our Large Print titles are designed for the easiest reading, and all our books are made to last. Other Magna Large Print Books are available at your library, through selected book-stores, or direct from the publisher. For more information about our current and forth-coming Large Print titles, please send your name and address to:

Magna Print Books
Magna House, Long Preston,
Nr Skipton, North Yorkshire,
England. BD23 4ND.

July 19
aug 29, 94

DEMCO